BROGNOLA HEARD THE DISTANT CRACK OF HIGH EXPLOSIVES

He touched the earpiece. "Barbara, what was that?"

"Grenade and small arms fire," Price answered. "The protesters who started for the security entrance have been hit. Secret Service is on the lookout for grenade launchers and assault rifles."

"Any idea who opened fire?" Brognola asked. He jogged to a nearby window overlooking the scene. Wisps of black smoke curled into the sky, a grisly grave marker for the brutal violence.

A police car racing to the scene suddenly erupted, bursting apart under the force of a shoulder-mounted missile. Flames blew out the glass on all sides.

Secret Service guards at the gate took cover as automatic fire sizzled at the guardhouse. Even bullet-resistant glass and built-in steel plating did little to alleviate the incoming torrent of bullets.

Brognola grimaced as the sudden flurry of violence abated.

This was not going to be the last shot fired in this war.

Not if Stony Man Farm had anything to say about it.

D0378583

DON PENDLETON'S

STONY

AMERICA'S ULTRA-COVERT INTELLIGENCE AGENCY

MAN®

COLD SNAP

A GOLD EAGLE BOOK FROM

W☉RLDWIDE®

TORONTO • NEW YORK • LONDON
AMSTERDAM • PARIS • SYDNEY • HAMBURG
STOCKHOLM • ATHENS • TOKYO • MILAN
MADRID • WARSAW • BUDAPEST • AUCKLAND

Recycling programs
for this product may
not exist in your area.

First edition August 2014

ISBN-13: 978-0-373-80446-7

COLD SNAP

Special thanks and acknowledgment to
Douglas P. Wojtowicz for his contribution to this work.

COLD SNAP

CHAPTER ONE

Hideaki Isamu ran along the deck, knowing that Captain Katashi expected nothing less than absolute efficiency and timeliness from his crew. Isamu skirted against the railing, allowing other sailors to rush past him in the opposite direction, and the young man was glad for the perfect paint job. The last thing he needed was a sliver of old paint or rusted metal to rip open his palms as he glided along the rail before turning back and running full speed ahead.

Isamu stared out over the blue-gray waters of the Ross Sea. It was a magnificent sight. To the south, as far as he could see, was the white crust of the massive Ross Ice Shelf, a V of thick sea ice that stretched from the end of the bay to a mere 200 miles from the geographic South Pole. It was more than 185,000 square miles of ice between 50 and 150 feet thick. The *Saburou Maru* was miles off of the shelf, but even from this distance, the thin sliver of purest white was an unmistakable horizon, taking Isamu's breath even on a mere glancing notice. He was looking at a body of ice that someone once said was the size of France. Ignoring something that huge, that magnificent, would take some formidable willpower, but Isamu tore himself away and concentrated on his duty.

The announcement had spurred the crew to the proximity of a pod of whales. While the water was choppy, whitecaps forming bright scars against the rippling surface, he noticed the breaches of whales in the far distance.

The *Saburou Maru* was on its annual research trip down into the Antarctic waters, along with other ships in the fleet, to determine if there were enough whales present to continue sustainable whaling for Japan. Isamu squinted and made out that the humps were from Minke whales, small animals, less than thirty feet in length. As opposed to the other species such as Fin or Sperm, the Minkes were common.

Isamu recalled a number of more than half a million living within the Antarctic ocean, plentiful enough to sustain Japanese whaling. Those numbers had not diminished significantly in the wake of research catches, some 14,000 between 1988 and the present.

If they were that plentiful, Isamu didn't feel bad about going after them. Captain Katashi was the same way. Whaling was central to Japanese culture; it was in the blood of many a young man seeking adventure on the high seas. There were times when Isamu wondered why world opinion was so harsh on Japan when there were cultures out there that treated human beings as property and enforced female genital mutilation.

Priorities, Isamu thought. Minke whales were not in danger of extinction and human lives were far more important than—

Something shook the boat.

"What the hell?" Isamu asked.

"We need fire control crews to starboard aft!" Katashi said over the announcement system. "Emergency."

Katashi was a firm, calm man, but even Isamu could hear the slight tremor of urgency in his voice. Isamu was a member of the on-board fire team and immediately about-faced and started to a causeway that would take him from the port rail.

Catching a few whales would have to wait. His fellow

seamen were in trouble as even now the stench of burning paint, metal and…

Is that pork? Isamu wondered. Dread flushed through the sailor as he bolted into the passageway and took off. Some part of his mind drifted back to the tales of the south seas and how they likened the cooking of human flesh to the smell and flavor of pork; hence the name "long pork" for cannibalism. His stomach twisted into a knot as he ran, but he didn't allow himself to slow down. If there was a fire and someone was burning, then he needed to get there immediately. He was part of the fire safety crew and he'd allow nothing to slow him down.

As he reached the starboard deck, he immediately plunged into a thick, roiling cloud that hit him like a brick wall. A spasm of coughing struck him and Isamu stumbled back, hacking gunk out of his nose and throat in an effort to regain his breath. He reached into his pocket for a rag and pressed it over his nose and mouth to form an improvised filter, but as he leaned out, the charcoal-gray smoke made it impossible to see more than a few feet toward the aft.

The grisly stench was stronger now and it was accompanied by screams of pain. Isamu cursed himself for being so impatient to get to the scene of the accident that he'd passed the fire-gear locker on the starboard side. He'd assumed that he'd prove able to get to the equipment locker on that side of the ship, and his haste now cost him. Rather than rush back and take even more time, Isamu relied upon his memory, feeling along the way to where he remembered the equipment locker stood.

Getting it open, Isamu reached in, found an oxygen mask and pulled it over his head, but only after the face piece was in place did he take the rag away from his mouth. No longer assailed by chemical smoke, his tears helped to clear his vision. Now with less of an excuse to be clumsy, he shrugged into a fireproof coat and tugged on his gloves. An industrial-strength fire extinguisher would get him moving toward the center of the disaster while others prepped the hoses.

Almost as an afterthought, Isamu grabbed up a walkie-talkie and plugged its jack into the firefighter's mask. Now he could transmit and receive, hands-free.

"I'm in gear. Heading to the fire with the extinguisher," he announced, following protocol. He'd screwed up once, and found himself floundering in the passageway. Another mistake would cost lives.

He scrambled toward the thickest of the smoke, the high-test extinguisher making him list with each step simply due to its weight. The bottle was heavy, seventeen pounds of mono-ammonium phosphate, which would give it sufficient endurance to move in and save as many of his shipmates as he could. The phosphate was a good neutral compound, perfect for dealing with anything from electrical to burning fuel. It would cut loose with a high-pressure cloud, more than enough to snuff out a large column of flames that he could maneuver through.

Sure enough, his first tug on the trigger quenched a section of deck, not only clearing a path for him to cut through to the main fire, but also allowing a couple of injured sailors to escape. Isamu waved and patted them on, careful not to touch any burned areas, for risk of exacerbating tissue damage to already injured skin. "Fire control, I have three coming in, severe burns, but they're still ambulatory."

"I read you," came the quick response. "We're prepping sick—"

Thunder crashed and Isamu suddenly lost his radio signal.

"Hello? Hello!" he shouted through his mask.

He couldn't waste more time. He gave the extinguisher trigger another squeeze, blasting more of the phosphate and smothering more yards of sizzling deck. As he did so, the smoke thinned, just for a moment, and he could see where a gigantic "bite" had been taken out of the ship, hot metal smoldering as a surging wave slapped it, a cloud of steam rising from the wreckage. The fires came back within moments, farther on, but because Isamu was far from the actual hole, he could see that the flames came from metal that was white-hot. For some reason the explosion looked as if it had originated two or three yards from where the hull should have been, but the harpoon guns that they used didn't have that much gunpowder and the magazine was elsewhere, closer to the bow.

A third thunderous impact shook the ship and Isamu whirled to see what was happening. Even as he did so, he noticed a low black object about four hundred yards away. At first Isamu thought it might be a whale from its sheer bulk, but it was too far out even to be a sperm whale. Another part of what made Isamu think it was a whale was the puffing smoke. It looked like the exhalation of a whale, the hot moisture of its breath expelled into frigid Antarctic air.

But another puff erupted. Something dark and small shot up and sailed through the sky toward his ship.

Hideaki Isamu had only a few moments to realize that the object on the waves looked reminiscent of an American stealth fighter, so famous and recognizable from countless video games and Japanese anime. He also recalled that there were ships—warships—that had a similar configuration. Comparable stealth craft had even been used in one of Isamu's favorite movies to destroy a Red Chinese—

THE YINGJI-82, *yingji* literally meaning "eagle strike" in Chinese, was a magnificent piece of weaponry. Though it was nearly 21 feet in length, because it was stored inside the trimaran's missile magazine, no camouflage paint was required to make it low profile. White with red piping and nose cone, the missile accelerated from the low-profile launcher and accelerated to 664 miles an hour in the space of a few seconds.

The YJ-82 was fired straight up, especially since the range and target were being guided by the launcher's own internal radar that currently painted the *Saburou Maru* with beams invisible to the human eye. The Eagle Strike—known by NATO forces as CSS-N-8 Saccade—had been designed from the ground up as an anti-shipping missile, complete with the ability to carry 360 pounds of high explosive to its target at speeds just below subsonic. The speeding munition rode on its turbojet at Mach 0.9 toward its target.

Though it was a current front-line surface warship and air-to-surface fighter jet weapon, the Yingji-82 wasn't exactly the newest in designs. It had begun its fighting history in 1989 and spread to the Middle East, particularly to Iran, thanks to sales by China in 1992. The weapon, though it hadn't been utilized in major military engagements, had proved its stealth in crippling an Israeli naval frigate in 2006. Hezbollah, supplied by the Iranians, hit the INS *Hanit* with a YJ-82 that managed to penetrate the warship's multilayered anti-missile defenses.

A Japanese whaling ship such as the *Saburou Maru* wouldn't stand a chance. The first round struck with enough force to make a forty-foot-wide hole in the aft of the whaler. Materials around the blast zone were heated up phenomenally, igniting any flammable objects in the area. On a warship, the flames would not have been so bad, as there was far more fire control equipment on hand and far less that would actually burn. On a whaler, which didn't expect torpedo or missile strikes, it was a churning inferno.

The Yingji-82 came down in close proximity to Hideaki Isamu, its semi-armor-piercing high explosives penetrating the interior of the *Maru*. Isamu didn't suffer at all as the detonation produced a sheet of force that instantly burst every single cell in his body. Neurons detonated under the pressure wave, and as such, Isamu literally had no means by which to experience the trauma that killed him outright, liquefying organs.

Others were not so lucky, as sailors were hurled into the frigid Antarctic waters. The poor men wouldn't last long, twenty minutes if they managed to keep themselves afloat. Unfortunately broken arms and legs or deep concussions rendered those seamen helpless. Unable to hold their breath, several already were gone, breathing in ocean water and drowning instantly.

Four missiles took apart the Japanese whaler completely, bulkheads torn asunder. The 150-foot craft groaned in agony, the swelling oceans producing enough stress on the threadbare keel to snap it in two.

The *Saburou Maru* was merely the first of the Japanese research whaling craft to be lost in the space of three days. Three more, including one factory ship, were destroyed, lost at sea.

BARBARA PRICE STOOD at the center of the Computer Room in Stony Man Farm. She was surrounded by a sprawl of computer hubs, each built and personally designed by the four master information-gatherers that made up the Sensitive Operations Group's cybernetic support crew. Between the four of them, if it could not be uncovered, it was beyond discovery.

Right now, Price was keeping her eye on the world map up on the video screen wall, also mirrored on her tablet computer.

In three days, four Japanese industrial ships had been lost. Casualties added up to nearly four hundred Japanese sailors; the rest of the whaling fleet being forced to abandon operations for the year. Already, the Tokyo stock market was reeling from the loss of manpower and matériel, even though no one had stepped forward to claim responsibility for the deadly attacks. The losses of the ships and manpower totaled up to $350 million U.S. dollars, adding another $24 million thrown into the mix due to the salaries of the crews not being paid out. At the thought of the damage wrought on four hundred different families, Price found herself feeling a little nauseated.

This was just the first round fired across the decks of the nation of Japan, and the carnage was on a scale of 9/11 to America, at least in loss of life. How many families would be forced into poverty and homelessness without wage earners? How many children would turn to crime to support themselves?

The effect on those people was of no interest to the twenty-four-hour cable-news cycles, no matter the political leaning of the network. Already cable news was bristling with the debate over the sinkings. On liberal channels, the mystery attackers were the vigilantes who finally struck a blow to end the barbaric practice of whaling. On more conservative channels, the debate turned toward unfair United Nations rules regarding national culture and business, as well as the economic impact on a national ally.

Aaron Kurtzman, Stony Man's computer genius, motioned Price to his side.

"The team and I have developed some intel on the missiles," Kurtzman told her.

Price took a look at the information as her tablet tapped into Kurtzman's research. Already things were tangling into a twisted web of conspiracy. The Chinese missiles seemed to have been routed through Iran.

Akira Tokaido raised his hand. "We've got developments at the White House!"

Price grimaced and brought up Tokaido's interface. Pennsylvania Avenue was alive and livid with anti-whaling protesters, all of whom were under surveillance by the army of Secret Service and Metro P.D. officers that secured the home of the leader of the Free World.

Of equal concern to Price was the fact that her superior and good friend Hal Brognola was also at the White House.

AMERICANS WERE BUZZING, especially since there was a Japanese delegation in Washington, D.C., visiting the White House. The President wanted to make a good impression upon the dignitaries, something that was made difficult by picketers parading across the lawn from the Oval Office, their placards decrying Japanese inhumanity to animals.

Harold Brognola, as usual, hung around the edges of the open meeting. As a major figure in the Justice Department, his presence usually went unnoticed, especially since he had the ear of the President across multiple administrations. His Justice Department position, however, was merely a smokescreen for his position as the liaison between the White House and the Sensitive Operations Group at Stony Man Farm.

The SOG was an extra-legal agency Brognola had helped to assemble person by person, carefully scrutinizing every support and field operative. While Stony Man operated outside the parameters of law enforcement or military, Brognola was aware that it would take a tight rein and an uncommon moral code to keep the ultra-covert agency from going the wrong way.

Indeed, Stony Man had battled not only foreign threats, but other agencies within the American establishment, rogue operations groups that didn't have the concern for innocent bystanders or were fueled by blind, bigoted hatred or simply unchecked greed.

Right now, Brognola was especially interested in what the Japanese delegation wanted from the President. The attacks on their whaling operation were at the forefront of the conversation and there was more than sufficient tension in their voices to make Brognola worried.

Stony Man Farm was already on full alert, especially since the attack on the Japanese ships was carried out by high-technology craft and military-grade missiles. The cyber crew at the Farm had picked up on Australian naval investigations of the sinkings. The Australians had discovered surviving pieces of them that implicated both China and Iran.

The Farm was on full alert, ready to allocate its resources to tracking down the vigilantes. There was a good possibility the action was going to be the spearhead of an international terror campaign. Iran's involvement already made Brognola tense.

"Hal?" Brognola's wireless earpiece was connected to his secure smartphone. It proved to be a means to prevent interruption of high-level conferences while allowing him to keep his thumb firmly on the pulse of an international crisis. The voice was Barbara Price's, the Stony Man mission controller.

"What've you got?" Brognola asked under his breath.

"We have the protesters under surveillance and a group of about twenty have wandered away," Price answered. "So far, none of them look as if they're armed, but confidence levels are low on that evaluation."

"Wandered where?"

"Toward the secure exit from the White House grounds," Price told him. "Secret Service chatter indicates they are aware of the potential threat."

"Good to know the Farm has both sides on watch," Brognola said. "Any idea of the identities of the protesters?"

"We're looking at a mix of Greenpeace and PETA," Price answered. "Known troublemakers for the group."

"'Breaking into chemical plants' trouble?" Brognola asked.

"On the nose," Price replied. "They have rap sheets, but none that actually equate to armed violence or bombings and sabotage designed to inflict injury. Still, there's a first time for everything."

"Keep me appraised," Brognola said.

The Japanese delegation made the motions of leaving; standing, bowing their heads, offering hands for shakes. The White House press corps took plenty of pictures and video of the activity, most of which would be run constantly in the background as B-reel footage while pundits from either cable news camp spouted their usual vapid commentary.

Over the drone of reporters struggling to get to the

front to ask their questions first, something popped in the distance. Brognola instantly recognized the distant crack of high explosives. He touched his earpiece.

"Barb, what was that?"

"Grenade and small-arms fire on the street with the protesters," Price answered. "The group that started for the security entrance has been hit. Secret Service is on the lookout for grenade launchers and assault rifles."

"Hitting the protesters?" Brognola asked.

"Metro P.D. is on the move and FBI Hostage Rescue is mobilizing," Price stated. "White House security has been raised to maximum."

"Any idea who opened fire?" Brognola asked, moving to a nearby window overlooking the scene. Wisps of black smoke curled into the sky, a grisly grave marker for where someone had struck with brutal violence.

Brognola had been to the site of such massacres, had gone through many more evidence photos, but was all too aware of the smell of spilled blood and burst organs, the moans and groans of the wounded and dying. Every instinct he had was to rush out there, but Brognola was not a young man, nor the fastest and fittest.

Younger men would—

A police car racing to the scene suddenly erupted, bursting apart under the force of a shoulder-mounted missile. Flames blew out through the glass on all sides, a billowing fire that vomited into the open. Brognola clenched his fists.

The gunfire continued. Secret Service guards at the gate took cover as automatic fire sizzled at the guardhouse. Bullet-resistant glass and built-in steel plating did little to alleviate the incoming torrent of bullets.

Brognola grimaced as the sudden flurry of violence abated.

This was not going to be the last shot fired in this war. Not if Stony Man had anything to say about it.

CHAPTER TWO

The American Vanguard National Fund's offices seemed like those of any other financial organization, though they were in downtown Baltimore, Maryland, only a few hours from Washington, D.C., rather than in physical proximity to Wall Street.

Of course, Rufus Schmied would not have wanted to be in New York City for the life of him. Baltimore itself was already stock-full of undesirable flesh trying to pose as humanity, but there was little chance that the 64 percent of the population who were black could ever hope to blend in with the society that Schmied sought to build. And the Jews held too much power in New York.

Schmied looked out the window on a city in which the rot was far too strong yet was a center of power in *his* state. Schmied didn't want to leave behind Maryland, which for the most part was pure outside the rotten core known as Baltimore. He'd even leave the city's demographics alone; after all, not counting the city, the state was fairly clean.

Big cities, with their "melting pots," were sources of violence and corruption. Farther inland, on the other hand, where Americans were still *Americans,* things were so much different, so much kinder and simpler, so much easier. Schmied didn't want to lose that.

After all, it wasn't the blacks' fault that they were crammed into housing projects that seemed specifically designed to make them accustomed to prison, or engaged in soulless, mindless rote learning that reduced their abilities to think constructively. Liberal policies, intended to give them a break, were nothing more than the morphine used to diminish opium or heroin addiction—the trade of one soul-crushing addiction for another.

The phone on his desk buzzed. "Mr. Schmied, your two o'clock is here."

"Thank you, Inga," Schmied replied, pressing the speaker button. "Please hold all calls."

"Yes, sir."

Schmied pulled the cable from the back of his desk phone. He opened a locked drawer and began to scan the room with a hand-held electronic device, even as the appointment walked through the door. Schmied put his finger to his lips, sweeping the area. He then took a small white-sound generator and pressed one of its speakers to the glass. The static vibrations would make even a laser microphone incapable of picking up their conversation.

"Don't you think that's a little much?" Warren Lee asked as he closed the door firmly behind him.

Schmied raised an eyebrow. "This from you?"

Warren Lee was tall, well-tanned, brown-eyed. If Schmied hadn't known the man was half Chinese and half American, there would be little to give away that Lee was anything other than a white man. It was uncanny, but then, Schmied had little problem with Asians. After all, they had their ties to the true Aryan race, as well. For them, except for those who had fallen under the fetish of communism in mainland China, life was honor and discipline, unlike the poor rats that teemed in American cities.

"Don't give me any of that," Lee grumbled. "I have to congratulate you on this morning's event."

Schmied nodded. "It was not my personal work. I merely set the balls in motion."

"And you threw a perfect strike," Lee told him. "The pins are falling exactly where we want them."

Schmied pointed to a seat for Lee, who sat across from him. Schmied poured a fresh cup of coffee for his visitor, leaving it black and setting it on the desk in front of Lee. He poured one for himself. Alcohol had proved the downfall of too many—the downfall of entire ethnic groups—so Schmied remained a teetotaler. Control was his drug. Anything that impaired his clarity was to be avoided like the plague.

"I'm pleased for your approval," Schmied said. He took a seat and crossed his legs, steepling his fingertips. Lee began to talk about the project they had allied themselves to accomplish.

Schmied smiled pleasantly, channeling his amusement. "Precious" Lee thought he was trying to convince the Fund that he was somehow part of a Taiwanese "interest" looking for a means of discrediting the Japanese economy. If there was one thing the American Vanguard National Fund possessed, it was the resources to thoroughly vet any person walking through their doors with a scheme.

Sure, Lee's bona fides seemed to be legitimate enough to survive moderate scrutiny, but Schmied had not transformed a hundred million dollars' worth of methamphetamine and automatic weapon sale profits into a multibillion-dollar bank by only making moderate inquiries. Laundering the business of biker gangs into a respectable banking conglomerate took attention and caution equal to the audacity necessary to raise that cash.

Lee spoke eloquently, pointing out how the AVNF could further increase its earnings by investment into the project, but Schmied knew exactly what he was putting his work into.

Hiring a highly skilled group of young men from Gehenna, Texas, dressed up as consummate professionals and equipped with the best weaponry money could buy, turned the sniveling milksops of Greenpeace and PETA into victims and national heroes. The Gehenna crew struck and disappeared, utilizing every ounce of intel they could to appear like a corporate security force taking vengeance upon a group of rabble rousers.

Already, donations to both groups had doubled, and the liberal cable stations were demanding the renunciation of diplomatic ties to Japan. Schmied's investments in Japanese businesses had quickly been sold off, filtered through dummy corporations, so that he wouldn't take a bath in his own stock department. He'd turned that influx of money around deftly. Everything the AVNF made would stay firmly in the pocket of true American patriots. Let China's SAD—the red Communist version of the CIA or the older KGB—continue to bluster and boast of the profits to be earned. It only confirmed the truth that the so-called socialists were simply common thugs, centralizing money and power for themselves. There was only greed, and SAD's greed was going to sate itself on the wounded, floundering whale that had been Japan.

Schmied was enjoying the crumbs torn off into the water by scavengers tearing at the bloody carcass. Now that the blood was in the water, every opportunist in the ocean was circling, looking for a bite of that thick, succulent blubber.

Schmied blinked and laughed at himself. The allusion to the dying whale must have been unavoidable, given the targets of those first anti-shipping missiles.

"Mr. Schmied?" Lee asked.

"I'm sorry," the "banker" answered. "I just had a mental image cross my mind."

"Oh?" Lee inquired. "What mental image?"

"Japan as a wounded whale. And you and I, Mr. Lee, are the sharks waiting to dig in for the feast."

Lee smiled. "I see."

"I just want to know what we can do to tie in the Iranians to one side or the other," Schmied said. "They will be an unavoidable link in the chain."

"Trust me, Mr. Schmied," Lee offered. "We have the perfect personages to take the fall for this."

Schmied tilted his head. "Let me guess. Iran is currently one of the nations exporting liquid natural gas to Japan, having doubled it in 2013. Someone is attempting to hurt Iran's petro-bucks, which means we can cast suspicion on Israel."

Lee's eyebrows rose in surprise. "How very perceptive…"

Schmied waved it off. "You sit behind a desk like this one, you know which way the money flows. Besides, one of the problems with Japan in international circles is its ignorance of Iranian sanctions. If anyone wanted to hurt Iran, taking a few points off the yen would be one of the best ways to do it."

Lee chuckled. "Most canny."

"Yeah." If there was one thing Schmied didn't appreciate, it was smoke being blown up his ass, and Lee seemed to have backed a foundry chimney between Schmied's cheeks.

The business speak was on autopilot, all the while allowing the AVNF president to channel his thoughts into what dilemma he'd run into if he hadn't kept the Chinese under tight wraps. So far, the Gehenna commandos were lost in the wind. It was a shame that a proud

American warrior patriot had to take escape-and-evasion precautions in the land of his birth, but then Schmied realized that America, as it stood now, was very far from that. So-called conservatives were engaging in invasions of privacy and propriety that they accused their liberal counterparts of doing.

Schmied had an enemy of his country, moving in close, assuming that he was clueless.

So Schmied would feed the bastard all the rope he needed. And, in the process, an economic powerhouse that had drained American money for decades would end up crippled. He had little doubt a political rival would take the blame, forcing the United States to become stronger, to stand up under its own power.

"I suppose you'll be needing something to show Iran as a victim, as well," Schmied said.

"We have something in line for that," Lee answered.

"Just make certain it's clean," Schmied told him. "We're skating a dangerous edge here."

The Chinese "businessman" nodded in agreement. "Don't worry."

Schmied bristled. "Don't worry" was the lie spoken by a man seeking to undermine you; a deception intended to disarm and leave vulnerable. The day that Schmied wouldn't worry was to be the minute he stopped breathing.

Lee's breathing would end long, long before that.

THE D.C. METRO POLICE were all too cooperative with Carl Lyons, Rosario Blancanales and Hermann Schwarz as the three men of Able Team arrived on the scene. The flash of Justice Department Special Agent badges garnered cooperation from the police who'd turned this stretch of side street into a crime scene.

Lyons, the Able Team leader, was a big man; six feet in height, fair hair contrasting against weathered skin that was drawn tautly across a broad-shouldered, muscular frame. The former Los Angeles police officer had very little body fat and his jacket was cut perfectly so that he could conceal a pair of powerful handguns—a Smith & Wesson .45 auto in a shoulder holster and an alloy-framed, 8-shot .357 Magnum revolver tucked into a pancake holster—just behind his right hip. Lyons was not someone who was known for taking half measures, and though he regretted leaving the long guns behind in the Able Team van, the two big guns were backed up by two Airweight revolvers, a knife around his neck, with another folding blade in his trousers' pocket and a Taser in a cross-draw holster.

Just because the violence had exploded and faded only a couple of hours before did not mean lightning would not strike twice.

Hermann "Gadgets" Schwarz was smaller than Lyons, shorter by two inches, but lighter than the former football player by a good piece. Schwarz was the definition of average, everything spectacular about him hidden beneath slender limbs, brown hair and brown eyes. Schwarz had been part of the elite U.S. Army Rangers, but his physique was one of sleekness and efficiency. He had strength in his arms and legs, but it was not tied up in the same bulging, rippling mass of musculature that the Able Team leader's bulk was carved from. Even so, Schwarz's greatest ability was his mind. He was a certified genius, having a vast array of scientific skills, being versed in areas of expertise as diverse as nanotechnology and various Eastern Tao's.

Lyons likened Schwarz to a hyperactive puppy, always throwing himself into each new project with glee and boundless energy. Whether it was designing a new homing system for a missile, hacking features in computer and telephone operating systems or discussing philosophy with Blancanales, Schwarz was rarely calm and still. Even when he said not a word, the genius was thinking, observing, applying his intellect with the skill and precision of a surgeon, dissecting the universe around him down to the last molecule.

Rosario Blancanales was the eldest of the three men. He looked older thanks to his weathered features, displaying more wrinkles than the others and his premature gray-white hair. However, doubts of the man's fitness for duty were dispelled by watching him move with grace and energy. Smooth of tongue and easy in manner, Blancanales often served as the spokesman and the negotiator for Able Team, earning him the dubious title of "Politician." Blancanales had been through the Green Berets' Robin Sage, and while he was no slouch in the application of force and violence, he was also masterful in the use of diplomacy and conversation.

Able Team possessed a dynamic of mind, body and spirit that turned the trio into one of the finest covert action teams in the world.

Once more, Lyons looked at the chalk outlines of murdered brothers behind the badge. D.C. cops and Secret Service personnel had lost their lives while attempting to prevent the cold-blooded murders of a group of reactionary protesters irate at Japan's appeal to the White House in the court of world opinion.

Lyons and Schwarz did not need to determine what to look for as they surveyed the site of the massacre. They'd been through this too many times, applying their knowledge, picking up hints and clues as to whom or what could have been behind the attack.

Certainly the Secret Service detail had given some details of the attackers, but Schwarz had military experience that allowed him to see things outside the box that law enforcement could think of. Hell, Schwarz had experience that allowed him to survey a battle and pick up almost impossible details thanks to his razor-sharp mind.

The whole universe was a box the genius could maneuver around and examine, peering into individual compartments and collating them with the barest threads of coincidence.

In the meantime Lyons had been to more than enough murder scenes to have an intuitive feel for the kind of attackers. Already he had a sense of focused rage. The men behind the attack were disciplined, firing short bursts, staying in cover and never staying still long enough to become a target. But there was something extra here. There was an underlying anger, a hatred of the protesters that went beyond the need to create dead bodies for the sake of a political message.

Lyons could tell just by looking at the wound patterns on the bodies in CSI digital photographs transmitted to his tablet.

It was one thing to shoot a man to end his life.

It was another to destroy the face of a human being, or to ravage the genitals of another with gunfire. There was both racial and sexual rage at work.

The three black men who were victims of gunfire—two protesters and one D.C. policeman—had been shot, but then also laid into with gunfire that shredded their genitalia. Lyons also noticed the destruction of the breasts of each of the women who had been shot. Five total. One woman survived by the grace of being hit from the side, the curve of her ribs deflecting bullets from her internal organs.

Lyons clenched his jaw.

The FBI's Behavioral Science Unit investigators were going over the scene and Lyons stood with them. The back and forth showed a level of violence reserved for hate crimes. Whoever was involved in the shootings had wanted to emasculate the black men in their sights, but at least two of the shooters displayed a deep misogyny, attacking the most feminine parts of the female protesters' anatomy.

Schwarz came closer to Lyons and the two Able Team investigators got to talking.

"This looks like a coordinated military assault," Lyons said.

"Looks like it indeed," Schwarz replied. "You've noticed the precision of the shooting, even in the instances where they're punishing their targets of opportunity."

Lyons nodded.

"The shooters have great marksmanship, but there's cruelty in there," Schwarz admitted. "This wasn't typical combat. I'm betting you noticed the injuries on the blacks and the women?"

"BSU is in agreement," Lyons told him.

Schwarz shook his head. "The vibe of this attack is all wrong for a hired kill. It's something pretty damned sick. These aren't ex-military, but they have been organized by a military mind. Their commander has found a hatred he could focus into a tool of opportunity."

"Paramilitary group. Not private security—too many of them are actual military or police. Someone with this kind of bigoted rage is not going to last too long on a force or in the service with that bubbling below the surface," Lyons said.

Schwarz shook his head. "For all the flack private military companies get, they have some strict psychological and background checks for their hires. Given the different cities, the different working conditions, bigots are not going to cooperate well with professionals no matter what their skin color."

"I sure as hell wouldn't want to be with them," Lyons added. "Add money, training and skill, and we've narrowed down the field considerably."

"White group. Definite cash. They're using actual 5.56 mm, not civilian .223 Remington," Schwarz noted. "And the missile looks like an FGM-172B."

"English," Lyons said.

"One of the two warheads developed for the SRAW—short-range assault weapon. It's a multipurpose fragmentation munition designed for anti-personnel as well as use against thin-skinned targets," Schwarz said. On his tablet, he called up the detonation of the police car as recorded on multiple surveillance cameras that watched the scene.

"We don't have good visuals on the shooters. Their heads were covered, as were their eyes, and they were driving fast enough to not give cameras time to focus," Schwarz added. "They could be any nationality short of Pakistani in skin tone. Also, no apparent tattoos visible, even with short sleeves."

"Skinhead gangs, bikers and such trend toward that, but only if they've actually been in prison," Lyons mentioned. "These could be free-born fanatics."

"I was thinking the same," Schwarz answered. "Like the Cosmic Church, which fostered the National Resistance."

"Which in turn gave birth to our dear friends, the Aryan Right Coalition," Lyons growled.

"We've got work to do on narrowing this down," Schwarz said. "I'm sending the data we've collected through to the Farm."

Lyons nodded. "Good. The sooner we get to smack answers out of someone, the sooner we get started."

Schwarz managed a weak smile. "Anyone tell you that you're sexy when you're a bloodthirsty avenger?"

"Not this week," Lyons answered. "But it's only Tuesday."

CHAPTER THREE

It was early evening when three members of Phoenix Force and *Dragonfin* went wheels up from Langley Air Force Base on board the C-17 Globemaster.

The C-17 was on loan from the United States Air Force Reserve, and the paperwork for the flight stated that the craft was taking supplies to MacMurdo Station, off the Ross Ice Shelf where the *Saburou Maru* had been attacked and sunk. With that cover, every subsequent trip would be off the books.

David McCarter overlooked the *Dragonfin,* running his fingers across its smooth, flat-black hull. The boat had originally been scheduled to auction after the Drug Enforcement Agency had captured it from drug smugglers. Its hold had carried two tons of cocaine. Even with all of that bulk, with its twin motors it was capable of 80 miles per hour. It was a new generation of cigarette boat.

Catamaran, McCarter reminded himself, not cigarette. The lads would have a fit over you misidentifying their little canoe.

His friends Calvin James and Rafael Encizo, both sturdy sailors—James tall and raw-boned, Encizo stocky and stout—had been overjoyed at the acquisition of a "go-fast" boat by Stony Man Farm.

Go-fasts were originally meant, and still utilized, in sports racing, but as with all things legal and legitimate, greedy men saw other uses for them. For years, drug smugglers had utilized the amazingly fast, low-profile craft for ferrying tons of drugs across international waters. While not as fast as a helicopter, "go-fasts" were still far swifter than any cutters or interceptor boats except for those craft also based on racing designs. For pure racing purposes, stripped down to cockpit, fuel cells and engines, the design on this particular catamaran hull projected a top speed of more than 200 miles per hour.

This particular beast had been specifically designed for long-haul smuggling and defense of its contraband. It was meant to counter U.S. Coast Guard Deployable Pursuit boats. To add to the survivability of cargo and space, *Dragonfin* was a twin-hulled craft. On the bottom there were two slim-line keels, where the Mercury drives were housed. Each was capable of 1,000 horsepower. For long range, the engines were equipped with four 200-gallon fuel cells. With a relatively sedate cruising speed, those cells would give it phenomenal range, but when it came to putting the throttle to full, they would tear along, as equipped, at more than 180 miles per hour. They sacrificed about thirty miles per hour with combat turrets for M-2 Browning machine guns, Mk 19 automatic grenade launchers and an M-242 Bushmaster 25 mm cannon, all operated by remote control.

With those weapons installed, *Dragonfin* could engage targets at up to almost two miles.

Aside from the turrets, *Dragonfin* had also been upgraded with a Kevlar polymer coating on the hull, which served to minimize the radar signature of the craft on top of the waves. Its sleek, almost space-fighter-looking design would also be hard to make out against the ocean, thanks to the dark blue mottled-camouflage patterns set into the coating. When they'd first seen it, it had been painted jet black by the smugglers, which almost was good enough.

Almost, however, hadn't kept the boat from being captured or appropriated by Stony Man Farm.

Underneath, there were streamlined housings for torpedoes, and *Dragonfin* had four of those deadly fish held in reserve just in case their targets had more than two inches of rolled homogeneous steel armor. The most important addition, however, was a communications system that would keep them in satellite contact with Stony Man Farm, allowing them real-time satellite imagery and telemetry to track any target they needed.

The Globemaster would give them near-speed-of-sound transit around the planet if necessary in their hunt for the attackers of the Japanese whaling ship.

James, Encizo and McCarter were to be the three-man crew for this journey. While the burly Gary Manning and the young, athletic T. J. Hawkins would be going to Japan to investigate possible intrigue in that country. McCarter's two friends, having spent years of their lives working with boats and diving, would be acting to help McCarter crew *Dragonfin*. It was a bit of a letdown, as both James and Encizo were adept at Japanese language and culture to some degree; James from the time he'd spent in Japan while in the United States Navy, Encizo from his close friendship with deceased Phoenix Force operative Keio Ohara.

As it was, Gary Manning had also had a good, close friendship with Ohara, often working hand in hand with the electronics expert; his skill with the language would be bolstered by a local asset of Phoenix Force's, a man named John Trent.

It only made sense, the Stony Man action and cybernetics teams had determined, that if there was a plot afoot aimed at discrediting Japan's credibility and destroying their ships, there would be clues to be garnered on Japanese soil. While McCarter and the *Dragonfin* crew went to the high seas to hunt and destroy the armed ships responsible for hundreds of sailors murdered, Manning, Hawkins and Trent would operate together and look for malicious agents on land.

McCarter didn't envy Able Team. The three of them were going after a group of sadistic murderers who'd tried to make it look as if Japan was smothering dissent with their whaling program with hired killers. The team had a handle on who might have been hired to make the bloody assault only a few hundred yards from the White House, but once again, they'd be diving into the deadly, murky world of American white supremacist groups.

Not that life on *Dragonfin* would be fun and games. The Antarctic Ocean was a cold place and while the ship had amenities for long-distance travel, thanks to the cocaine smugglers before them, McCarter and his allies would be spending twenty-four hours a day in their immersion survival suits, like those worn on arctic fishing boats. They'd also have to eat MREs—meals ready to eat.

For now, though, McCarter and his partners would be heading to the Ross Sea and, hopefully, the trail of the ship killers would not have gone too cold.

McCarter grimaced at that thought. The Ross Sea is as cold as hell. An' us lucky blokes have to find a needle in that haystack.

GARY MANNING WAS glad that this was a private jet, allowing him to spend time working on his tablet computer, checking stock news, paying particularly close attention to the Tokyo exchange. While the Farm's cybernetics crew was giving a token effort toward monitoring any unusual purchases or sell-offs in relation to Japan's economy, they were also working on trailing the money for the hired gunmen, analyzing intel on fugitives and scanning the Antarctic and Pacific oceans for signs of the marauders and their Iranian-owned, Chinese-designed, ship-killing missiles.

Manning knew that if there was one thing the members of the Stony Man action teams were chosen for, it was for more than just their raw ability to aim a gun and fire. The members of Phoenix Force and Able Team had among their numbers experts in multiple fields. Here, though they were a tad underutilized, Manning's business acumen would come in handy.

He looked in parallel market listings, utilizing his data from the S&P Asia 50, which allowed him glimpses at Japan's Topix and Nikkei 225, and the dozens of markets in Singapore, such as the FTSE group. Singapore would likely be the source of insider trading on any pan-Asian economic assault, since the FTSE had twenty markets in Southeast Asia itself, covering China as a proxy.

Being thorough, he also glanced at Australia's S&P indexes. There were plenty of forces in the world market that would like to see Japan take a few shots to weaken the yen, and not all of them had to do with Communist China, which had its own trinity of indexes for international trade. Capitalism, Manning found, was still a major factor on what should have been the worlds behind the Iron and Bamboo curtains. Money and resources still made the world go around, still got things done, and no amount of socialist idealism—of which the Soviet Union was hardly an exemplar—changed the balance of supply and demand.

There was movement behind Manning and he looked into the face of the Texan joining him on this journey to

Tokyo. Even Thomas Jackson Hawkins, with his staunch military background—as both a member of the 75th Rangers and the Special Forces Operational Detachment Delta—had skills far and beyond merely being a gunman. It had been a while since Phoenix Force had had an electronics expert on the team, and Hawkins was up to date on twenty-first-century communications technology, as well as being one of the finest parachutists and airborne deployment specialists in the world. Hawkins was also the youngest member of the team, the most recent addition to the five-man "foreign legion" of the Sensitive Operations Group.

Hawkins chewed on some gum, which Manning was glad for. Inside the jet's cabin, Hawkins's preference for a pinch of "chaw" would have made him more than a little nauseated. Fortunately, T.J.'s training and discipline allowed him to swap out the ugly chewing tobacco for something that didn't smell so much, nor require a cup to spit the gooey sap into.

Gary Manning was the second oldest member of Phoenix Force, right after Rafael Encizo, but he looked as if he only had five years on Hawkins due to the fact that Manning was a fitness fanatic. Underneath Manning's suit, tailored to make him inconspicuous and innocuous, his body was sculpted muscle from regular five-mile, early morning runs and weight-lifting sessions where he could bench press up to 515 pounds. At six feet, with close and neatly trimmed hair, Manning's age was indistinguishable, even by friends who knew him closely.

"You have the body of an eighteen-year-old football player and the brains of a seventy-year-old banker, hoss," Hawkins noted, looking at the trade numbers scrolling across Manning's tablet screen. "You have to give me an app for that."

Manning shrugged. "I didn't become a millionaire by not knowing my way around the market, Hawk. And no, import-export was not a code name for drug dealing."

Hawkins smirked. "Never crossed my mind, Gary. Picking up any trends?"

Manning frowned as he pored over the numbers. "Some of these economic moves are pretty damn subtle, so I have to go over months of data."

Hawkins nodded. "Stop all this thrilling action. My heart can't take it."

"Did I mention I was a millionaire?" Manning asked. "I like going over data."

Hawkins shrugged. "How many hours until Tokyo?"

"Ten," Manning returned.

Hawkins sighed. "I'll get some early sleep, then check out our gear."

"Do what you have to," Manning said, returning to the numbers and trends on the screen. He used his stylus to mark points that might have links to avenues of potential insider trading or hedging of bets toward the economic disruption of Japan. Attacking any of the G8 nations with intent to cause financial ruin was not merely a risky proposition, it was also potentially suicidal. Many of these manipulative plots could backfire, turning a profit into their own nosedive.

The Soviet Union had attempted such a plot against the United States's economy and found itself taking a bath, destroying the integrity of its own monetary value.

Manning felt bad for Hawkins, as the Texan was a man of action. While the Canadian himself was someone who was equally adept in the rough and tumble of field operations, Manning's talents could be used, at least in this instance. Like Hawkins, Manning's brain was always in motion, always looking for patterns that would indicate hidden dangers, but inside the belly of a jet, there was only waiting, at least where Hawkins was concerned.

It couldn't have been easy, but the Texan closed his eyes and was immediately off to slumber.

If he couldn't keep his mind active, Manning knew he'd store energy, rest and prepare himself. They'd already been an hour on the plane and T.J. had read up on as much Japanese culture as he could endure, had enough refreshers on common Japanese phrases and been in on plenty of briefing on foreign intelligence services at work in Tokyo, their current destination.

Manning and Hawkins were "stuck" with the job of being boots on the ground in Japan for the certitude that there would be elements of the anti-Japanese conspiracy active in that country. Manning's business knowledge would give the two of them a head start on looking for angles and leads.

Would it be good enough?

Manning dismissed that thought. It *had* been enough before. Stony Man worked simply because the covert agency, despite its incredibly small size, utilized every asset it could assemble.

Thinking outside the box, while being intimately aware of the makeup of said container, was one way in which the teams could intercede and defeat threatening forces.

So far, it had worked.

Manning didn't intend to fail for lack of effort.

BARBARA PRICE WAS glad that Phoenix Force was off and away, and before the day was over, one half would be in the Ross Sea, seeking out the lethal marauders. Manning and Hawkins were on their way to Japan to seek out potential suspects working within the country. Able Team, at home, was on the hunt for those who'd staged a massacre mere hundreds of yards from the President and a contingent of diplomats.

As it was, the international scene and local press were talking about the White House crisis and how Japanese "big business" had the nerve to murder honest Americans in the middle of its capital city. That point of view was coming from the left, looking for a "good war," while the right buckled down on how the U.S. administration was antibusiness and was using the crisis for the sake of painting "job makers" as the criminals.

Price wrinkled her nose. Once upon a time, there was such a thing as a news cycle, where events were reported and later analyzed to find meaning. But now, in the parade of propaganda, the truth was lost. American was pitted against American, leading the more paranoid of commentators to foresee a civil war. Such a fomentation of hostility, where one wing of philosophy saw the other as utterly evil, despite evidence of the truth, was an abomination that Stony Man sought to battle. Far too many times the teams had seen an attempt to manipulate public opinion to the point of fracturing societies, to inspire wars between nations. Such trickery was so commonplace, Price had developed an armor against leaping to unfounded accusations. She didn't develop an opinion without conclusive facts.

The Stony Man intel would never be allowed into a court of law, but their evidence was always succinct and conclusive to the point that when they took action against the guilty, there would be no mistakes. Every time Able Team and Phoenix Force went into action, they battled with clear consciences. Their foes were not scapegoats, but those who actually acted to harm innocent noncom-

batants or the madmen who sought to secure profit and
power from acts of terror and mayhem.

Then again, Price knew that her job wasn't to sell com-
mercial time to fatten the pockets of media moguls. Her
job was to help protect America, her allies, the whole of
the world at times. She and the cybernetics crew looked at
raw data and events. They could tell that poverty and or-
phanhood were factors that gave violent gangs and terrorist groups thousands of recruits yearly for their personal
shock troopers. Hamas soldiers didn't stem from Israeli
occupation, but from the poverty caused by the strife in
the region. Poor and homeless, often growing up without fathers or mothers or both, these young people were
ripe for transforming from "victims" into "avengers."

Smart, devious bastards located a bumper crop of
foot soldiers to twist to their cause, and they swooped
in, forming modern-day groups such as the Ku Klux
Klan, the Bloods, the Islamic Jihad. Give a man without
life a target for his anger, a reason for his failures, and
you could fill an army's ranks. Trailer parks. Occupied
slums. Inner cities ruled by drug lords. Nations deprived
of education.

Because of this continuum of ignorance, of fanned
prejudices and hatreds, Stony Man was perpetually at
war.

There were billions of humans on the planet and hundreds of potential holes from which the greedy, the sociopathic and the murderous could draw upon. Finding
dupes, already led astray by fake news and overhyped
political commentary, turned the world into a factory for
fanatics and maniacs.

Price sometimes wished that she could arrange for
the cyber crew to crash some of these news stations,
bankrupting them and obliterating their influence upon

the American public. Liars of left and right persuasions would suddenly have nothing else to work with. Unfortunately such an act would be the ultimate in government censorship.

While the alarmists bellowed "Fire" in a crowded theater, pushing people to trample their neighbors in panic all for a profit, Price would not violate the Constitution in that manner. Freedom of speech also applied to blind stupidity, bigotry and prejudice, as well as lies.

"So we save the world from itself, one brushfire at a time," Price muttered.

"Feeling disgusted by the news coverage?" Kurtzman asked. The wheelchair-bound genius had rolled past her to a coffeepot to refill his mug with a splash of the black, oily, high-octane gruel they jokingly referred to as coffee. It tasted terrible, but it packed the punch of a rocket launcher, enabling the cyber team to withstand hours of hacking and data research.

Price glowered.

"I know. I know. It's not news," Kurtzman amended. "But not everyone has access to raw data like we do."

"No," Price answered. "But that's still not an excuse for willful deception of millions of viewers."

Kurtzman shook his head, agreeing with her with a simple frown. Thickly bearded and with arms and a chest of solid muscle, the leader of the cyber team had earned the nickname "Bear" long before he'd taken a bullet to the spine. Price was reminded of the tales of Native Americans, granting bears great, nearly mystical wisdom, as well as patience. Kurtzman had a calming effect on her. "Unless we catch these people actively destroying Americans, we can't go after them. But when they do, we'll drop on them like a ton of bricks."

Price took a deep breath. She poured herself a mug of

the crap they called coffee. She'd need the energy, despite the fact that she had a thermos of homemade java, creamed and sweetened to her particular biases. "Sometimes, though, you have to wonder if these crazed morons aren't just deliberately shoveling fuel onto the fire."

"I know how you feel," Kurtzman told her. "That's why I always cast an eye toward that avenue. One day, we'll strike gold."

Price narrowed her eyes. "I'll settle for last blood."

CHAPTER FOUR

Rosario Blancanales drove the Able Team van, a mobile headquarters for the team that also served as armory, electronics locker, communications nerve center and occasionally the biggest hunk of cover that they could find. The van, on the outside, resembled any other generic professional van, complete with the stylish logo of an official-sounding company. Dark brown, with gold-colored lettering, the delivery vehicle was invisible and unnoticeable in residential and professional neighborhoods. The official term—aluminum walk-in van—had become so much a part of the public consciousness that the vehicles, for all intents and purposes, were ignored, unless rolling up for a specific delivery.

However, Able Team's van was made of much more than aluminum. Inside the outer shell there were sandwiched layers of Kevlar weave and carbon fiber sheets. It wasn't Chobham armor, but Carl Lyons and Stony Man Farm armorer John "Cowboy" Kissinger had fired at the interior plating with everything up to a .50 BMG rifle and the shell held together.

In terms of a communications suite and computer center, Hermann Schwarz and the rest of the Stony Man cybernetics crew had developed the "Suitcase." Utilizing solid-state drives for instant startup and file access, as well as lack of vulnerability to electromagnetic interference, the case contained the most powerful satellite uplink in the smallest size possible. There were few places on Earth the team couldn't reach twenty-four hours a day.

Combined with powerful processors and having a satellite computer link to the Farm, the case could provide real-time data and electronic intel from anywhere around the globe. A second variant of the Suitcase had been installed on *Dragonfin,* the rocket-fast catamaran Phoenix Force had taken to the Ross Sea.

Surveillance devices were stored in the van in out-of-the-way cabinets behind a camouflage made from cartons, wires and stray screws and bolts. Firearms and ammunitions were similarly obfuscated. The Able van was as close to a golf bag full of rifles as Blancanales once joked about. Sniper rifles, full-auto M-4s, grenade launchers, SMGs, shotguns and pistols were set up for each of the team members, including sufficient ammunition for each. The heavy armor was not merely for protecting the team if it came under attack, it was also to shield and protect cakes of high explosive and compact shoulder-mounted munitions.

The last thing that Stony Man Farm needed was a van equipped with so much firepower to take a wrong bullet or a bad hit and blow up half a city block. It helped that the high explosives were kept in a fireproof container and that modern plastic composition explosives didn't detonate due to shock or to heat. The detonators were even better protected and would only generate sufficient force to activate the C-4 if inserted within the puttylike explosive.

Blancanales was not unarmed. He had his Able Team-issued sidearm, a Smith & Wesson MP-45 with a threaded muzzle addition and a knob to protect the threads. In a moment, if necessary, he could put a suppressor on the M&P and be ready for stealth without giving up stopping power. Since he was on driver duty, he wore it in a shoulder holster, balanced out by three 10-round magazine pouches on the other side under his jacket, with the option of swapping them out for 14-shot extended mags.

Blancanales had originally been a fan of the Colt Government Model .45 for his military career, but the MP's thumb safety worked exactly the same as his locked-and-cocked Colt, held three more cartridges in the magazine than the Colt and was much lighter and handier than the steel-framed pistol. With the trigger made crisp yet reliable, the handgun was accurate. The only thing he'd given up was a half inch of barrel length, which was returned to the pistol by its suppressor-ready pipe.

It wasn't a rifle, but Blancanales didn't feel undergunned with more than forty rounds of hot .45 ACP hollowpoints ready to launch at the flick of his thumb.

Tucked down next to his leg and well out of sight from anyone peering into the cab of the van, Blancanales had a longer range weapon: a KRISS submachine gun, also in .45 ACP. With the presence of its folded shoulder stock, it had the potential for better accuracy at longer range. In its stowed condition, it was the size of a small briefcase. With the stock snapped out, it was twice as long, but a stable, tack-driving weapon capable of hammering out bursts of heavy slugs that could knock down a target with authority out to 150 yards, much like the old Tommy guns and M-3 Grease guns of World War II, except in a lighter, more concealable package.

Out of sight, but not far from reach, was the main weapon Blancanales would employ if things went wrong. It was similar to the M-16 he'd utilized as a Ranger, but the official U.S. Army designation was the Squad Designated Marksman Rifle—SDM-R for short. It was not a compact weapon, complete with the full 20-inch barrel that originally rode on the M-16, which gave Blancanales confidence in its 5.56 mm rifle round. That length gave it an effective range of 660 yards, which the ACOG—advanced combat optical gunsight—on top could easily handle using its 1.5-6x magnification.

Having reached their destination, Blancanales hung back in the van, this firepower on hand, keeping over-watch for his partners, Hermann Schwarz and Carl Lyons, as they approached the small clubhouse. The two men were Caucasian, Schwarz with tousled brown hair and a thick mustache, Lyons tall, blond and blue-eyed. Even with his skin burned to a deep tan, Lyons was an Aryan's dream.

However the men in the clubhouse were members of the Heathens Motorcycle Club, an all-white outlaw gang that stretched from Maryland to New York with more than five hundred members. Blancanales had learned all the facts about the Heathens thanks to Lyons's nearly obsessive need to study up on their potential opposition.

The Heathens had formed ties with the White Family, another East Coast gang started within the prison system of Maryland. White Family members released from prison could always find a safe haven at a Heathens club-house if they couldn't reach an appropriate Arrangement compound. The Arrangement was the name chosen by the Maryland "alumnus" of the federal prison system, and where they recruited young, disenfranchised white men and women to the cause of a "strong, free society."

That wouldn't have been a reason to hate them, but the Arrangement wanted a society where all Hispanics were treated as if they weren't American-born citizens, like Blancanales's younger siblings or other naturalized citizens such as himself. Yes, he and his family had come to

America on a rubber raft, braving a rough, terrible ocean, but they'd immediately gone to the effort of achieving citizenship.

The Heathens were in a serious conflict with the Khan's Hispanic biker gang from down the coast, so their allegiance with the Arrangement was their ticket toward armed conflict. The Arrangement benefited, as they were able to cook tons of meth that the Heathens readily distributed. The Heathens also were able to bring in the kind of weaponry the Arrangement could utilize in its war for national "purity."

Lyons and Schwarz were each adorned with motion-picture-quality tattoo appliqués on their arms and necks, identifying them as part of the RLR West Coast gang Lyons had blown through on a prior mission—the Reich Low Riders. It was a risky proposition, but the two of them were rough and tumble, and had gone through this ruse before. The presence of the adhesive, skinlike swatches that made them look all inked up, would help. Few in law enforcement would actually attempt to wear prison tats.

And if things didn't work out, well, Blancanales was Able Team's designated marksman and well-equipped for the task.

But Able Team was there for information, not a body count.

ON POINT, CARL LYONS stank of sweat and gasoline. He was clad in dingy, dirt-ground jeans, scuffed boots and a hole-riddled T-shirt underneath the denim vest that sported his colors and Los Angeles "rocker."

Hermann Schwarz had gone for a leather jacket rather than the denim vest. He also had spurs clamped to the heel of one of his boots. The stirrup that connected the spur to the boot was solid steel, as was the bar surrounding the multi-tined star on its axle.

Lyons knew men who wore spurs. A spin kick with one of those would slice a face in two or rend someone ear to ear. It was the perfect accessory for a biker thug, and Schwarz was adept with kicks. Even as they walked in, more than one set of eyes dropped to the jingling metal on Schwarz's right boot. Cold recognition flared in their faces.

One man spoke up as the two Able Team undercover operatives entered. "RLRs? You're far from home."

"Would have thought this a safe harbor," Lyons returned. He sized up the speaker, well more than six feet in height, with a reddish-blond beard and a scalp that was cleanly shaved, not even stubble on top. Lyons himself was a big man, but this guy had between twenty-five and forty pounds on him, depending on what he was like under his riding gear. Like Lyons, his arms were bare, displaying not only ink that told tales of his life as a biker and in prison, but muscles like knotted oak branches. Leather straps surrounded the man's wrists and his green eyes glared with suspicion and hatred.

"Our berths are full, California," the Heathens leader said. "But you can sit for a drink if you behave."

Lyons sneered, looking the bald man over. "Behave?"

"No crippling, maiming or killing. You'll get it back proper for every punch in the face," the biker told him.

"You guys are no damn fun," Lyons grumbled.

The leader laughed. "I'm Crunch."

"Irons," Lyons returned, holding out his hand. The two met halfway, tugging each other close with knuckle-cracking grasps and slapping each other on the shoulder. Conversations and music rose from the tension. "This is Geek."

Crunch looked Schwarz over. "Why 'Geek'?"

"Take your pick. I like chicken heads and I like radios," Schwarz answered. "Why do your prospects look so squirrelly?"

Crunch rolled his eyes. "There's heat coming down all around this part of the state since that shoot-up in D.C. An' for some reason, the pigs think one of us might have been involved."

"Heat over a buncha seal-humpin' hippies?" Schwarz asked in his Geek guise.

Crunch shrugged. "I'd take a piece of that pussy action myself, but cops got smoked, too. Them's the ones which got the bacon sizzling."

Lyons shook his head, as if in agreement with the disgust over such a fuss over the protesters. Of course, being a lawman for most of his adult life left him with a queasy disdain for this smelly asshole Crunch and his slurs against fallen lawmen, especially those who had been gunned down in the performance of their duties.

Still, he was thankful to Crunch for reminding him that the men around them, despite their "welcoming" demeanor, were nothing less than thugs who had no regard for law or civilization.

"What brings you two here?" Crunch asked.

"We're feeling too naked," Schwarz answered. "Hoping for something more than pistols. A friend said this is a good place to go."

Crunch narrowed his eyes toward Geek. "A friend?"

"Bones," Lyons returned. "Heard of him?"

"He got pinched a while back," Crunch said. "But he's got some cred here in the east."

Of course Bones has cred here, Lyons thought. I went over his rap sheet specifically in case I needed to infiltrate you animals ever again.

"How do you know him?" Crunch added as a question.

"I prospected under him," Lyons said. "He jumped me in, too."

Crunch nodded.

Lyons had done his homework on this particular thug, having placed him from the files he'd studied in preparation for this infiltration. Crunch had been born Alphonse MacCafferty. The Irish was evident in his beard and the few splotches of freckles that showed through the sleeves of tattoos up and down his arms. Crunch had plenty of tags for assault, but he'd managed to beat drug and arms traffic raps, thanks to Arrangement-supplied lawyers. He'd also been a person of interest in at least four murders, but nothing had stuck to the bald biker.

The .357 Magnum on his hip, a Blackhawk single-action revolver, showed he meant business in terms of ending a shootout with a minimum amount of stops. Lyons had his own Ruger, the double-action GP-100 with a six-inch barrel. Crunch eyed the revolver and nodded with approval, making Lyons feel nauseated. He didn't allow it to show in his features, though. He'd spent time working as an undercover agent for the FBI after his stint with the LAPD, and his control was ironclad. But when it came time to break this little clubhouse open, Lyons had plenty of fuel for his berserker rage.

"Good to see at least one of you queer-coasters like American iron," Crunch said, acknowledging the weapon on Lyons's hip, then looking askance toward Schwarz and his shoulder-holstered Beretta, unmistakable for its magazine base pad and the lanyard ring behind it.

Carrying or riding anything that wasn't American-made was forbidden among bikers, which was why they'd pulled up in a rented Jeep Cherokee rather than rented "rice burners" aka Japanese-built motorcycles. As big and brawny as Honda could make a motor bike, it still was not an American-made Harley-Davidson. There wasn't one of these men who would spare more than a second glance at a foreign-made weapon or vehicle.

Schwarz had a Beretta M-9 A-1, which thankfully had Made in the U.S.A. scrawled on its slide, even though Lyons was fully aware that some might turn up their nose at him for carrying a gun with an Italian name.

"What part of 'Made in the U.S.A.' don't you understand?" Schwarz asked nonchalantly. He twisted the cap off a beer and took a drag on it. "'Sides, good enough for Uncle Sam, good enough for me."

Crunch shook his head. "Stupid European guns. Not even in a proper caliber."

"So give us something," Lyons returned. "We've got the cash."

"What are you looking for?" Crunch asked.

"I'm not looking to screw around with follow-up shots," Lyons answered. "I'm here for 'fast-and-dirty and then get the hell home.'"

Crunch nodded. "You want 12-gauge air-conditioning, then."

Lyons smirked. "You get me, brother. You really get me."

"What about the guy with the pellet gun?" Crunch asked.

"He digs .22s," Lyons said with an eye roll.

Crunch leered over at Schwarz. "Poodle shooters and pasta pistols. You need a new partner."

"Despite his wimpy tastes, I'll keep him," Lyons returned. "He might have to shoot someone five or six times, but he always has my back."

"That's a good reason to keep him around," Crunch

said. "Listen, even our semi-only ARs are pulled for important stuff. I only have shotguns."

Lyons narrowed his eyes. "Things that bad, eh?"

"You have no idea, and you never will," Crunch returned. "Don't dig in our business."

Lyons shook his head. "I don't shit where I eat."

"That's a rare admirable quality," Crunch said. "Rucks, go get these two a couple of 870s from the locker. How much ammo you gonna need?"

Schwarz spoke up. "Twenty apiece. If we need more than that, we're dead, anyway."

"Says the faggot who needs fifteen in a clip," Rucks chuckled.

Schwarz was not the biggest or strongest member of Able Team, but he moved with such fluid grace and swiftness that no one in the clubhouse even saw him go from lounging on his tilted chair, heels crossed on the table in front of him to standing over Rucks, pushing the biker's head to the floor with one hand. Lyons knew the move that kept the smart-mouth pinned. He could see Gadgets's two first knuckles up under Rucks's Adam's apple, the other two fingers extended and pressed against the nerve junction under his jawbone.

The Heathens wise-ass now had trouble breathing, his airway pressed down upon. The real paralyzing pressure, however, came from the ring finger and pinkie jammed against the cluster of nerves and juncture of blood vessels at that part of his body. Rucks's eyes were wide, his mouth moving, gaping like a fish out of water.

"You better be talking about a cigarette," Schwarz growled as he loomed over the biker.

Rucks croaked, the knuckles paralyzing his larynx, even as Lyons knew the blood flow to his brain was being interrupted. A few more moments and he'd be unconscious. It wasn't as if Schwarz cared if someone thought he was gay, but in the role of a bad-ass, government-hating biker thug, the merest mention of his lack of manhood should have made him fly off the handle.

Anchoring a man to the floor by his throat with one hand wasn't flying off the handle, but eyes widened all around the scene.

"Now you know why he only needs small stuff," Lyons said nonchalantly. "Twenty sounds right."

"Have your boy let my man go," Crunch said.

Lyons nodded to Schwarz, who stood back. Rucks rubbed his throat, looking up at Schwarz.

No, Hermann Schwarz was not a big man, but he was a master of Monkey Style Kung Fu, which meant that he kept his body far more limber than anyone of his relative mass and fitness should have been. The Monkey Style was loose and agile, matching the speed and limberness of Schwarz's mind and body. Sure, Lyons snapped dimension lumber with a single punch with his choice of Shotokan Karate, but he didn't think of his friend as a weak link, either.

"You okay, Rucks?" Crunch asked. He hadn't taken his eyes off Lyons. The bald biker was not going to give the undercover Able Team leader an opening due to a lapse of attention.

"Feel like I swallowed a pool ball," the Heathen croaked.

"You're lucky you didn't swallow your own ball sack," Schwarz told him.

"Someone get these two assholes their guns and ammo," Crunch said. "I'm getting sick of looking at these left coast pricks."

Lyons pulled a fat roll of bills from his jeans pocket.

"No. Screw it," Crunch muttered. "The RLR will owe the Heathens."

Lyons's lip curled. "And we were getting along so nicely."

True to Crunch's word, a pair of 870s and several boxes of shotgun shells were loaded into a nylon bag.

"Now blow," Crunch grumbled.

"That we'll do," Lyons returned, hefting the bag.

We'll blow you straight to hell.

THOMAS JEFFERSON HAWKINS didn't know which made him feel more naked: the lack of firearms concealed upon his person or the hostile glares when Tokyo citizens heard his Texan drawl, even if it was subdued. Both he and Gary Manning did their best to appear as innocuous as possible. So far, their mission was low-profile advanced intelligence gathering, seeking out signs of the conspiracy in Japan itself.

Unfortunately, Hawkins, even though he had a fairly good tourist vocabulary in Japanese, still had a tiny bit of that twang. Right now, the Land of the Rising Sun didn't want to suffer the presence of Americans among them. Manning, on the other hand, was less conspicuous in his mannerisms and speech. He already had a voice that sounded neutral, more reminiscent of a voice-trained news announcer who buried drawls and speech shortcuts to be accepted nationwide. As a Canadian, it was no effort for him to return to a more thick-tongued, long-voweled "Great White North" pattern of speech that divorced him from the United States of America.

Even with that, Canada was scarcely a close ally of the Japanese in regard to research whaling, even though their interaction with the nation was minimal thanks to the

U.S. and the Commonwealth of Independent States taking the brunt of any Japanese whaling in Arctic waters.

Hawkins might not have had a concealed pistol, but he was far from unarmed. Tucked inside a waistband sheath was a combat knife, while on a thong around his neck, blade up, was a talon-hooked Karambit knife.

The knife, sheathed and concealed at his waist, was an old U.S. Army Ranger favorite, the Fairbairn-Sykes. But rather than the weak-handled original, Hawkins went with the Emerson Knives' version of the fabled Ranger fighting blade. Made from one whole piece of steel, the eleven-inch-long fighting tool was slim, flat, ideal for keeping hidden, yet swift into action. A 650-pound test para-cord made up the handle, providing a sure grip and, in a pinch, a length of cord that could hold Hawkins's weight, plus that of and two other men. Double edged, with a point swelling then narrowing to a waspish waist, the F-S blade provided plenty of cutting edge for only six and a half inches of finely honed steel, and a spine tough enough to hammer through an automobile door.

The Karambit was curved like the letter *J*. The inner arc of the blade was serrated and sharpened all the way to the deadly, piercing tip at the end of its hook. As a tool, it reaped rice. As a knife, it adorned the personal battle kits of warriors as far spread as Thailand and the southern Philippines

Gary Manning, Hawkins's Phoenix Force partner, had traveled the world in the course of his various business ventures and had fleetingly even been to Southeast Asia as part of an "armed observer" mission in the Golden Triangle for the Royal Canadian Mounted Police. Manning's Japanese language and custom familiarity had been vastly enhanced by his close friendship with the late Keio Ohara.

Manning, on the experience of both Ohara and fellow Phoenix Force member Rafael Encizo, had chosen a traditional Japanese blade. Two in fact. The first was a full-length, six-inch Cold Steel Tanto knife. With a chisel point and a rigid, thick spine the Tanto had served Encizo in countless knife battles with unfailing reliability, strength and dexterity. A smaller version was on a nylon strap around Manning's muscular, bull-like neck. Built with a two-inch blade, it looked as if the knife had been punched in the nose and had swollen to three times its normal thickness, but its edges were every sharp. As a backup fighter, it was sturdy yet unobtrusive, giving the burly Canadian more than enough deadly punch if necessary.

The two men, relatively secure with at least their fighting knives, still knew the best weapons in their arsenals were their alertness and the knowledge gained through dozens of ambushes and years of accumulated experience in the dark, dangerous back alleys of the globe. Right now, both men cautiously made their way through a literal alley in Tokyo, far from the neon-splashed streets that made the city synonymous with ultramodern and high technology. Here, just a few yards from automobiles run on lithium batteries and storefronts packed with the latest in electronics, streetlights came in the form of rare rice-paper lanterns lit from within by candles and security relied upon the alert nose and ears of a guard dog.

As assuredly as the two warriors of Phoenix Force were currently operating without benefit of firepower, history showed that the presence of assault rifles and shotguns would not be tamped by Japanese law. Tokyo was a city where air-soft replicas of the latest in frontline rifles was commonplace to the point where professional teams formed to engage in mass simulated gun battles. Hawkins and Manning simply knew they didn't want to risk an engagement with an already edgy and on-alert Tokyo law-enforcement community. They could not risk the attention that guns would bring, not when they were here in a wholly unofficial status to meet with a NOC—a non-official cover agent for the Central Intelligence Agency.

Whoever was working the angles of ruining the Japanese international image and national economy had made certain to work within operational security parameters that precluded any form of electronic communication. The NOC, however, had raised a report about RUMINT—intelligence gathered by rumor, in the parlance of normal, non-spy folks. It was a slim lead, one that had only been spotted through the tireless perusal of Huntington Wethers. A former cybernetics professor at UCLA, Wethers was now one of the computer wizards back at the Farm. He was nothing if not meticulous in looking for every possible thread of information, especially those that frayed and fell by the wayside of official investigation.

In Phoenix Force's line of work, they knew that sometimes rumors were true. The five members of this world-spanning team had become urban legends in their own right, often identified as either members of a CIA black operations group or a special SWAT team under the aegis of INTERPOL, both of which were far from the truth. It was the blurry line between official backing that allowed the Farm's commandos to board U.S. military aircraft bound for war or to be assigned to federal law-enforcement task forces and "unsanctioned" operations that kept their hands from being tied as they did not fear the diplomatic fallout from bringing down corrupt "allies" or rogues from within the United States govern-

ment. Stony Man Farm had been developed specifically
to avoid the entanglements of agency jurisdictional pride
or the public face of international allegiances with those
to whom human rights violations or the support of criminal or terrorist enterprises was not a point of concern.

Phoenix Force and Able Team were highly agile,
quickly deployable teams that answered to the law of
their own consciences. While special interest groups
turned congressional debate over resolving issues into
an endless circle of inane logic and politically advanta-
geous rhetoric, the Farm's cybernetic apparatus could
burn through the internet, seeking out the true trails of
evidence leading to the guilty. Able Team or Phoenix
Force, or often both, would then be dispatched to properly solve the problem.

Those solutions usually ended with cold-hearted,
greedy or fanatical murderers torn asunder by precision
gunfire, all while minimizing the risk to noncombatants
and bystanders as befitting a Stony Man commando. It
was far more than a matter of pride that none of the Stony
Man operatives had ever intentionally harmed an innocent person in the course of a mission. Be it combat or
grim laser-precise direct action, the only ones who died
were those who had innocent blood on their hands.

"Something feels wrong," Manning murmured under
his breath. Fortunately the hands-free communicator built
into his nearly invisible earpiece allowed him to be heard
loudly and clearly by Hawkins.

The Texan himself was also aware of a feeling of
dread, of a potential for doom that hung in the air. He'd
picked up a familiar scent wafting through the night air as
he and the Canadian had made their way toward the small
house owned by the NOC. "You catch a whiff of that?"

Manning, in the dim light of a distant rice-paper lamp,

frowned deeply, his features darkening in the lengthened shadows. "Dead body."

Hawkins scanned the small cube home of their contact and noticed that one of the windows was cracked open only slightly. He moved closer to the sill and took a deep sniff. It was with a queasy certainty that he could tell the exact length of time the corpse had been moldering inside the house just by the faint odor leaking through a window left ajar. "Seven hours."

Manning nodded agreement with Hawkins's assessment. The brawny man went to the door and, deftly drawing the Tanto from its sheath, hammered the chiseled point into the doorjamb just off to the side of the door handle and lock combination. Against wood and brass, and focused by the sturdy knife, Manning was more than adequate to open the locked door with the sound of a sharp crack in the space of only a moment.

Hawkins had his knife out, the Karambit held with his trigger finger through the loop, the wicked talon of the blade sticking out from the bottom of his fist. The grip was rock-solid, making it nearly impossible to pry from his grasp. He also produced a powerful LED Surefire pocket-size flashlight. He was to take point and would only activate the switch when he absolutely needed to illuminate a target.

Neither Hawkins nor Manning had anticipated the need for night-vision goggles, so the less they used their flashlights, the better their natural senses would allow them to maneuver in the darkness. Less utilization of flashlights would also lower their profile.

Like it or not, if the Tokyo police showed up to a house with a corpse inside, Hawkins and Manning had both illegally broken into the dwelling. Suspicion over the death would fall on them.

Manning clicked his tongue and Hawkins glanced back at his partner. The Canadian had had the foresight to bring along latex gloves to minimize the chances of leaving behind fingerprints or DNA. Hawkins pocketed the knife and sheathed the Karambit swiftly to free up his hands for donning the gloves, then quickly rearmed and readied the light to scan the shadows if necessary.

"Won't have much time," Manning mused softly. "The door cracking open will have been heard by someone."

"This doesn't seem like an area with a lot of 9-1-1 callers," Hawkins said, following his nose to the body.

The Texan came to a halt, seeing the outline of the body on the floor.

In life, her name had been Veronica Moone. At least, that was the name given to her nonofficial cover. She'd been there in the guise of a young college graduate traveling abroad, living in Japan, sometimes working as a translator and sometimes teaching American English to local students. The ruse had given her plenty of room to move around, allowing her to travel to different Japanese cities for schools or businesses needing English translators. Invariably she'd had an inside edge for identifying potential threats to those global corporations.

In her role, either speaking to the parents of grade-school students or conversing with young businessmen looking to make it easier for themselves internationally, she could pick up details and information with far greater precision than the most advanced satellite imagery.

Moone wasn't the name she'd been born with, Hawkins doubted, any more than their cover names were real.

Seven hours and her body was still in rigor. Kneeling beside her, he used what little ambient light was available to look for signs of injury. Barring that, he cupped his fingers over the lens of the flashlight and the glow between his fingers and a gleam he let loose to splash over her body. Shielding the light from being visible through the windows gave him immediate illumination, both figuratively and literally.

A line of bruising on her throat, marked by a large knot of blackness over her windpipe, revealed the tool of her death as being a garrote.

Manning took a glance, then frowned. "Silk scarf with a coin knotted into the middle."

"Or para-cord around a large chain link," Hawkins said, though he didn't really believe that. "Why in hell would someone kill her along the lines of a Thuggee killer?"

Manning's shrug didn't give Hawkins any good vibes. Unfortunately, Manning's familiarity with the cultlike murder/assassination was only too much of an indicator of how often different killers resorted to techniques such as these. Hawkins hadn't been on the team in one instance where the masterminds behind a new Thuggee cult had gone so far as to create an animatronic statue of the Thuggee's deadly goddess Kali, complete with a compact microwave laser unit installed in her elaborate headdress that could kill with a single robotic glance.

"The Thuggee, the Assassins, the Ninja, they're all effective, and the more they appear as something either cultlike or outré, the more layers of obfuscation fall between the murderer and the victim," Manning said. "We're likely the only two people in this city, or even Japan, who could have figured out that Veronica here was murdered because she was a CIA operative instead of just a poor unlucky victim of a death goddess fetishist."

"Striker ran into some Thuggee like this a while back, too, only operating in the Middle East," Hawkins returned. "And let's not forget England and the so-called Ripper killer."

"Makes you wonder if fifty to a hundred years from now, some hush-hush group disguises their disposal of witnesses as the work of a fiend with a machete and a hockey mask," Manning mused.

Moone, her mousy-brown hair cut short, but not boyishly so, might have been more attractive if all the blood had not drained from the right side of her face, leaving it gaunt, and settled into the left side, rendering it bloated and discolored. Her hazel eyes glinted in the shielded light, her having died with them open.

"Not a real Thuggee. They always close the eyes of their victims," Hawkins noted.

"Obfuscation, obfuscation," Manning repeated grimly. He turned away from the scene and moved toward the back of the house. The front door was locked, and there might have been another exit.

Hawkins knew that the death she suffered would not have been easy or gentle. The coin in the center of the garrote would have crushed her windpipe, so even if the pressure had been released, she would have had no chance of getting another breath. The strangling cord had been pulled tight, but there were no signs of fists balled up against the underside of her mandibles, meaning that while she'd suffocated, her brain had received blood. Moone wouldn't have passed out.

A crust of dried tears pooled at the corners of her eyelids. Her end had been slow. Cruel. Meticulous.

All to cover up a conspiracy. This woman, who genuinely had taught people a language they'd wanted to learn, had been murdered. She'd gained information about what might have been a clue as to why shiploads of Japanese whalers died in a salvo of ship-busting missiles. Hawkins normally had a low opinion of those who engaged in wanton murder, but so far the logic of these brutal deaths escaped him.

Certainly, Hawkins had more than a little passing concern for the smart, almost relatable giant mammals of the ocean. Even as a good-ol'-boy hunter, he believed in conservation, not sloblike slaughter. He couldn't fathom the slaughter of an endangered animal just to make a rug or to simply get a piece of rhinoceros horn to enhance the strength of their own horn. Be that as it may, the Japanese sailors killed on the factory ships were not killers. They'd simply been working jobs to feed their families.

However, many in the world saw the deaths of "evil Japanese hunters" as a cause to rejoice. Those who simply wanted to protect an endangered species, and the lawmen who sought to protect their freedom of speech, had also been slaughtered.

Dead was dead, so it shouldn't matter, but Hawkins was offended. He was raised with strong values of what was right and what was wrong. Being murdered for doing your job was in the wrong column, so he sympathized with the Japanese sailors, and even more for the widows, orphans, surviving siblings and parents of those who'd died at sea.

Moone was a covert operative; she'd known that any one of her investigations could have brought her to a violent death. But seeing her lying there, murdered in this manner, Hawkins felt a pang of guilt for her. She looked innocent. She'd tried to do right by her country. She was a sister in arms. A face to which he could attach the statistics of those murdered.

Movement out in front of the house brought Hawkins's attention back to the present and he rose from beside the dead girl. The light had instantly been smothered by his hand and he made certain the toggle switch was turned off. "Gary?"

"I'm out in the alley," Manning answered over his hands-free com.

Hawkins padded in the direction his friend had gone. "Movement through the front door."

"I'll circle around," the Canadian returned. "Stay put unless it's a badge."

"Yes, sir," the Texan replied. He perched in the shadows by the back door, making certain that his presence was unseen in the frame of the partially open entrance.

Tense, he waited to see who would show up on the doorstep of a murdered girl. And just in case, he had both knives out and ready, hoping to greet the assassin.

CHAPTER FIVE

The door swung clumsily on its hinges, the shattered lock giving no resistance as it was pushed open and reached the apex of its usual swing with a slam. No flashlights sprayed their glare, no echo beyond the entrance to Moone's kitchenette. T. J. Hawkins was familiar enough with police procedure to know that cops would not enter a darkened house without lights. Sure, the glare would make them an obvious focus, but in dim conditions as in Moone's almost empty home, the blaze of LED bulbs would actually do more to blind an ambusher than anything else.

As well, police officers would also call out to inquire if anyone was in trouble within.

The bastard or bastards at the door were most likely not cops.

That meant that he and Manning had made contact with an enemy. Hawkins subvocalized confirmation to his partner. "Close them off."

"On it," Manning returned.

Two syllables and Hawkins knew there was nothing that would stop the big Canadian from coming to his aid short of a wall of blazing death. And even then, Manning's combination of genius and brawn would likely find a way to punch through that barrier, as Hawkins had come to know the Phoenix Force veteran.

Even as Hawkins thought of the difference between how police and criminals would enter a house with a broken door, he replaced the small Karambit in its sheath, drawing the pocket flashlight, thumb over the cap switch. The tiny light would prove useful, not only in the prevention of mistaking Moone's CIA contact with a murderer, but also blinding them in the darkness if they truly were here with murderous intent.

The first figure lurched into view and Hawkins hit the switch, blasting him in the face with 320 lumens of brilliance. The painful blue blaze made Hawkins's target throw his hands up to shield his eyes and, in a moment, Hawkins could discern the brief flash of Korean features as the man backpedaled. Hawkins could also make out the gleaming silver finish of a Desert Eagle in the intruder's hand. Normally this would have been all the justification any member of Phoenix Force would need to use their weapon to kill the armed opponent, except for two things.

T. J. Hawkins was a member of Phoenix Force, and had been chosen not just for his willingness and ability to kick ass, but also his quick wits and swift decision-making. While Hawkins had allies who regularly used the Desert Eagle magnum autoloader—Mack Bolan and Gary Manning chief among them—he had yet to see a five-foot-one Korean woman pick such a large and unwieldy weapon as her primary weapon. Hawkins held off on utilizing the Ranger knife, instead using the flat of the blade as leverage to hook the woman's gun wrist and tug powerfully.

Her grip on the pistol broke, and instead of the clunk of heavy, high-quality steel impacting the wood flooring, it was something lighter. Hawkins also realized that the gun in the woman's hand was not cocked. The Desert Eagle was a single-action design, with a slide-mounted safety. Carrying the gun with the hammer down was no way to use it, not without clumsily thumbing back the hammer to make it fire.

The woman had been given an air-soft replica of the pistol, likely in an effort to get her shot to death. Hawkins killed the flashlight, then swept the girl behind him. The last thing Hawkins wanted to do was to bring harm to an innocent bystander. Even as the woman dropped to the floor, the Texan was aware that she'd discovered the dead body.

"Veronica!"

The figure behind her was five-foot-six, judging by the size of his shadow, and there were yet two more in the group, both about the same height as the man in the lead. Hawkins had about five inches on all of them, and from the looming shadow behind them, Manning was about to be on hand immediately.

There was a grunting curse and Hawkins could only make it out to be an Oriental dialect. It didn't matter what the source of the epithet was; he saw the unmistakable motions of someone raising a pistol to shoot. Hawkins clicked his flashlight on and in an instant this man, armed with what looked like a SIG-Sauer P-228, winced and half turned away from the brilliant glare of the light. The man must have had his finger on the trigger as the crack of a 9 mm round added an extra bit of flash to the darkened room.

This bastard was armed and intended to kill. With a flick of his wrist, Hawkins lunged. The broad point of his dagger hit the man just off center of his nose. The crackle of face bones and the sudden surge of paralysis striking the gunman informed the Texan his aim was true. Six inches of steel embedded into the killer's brain. Unfortunately the blow was so powerful it lodged the knife there, ripping it from Hawkins's grasp.

Behind the dying man, Manning grabbed one of the other two in a head-scissoring arm lock. The smaller Asian gurgled, sputtering, attracting the attention of the center man, who suddenly realized he was not beset on both sides by relative giants.

Hawkins didn't go for the Karambit on its thong around his neck. There was a good chance these killers might have good intel on what was going on, on why it had been so vital to murder an American English teacher. Rather, he punched forward with the end of his flashlight. The Surefire model that Hawkins carried had a crown around its lens, a high-impact aluminum ring that not only could be used for protecting the lens of the flash, but also could be used as an impact weapon. The crown design, with semicircular scallops taken out of the perimeter, had been designed to snag skin rather than slip off, as well as to increase the force of the punch.

Hawkins slammed it at the corner of the man's jaw, spiking into the juncture of nerves and blood vessels running through the neck to feed the man's brain. With a single blow, the Texan laid him out.

In the meantime Manning had taken his opponent in a sleeper hold. Deprived of fresh blood and oxygen to the brain, his man had also passed out.

It was all over and done, but time was no longer on Phoenix Force's side. The first of the men had fired a gunshot. If the bursting of Veronica Moone's front door hadn't inspired this neighborhood to call the police, that act of violence would.

"My knife is stuck in his face," Hawkins told Manning. The Phoenix veteran nodded and applied his strength and leverage to the task of retrieving the weapon as the Texan turned to the Korean girl.

"Don't hurt me," she whimpered.

"It's okay," Hawkins replied with a soothing drawl. "I don't want to see you hurt, either. Are you all right?"

"They killed Ronnie," the woman said. She was numbed.

Hawkins rested an arm around her shoulders. "We need to go. Can you come with us?"

She nodded.

"You speak Korean?" Hawkins asked. It wasn't a foolish question. There was a population of Koreans who lived in Japan as a minority, but some of them might not have kept true with their ethnic origins. Back in Texas, Hawkins had met enough Hispanics who denied their cultural heritage, preferring to live within the flow of Texan ethnicity. They were third- and fourth-generation Americans.

"Yes," she answered. "They gave me a gun…"

"I know," Hawkins said, helping her to her feet.

"Hey," Manning whispered. Hawkins turned and found his knife being handed to him, handle first, the blade wiped clean. "Their car is outside."

"Enough room for us?" Hawkins asked, sheathing his knife.

"Just four," Manning responded.

"Take her. I'll catch up on foot," Hawkins replied. He turned to the Korean girl. "Follow this man. We both want to protect you."

She looked doubtful at first, but when Manning threw one of the goons over his left shoulder, then picked up the other unconscious man as if he were a duffel bag, she nodded.

"Don't dawdle," Manning suggested to his younger partner.

Hawkins shrugged. "Just enough to throw them off your trail."

Manning nodded, knowing what his friend intended.

With that, Manning and the girl were out the front door. They piled into a minivan, emphasis on "miniature."

All need for stealth past, Hawkins turned on the lights and examined the small home, now the worse for a second corpse. He couldn't help but think that he'd failed Veronica Moone, but was also aware the young woman would have secured information somewhere. He mentally went over all the trade craft he'd learned and developed since becoming an operative for Stony Man Farm. The CIA NOC would have had to secure what notes she'd assembled in a place that would not be obvious, even to trained intelligence agents, but could be accessed quickly in the event of an emergency or a swift exit.

When the Koreans came to kill her, one of her first thoughts would have been about the information she'd stored away. He examined the room once again and then looked at the dead woman's posture on the floor. She'd been dragged into the kitchen by the garrote that had crushed her windpipe. One of her shoes was in the living room, on a small rug. Hawkins thought that maybe she'd hidden her info somewhere in the relatively Spartan living area, but immediately dismissed that. She had been moving away from the kitchenette. Hawkins turned and scanned the shelves.

Two bags of rice caught his attention. One was open, partially used. The other didn't look as if it had been opened, but the sack holding the rice had been taut, pillowlike. Hawkins went for the more stuffed bag and saw that its top flap had been secured by a swatch of duct tape.

"If your cell phone ever gets wet, put it in a container of rice to dry it out," Hawkins murmured aloud. Considering Japan was a nation that had experienced its fair share of traumatic tidal waves, it would also prove a smart place of storage for small electronics that could hold data... He tore open the bag and sifted through. After a few moments he felt something inside. It was a PDA. Just to make certain, he rummaged through the rice some more and came away with four thumb drives.

Hawkins pocketed the items, then frisked the corpse of the murderous Korean who'd nearly shot him. There were no pieces of identification on the man, not even clothing tags. There were, however, two spare magazines for the Norinco copy of the SIG-Sauer P-228. He pocketed them, picked up the pistol and depressed the decocker, lowering the hammer and returning initial trigger pull to a drop-safe, flinch-resistant twelve pounds of weight. He pocketed the pistol and noticed the flicker of red-and-blue flashes through the open door.

The time to leave was now and he opened the back door into the alley. Hawkins's sudden arrival startled two cats *in flagrante delicto* and the animals leaped away from each other, yowling in protest. It almost would have been funny, but the feline racket and their flight sent garbage can lids toppling with a gonging clatter. The police out front would no doubt have heard the noise.

Hawkins produced the NP-228 and fired two shots into the kitchen floor through the doorway. That racket would most assuredly have drawn attention, but it would also freeze the Japanese policemen where they stood. Once again, the Texan's familiarity with police procedure, most specifically Japanese procedure, meant that he would not have to worry about inciting an international incident. The cops out front would be loath to open fire immediately, for fear of harming a possible hostage or out of concern that bullets would cut through one building and harm someone in a nearby structure.

With that lead going for him, Hawkins made the pistol safe and took off down an alley between two houses. Vaulting short fences was little effort for him, and he wove through the neighborhood as fast as he dared without attracting further attention to himself. It took him twenty minutes before he allowed himself on the main street, circling back to where he and Manning had parked their rental vehicle. The wisdom that kept them from parking too near to where they were going had served them well. The car was undisturbed, even though it was likely a half dozen police cars had driven past it.

Hawkins slid behind the wheel, fired up the engine and took to the streets back to the safe house that had been set up for him and Manning. Along the way, he took care to ensure that he wasn't trailed, either by the law or by whichever Korean murderers had been waiting in reserve. The three men might have been bowled over by the pair of Phoenix Force veterans, but that didn't mean they were incompetent. There could easily be backup agents elsewhere, but so far, Hawkins seemed to have lucked out.

Even so, he engaged in evasion techniques twice during the drive to the Phoenix safe house. Getting sloppy and complacent was a certain path to being shot dead. It was attention to details that had allowed the two members of the team to capture prisoners and to find a friend of the murdered CIA agent.

"That's the assumption," Hawkins mused. He would have to plug the devices into their sat case—a briefcase-size computer unit with USB and fire-wire ports and several sizes of flash-card data reader slots—to be sure. Through it, Able Team or Phoenix Force could instantly transmit data to Stony Man Farm for investigation. Built-in filters would catch any viruses or logic bombs hidden in potentially sabotaged data, just in case the Koreans had wanted Hawkins and Manning to find the drives and PDA.

"What's your status?" Hawkins asked through his hands-free communicator.

Manning's response was swift. "Prisoners secure. Girl quiet. No law-enforcement interception. No tails."

"Good news," Hawkins replied. "Found the agent's stash of data and her secure device. No tails here."

"Remain sharp," Manning told him.

It would take a while for Hawkins to arrive at the safe house, but that allowed him time to continue searching for possible enemies. While he would have liked to forward Veronica Moone's intel to the Farm, haste would not just make waste, it also would leave him more vulnerable to being wasted.

When he finally pulled up to the safe house—actually an abandoned store along the waterfront—he made sure the car was well hidden. The minivan was also there, empty and locked down.

Hawkins looked over the appropriated pistol. He still hadn't taken off the latex gloves he'd been given when he and Manning had discovered the crime scene. He didn't remove them, hopeful that he'd find fingerprints of the dead man on the gun itself. His instincts told him the three men might have been North Korean agents, especially since they'd reverted to what he assumed was Korean when they'd cursed in surprise at Hawkins's attack. There was still a possibility that the three men might have been South Korean, as well.

If there was one truism in Southeast Asia, old grudges clung to the peoples as if they were strangling vines. Though World War II was years before, Koreans still held an enmity toward Japan and the violations of human rights inflicted upon the whole of the peninsula during their imperial expansion. People had been reduced to slave labor; thousands had been tortured or had died of overwork. In Korea, as well as China, the Japanese military had sated whatever desires their troops had had with gigantic rape camps. The men didn't need to be North Korean to hold a grudge against Japan.

Hawkins stuffed his hand into his jacket pocket, where he kept the appropriated combat pistol. He doubted that three people could get the drop on someone as strong and smart as Manning, but he didn't want to take any chances.

"It's me," Hawkins called out as he entered, unlocking the door ahead of him. As soon as he was through, he closed the door firmly and reset the locks. He saw Manning standing, arms folded. "No trouble with the prisoners?"

Manning shook his head. "One did try to escape. I put him to sleep."

"Good," Hawkins replied. He pulled the NP-228 from his pocket and laid it on a nearby table. "I'm going to strip this, open up some liquid cement and see if I can find any good fingerprints."

"Smart idea. I've got the prints from the others in the ether back to Stony Man," Manning replied.

"Can't hurt to be completest," Hawkins added.

Manning looked back. "The girl's name is Min-seo Geum."

Hawkins already had the SIG stripped down to parts. He poured a small cap of Super Glue and placed it under a trash-bag-improvised tent. The process was an old forensic trick at gleaning fingerprints from most surfaces. The oils that caused the surface transfer that formed a latent print would attract the fumes from the glue, producing a visible pattern that could be photographed. Hawkins hoped the flat sides of the pistol's magazine or the outside of the slide would provide enough for identification, but just to be certain, he stripped the bullets from the magazine.

People might think of putting on gloves for firearm handling, but few professionals were paranoid enough to wear gloves while feeding ammunition into their appropriate magazines on a clandestine operation.

Hawkins turned away from his fingerprint-gathering project and produced the PDA and thumb drives that he'd discovered. "Is she all right?" Hawkins asked.

Manning nodded. "She's been having a good cry over her friend. She was a teacher at the same school. They were once very close."

Hawkins raised an eyebrow. "Roommates?"

Manning nodded. "And quite a bit more."

Hawkins sighed. "And I threw her on top of a woman she loved…killed like that…"

"The other option was to let her get shot in the back," Manning offered. He took the thumb drives and looked over the PDA. "I have a wire for this device on the sat case."

"All the better," Hawkins replied. "The more we know, the more we can get to taking down the fucker who killed Veronica."

Manning glanced at him. "We never knew her."

"She was working for our side," Hawkins replied.

Manning nodded, then rested a hand on his shoulder. "Don't let it get too personal."

Hawkins frowned. "I'll keep my head. But that doesn't mean I won't take satisfaction in taking theirs…"

The Canadian Phoenix vet left the younger man to his task. Manning had faced his losses over the years and had made enough missions personal. Every member of the team had. And sometimes, that personal investment was enough to take an impossible battle and push them over the top to victory.

But in the end, it still never quieted the ghosts they vowed to avenge.

CHAPTER SIX

Blancanales shadowed Schwarz and Lyons as they drove away from the clubhouse, giving his friends a head start just in case the paranoid Heathens club members sent someone to trail them. He'd waited and, through use of the rear-mounted camera, made certain he was not being followed.

The last thing they needed was to be ambushed as they reassembled and prepared for a hard entrance.

Blancanales had been tuned in to his friends as they'd made their infiltration of the clubhouse; he'd heard everything, thanks to built-in, Schwarz-designed zero-profile microphones and the surveillance equipment intrinsic in the Able van. His teammates wouldn't have been able to hear him, but there was not an interaction that didn't resound loud and clear in Blancanales's ears.

Had things gone wrong, he was on sniper overwatch, ready to provide cover for his partners. Now, he was providing further support for his brothers in arms as they fell back to begin their assault.

When Blancanales opened the rear doors of the van, Schwarz was already tearing off the latex of his false tattoos from his neck and shoulder, crumpling the mass up in one fist. He whipped them into a small waste basket with a grimace.

"Bad mood?" Blancanales asked.

"Having to sound like one of those homophobic

assholes?" Schwarz growled. "I feel like puking my guts out."

"They've got the shooters locked down in their headquarters," Lyons said. "They kept too calm a profile. Even when Gadgets made a move against one of their own, and not a prospect, Rucks had full rockers and patches."

"The prospects outside were edgy and stayed close to more than a couple of trash barrels out front," Blancanales returned. "Those were the right height for stowing some ARs, especially if they were clean on the bottom."

"Lid in place, yeah," Schwarz noted. He went to one of the banks and opened the digital surveillance files. He maximized the thermal imaging camera and made a quick count. Thirty prospects were outside the clubhouse, surrounding it. Inside, it was a little more difficult to see true heat signatures through the walls. Even so, he got general numbers and groups off the colored blobs.

"What odds are we looking at?" Lyons asked, looking over Schwarz's shoulder.

"The place, from your and my observations, should only have about twenty guys inside. But there are major concentrations of heat sources in the basement and on the third floor," Schwarz said.

"They split the shooters into two groups?" Lyons inquired.

"Or they have much more than a safe house set up in the clubhouse," Schwarz said. "The top floors can either be a grow house—in which case, it's highly unlikely that any shooters are going to be kept on the premises—or a server farm."

"That much computer equipment atop a biker hangout?" Lyons asked.

"You would be surprised at what bikers get into these days," Schwarz answered. "Identity theft, getting their old ladies into law-enforcement support roles to grab intel from cops..."

"I know all about the latter," Lyons noted. "We've encountered the results of that kind of infiltration before."

Blancanales nodded. "Good people end up dead because of lax background checks on whom a sheriff's department hired."

Lyons's scowl remained deep. "So the Heathens are using a lot of computer power. For what?"

"I'm going to see if there's a Wi-Fi signal," Schwarz said. "We hack into that..."

"Don't explain. Just do," Lyons returned. "In the meantime, I'm going to see what's going down in the basement."

"And just how are we going to do that?" Blancanales asked.

"The hard way," Lyons answered.

"Then why am I even trying to crack into whatever files they have?" Schwarz asked.

Lyons smirked. "First, you're just grabbing their signal and handing things over to the gang back at the Farm. Second, I'm not going through the clubhouse's armed forces, but directly into the basement."

"This ain't a Minecraft game, Carl," Schwarz said. "We just don't whip up some pickaxes and dig through the earth."

"Pickaxes are for people who don't know how to cook up low-velocity breeching charges," Lyons returned. "While we're going through the bottom, Bear and whoever he has on data-cracking duty is going through that server farm, as you call it."

Schwarz nodded. "I've got just the thing, if you've got sewer access to get into it."

Lyons clapped Schwarz on the shoulder. "You know me. I'm the hard-core Boy Scout. I'm always prepared."

With that, he laid down his tablet at Schwarz's elbow. Schwarz picked up the device and saw that Lyons had indeed done his prep work, pulling up records on the maintenance and access tunnels in the area of the clubhouse.

Schwarz even spared a wry grin as the path they were to take to the basement of the Heathens' local headquarters had been mapped out by the Able Team leader. "So do we just bust in the hard way?"

"First, we take a peek in. Fiber-optic cam," Lyons said. "Once we know who and what's up, we blow our way in, take prisoners and kill anyone else coming into the basement. How is your penetration of their cyber security going?"

"It's going," Schwarz answered, seeming a bit evasive. Lyons picked up the concern on his features.

"Not well?" Lyons pressed.

"There seems to be a damn good reason why the Heathens are off the grid," Schwarz returned. He frowned. "They've got some great anti-spyware, and it's turning back on my system."

"How bad is it coming back to us?" Lyons asked.

Schwarz's face screwed up tightly for a few minutes as he opened up applications and began moving the mouse around the screen. He seemed to be throwing black screens of green neon code against a square of darkness in the center of the monitor. His concentration was complete, fingers of one hand moving swiftly across the keyboard while he was selecting and dragging with the mouse. Lyons couldn't comprehend what was going on, other than that these motions were last-second efforts at deflecting the cyber counterattack on their system.

Lyons could only hope that as fast and furious as the

Heathens' electronic security was, Schwarz somehow was keeping the bikers in that clubhouse from detecting the attempted infiltration of their system. He didn't voice that concern, however. Schwarz was working feverishly and anything might distract his partner, leaving Able Team out in the open and a vulnerable target to the Heathens.

Lyons was sure the bikers wouldn't be a match for Able Team, but every moment spent exchanging fire with the outlaws would buy the death squad vital moments to escape and find another place to hide out.

The team had come too far to let the murderers of innocent protesters and D.C. lawmen escape.

"Got it." Schwarz breathed out with relief. "They didn't detect me."

Lyons waited a beat.

"No 'I hope'?" he asked Schwarz.

"No." Schwarz nodded in agreement.

Lyons let a breath out. "Small favors."

Blancanales already had the GPS map out, pointing them toward the sewer access tunnels. The entrance was out of the way and large enough for each of the three men to fit through with full gear. Schwarz already had his drill ready for the fiber-optic camera. The bit on the end of the tool would be silent, thanks to a high-power, high-efficiency electric motor and a tungsten borer.

With his remote key fob, he armed the security system on the Able Team van; a selection of high-voltage shock leads, tear gas dispensers, as well as electronic shutdown of systems that would not activate, even with conventional hot-wiring means. If someone could break into and start the van, they were welcome to it.

Moving swiftly, their gear secured so that nothing clattered or snagged, the three men slithered into the man-hole down to the sewer.

Lyons took point, as he naturally did. The big, blond ex-LAPD cop always chose to be the first down a tunnel or through a locked door. When they operated in South American jungles or in hostile shanty towns in Sri Lanka, it was his instincts, his attention to detail, that got the three of them through all manner of ambushes.

And since Able Team was going into close-quarters warfare, Lyons performed the heavy-duty, close-quarters artillery role. The weapon he held looked like an M-16 with four rotating tubes under the long barrel and no magazine well. It was a SRM Arms Model 1216 shotgun. Each of the four tubes rotated and held four shells, making the combined unit a 16-shot magazine of 12-gauge ammunition. Lyons wore two spare quad-tubes, sheathed over one shoulder akin to a quiver of arrows. Reloading was quick and certain, and though Lyons could have gone with one of two shorter barreled models, the Able Team leader wanted all the power of the 18-inch tube and the full load of 16 rounds on tap.

When the shotgun ran dry, then would come time for the 6-inch Ruger GP-100 and its balanced partner, the Smith & Wesson MP-45 auto with extended 14-shot magazines replacing the more concealment-friendly 10-rounders.

On top of the SRM, Lyons had an M-26 Modular Accessory Shotgun System, a magazine-fed, bolt-action shotgun. The device was loaded with neoprene rounds, meant for stunning and battering subjects into unconsciousness. Blancanales had another of the MASS shotguns, so once Schwarz breached into the basement, the two men would hammer the hidden death squad into senselessness.

And if any of the cold-blooded murderers shot back? Schwarz would be on their heels with his AAC Honey Badger PDW. The spray of .300 Blackout rounds was ballistically equivalent to the fabled old AK-47 bullet and possessed a hell of a lot more energy and penetration out of a 6-inch barrel than a traditional .223 Remington out of such an attenuated machine pistol. With a short tube, the standard M-16 caliber would not carry enough energy or momentum to do much in close-quarters combat. The .300 AAC Blackout took the world-famous 7.62 mm COMBLOC round and shaped the casing to fit the M-16 platform. With a bullet two to four times as heavy as the 5.56 mm, the Honey Badger could develop more punch out of the stubby nose of the machine pistol. Out of a standard rifle barrel, the Blackout was stabilized for long-distance shots beyond what the normal M-16 could manage and still deliver deeper and larger wounds than the normal counterpart.

Blancanales also carried one of these stubby Personal Defense Weapons. The two men had foregone suppressors, instead putting in electronic earplugs that deadened the pressure against their eardrums of gunfire inside a building. Lyons had a pair himself, and was glad for the protection. His shotgun would be loud, and in many cases, even the bellow of the weapon in the same room produced enough overpressure to knock people senseless.

The three warriors only had a few hundred feet to go, twisting through the narrow tubes. They had to stoop much of the way, but the route Lyons had mapped out for them never grew too small or too clogged to navigate. After all, it was Lyons's plan, and despite seeming like a rampaging maniac while tearing through the opposition with a high-capacity shotgun, he was a team leader who believed in preparation and planning. Getting in and getting out were part of his everyday thoughts ever since joining Able Team. That level of alertness and prescience went from stopping in a mini-market for a beverage to super-max prisons and presidential-level accommodations.

If he knew he was heading somewhere, he liked to know the perimeter, the weaknesses and strengths of the defenses, how easy it would be to get out, how difficult it would be to hold the line against an enemy's assault.

The GPS led them right to where Lyons wanted the team. He pointed to where he wanted the quick sneak-and-peek into the basement.

With deft swiftness, Schwarz brought up the tungsten-tipped drill. For a moment Lyons was afraid the tool was not working, until he noticed the dust ejecting from the hole and a dull, rumbling crunch as the tungsten screws tore apart and ate into the stone.

Schwarz gave his boss a wink as he continued pressing the drill into the wall until he reached a depth he wanted and withdrew the bit from its hole. He swiftly pulled another gunlike object, but this one had what looked like a stiff section of fishing line poking out of its nose.

The electronics genius fed the clear fiber-optic cable through the aperture, then activated a cell-phone-size screen. Lyons and Blancanales were able to see the screen and almost instantly the three members of the team could see a group of men in a room. Bunk beds lined either side of the small area, and they were full of sprawled, listless men. Several sat around a small card table, smoking cigarettes and trying to distract themselves with a card game in the harsh orange glare of a naked lightbulb hanging in the middle of the ceiling. Assault rifles leaned on either side of a heavy metal door, and more than one of the men had a pistol in his waistband.

They could not hear or smell inside of the room, but even without breathing the air where the gunmen hid, Lyons could taste the sweat, desperation and impatience. Stale beer, cigarettes and bags under their eyes were more than sufficient evidence of the ugly tension. However, the guns resting against the door was evidence that they would concentrate their attention on the door, not the walls behind them.

"This is the group," Blancanales said. "The rifles match the weaponry on the surveillance footage used against the protesters and the Secret Service."

"Wire the wall," Lyons said. He made certain that his M-26 MASS was loaded with its less lethal rounds. While he didn't care if one or two of these murderers died, he still wanted to take prisoners to find his way up the food chain.

Schwarz had the explosives set up. The shaped charges had been assembled in pre-formed webs and nets. The high-velocity detonation cords were formed so that they'd direct incredible amounts of energy and pressure against the stone with efficiency and razor-sharp cutting power.

A side bonus of this particular setup was that when the wall-breaching charge went off, all of the dangerous force would go into the wall and not splash back against the men of Able Team as they sat on either side of the explosive webbing. Schwarz nodded for Lyons and Blancanales to step back, only a few feet, just to avoid shrapnel and faces full of dust, despite the armored goggles and faceplates that they wore. Just because the backblast would be minimized, there was still a small risk of injury.

Lyons nodded.

Schwarz depressed the detonator stud.

The slicing energy of the breaching charge slashed through the wall. It wasn't a thunderous crash, more like the revving of a muscle car ready to race. Either way, people would know what was going on, even if they were on the floors above.

The roar of the det cord burning through ended, and Lyons and Blancanales whirled out on the end of that snarl. The cloud of dust from the collapsing section of wall sliced free was thick, but Lyons and Blancanales had the benefit of knowing where the men inside were positioned, thanks to the fiber-optic camera.

Lyons triggered, then worked the bolt on the 12-gauge MASS, punching high-density baton rounds into the center mass of anything standing in the mist. Backlit by the naked lightbulb, the gunmen were easy targets, especially since jets of dust and ejecta had left them blinded and stunned. Lyons felt the section of fallen wall shift beneath his feet and heard a groan issued from below him. The breach had landed atop someone's back, and the movement accompanied a wet, ugly crack that turned the low moan into a higher screech.

Blancanales's magazine-fed MASS hammered out thunderbolts of rubber, grunts of pain signaling the fall of another of the hired gunmen.

Lyons fed in another magazine, looking to anchor anyone who hadn't been outright knocked out. Blancanales and Schwarz immediately set to work with cable tie wrist bindings for the battered men, jamming rags into their mouths and taping their lips to keep them from calling out for assistance.

Certainly, the Heathens upstairs had heard the booming of the pair of magazine-fed shotguns, so they would be on their way down quickly.

Lyons opened the metal door and glanced toward the stairwell. It was now his job to act as area defense for the others as they made their choices among the downed gunmen.

There had been eight, but one of them had been flattened beneath the collapsing wall from the sewer. He seemed in healthy condition, except for an arm that had been twisted at an obscene angle. They wouldn't choose him for snatching. They could load about four men into the drag-bag they had laid out in the sewer and slide them down the tunnels to return them to the van.

Three would be left behind. Lyons left them to that while his electronic earmuffs picked up the clatter of hard biker boot soles on concrete. The Heathens had recovered from the thunderstorm that had struck their basement.

Lyons doubted that the bikers would leave their guns behind. As soon as he saw a pair of leather-clad legs on the stairs, the Able Team leader cut loose with the 1216. A burst of buckshot struck the man at knee level, shredding his leg and removing any hope of standing. The Heathen suddenly toppled, crashing to the basement hallway floor in a tangle of limbs, smearing blood and chunks of greasy meat behind him.

Another leg swung into view and this time Lyons smashed the man's ankle with a 12-gauge sledgehammer of pellets. This guy tumbled, but someone above him must have grabbed an arm, because he was hauled up and away from the meat grinder that the bottom of the stairwell had become.

Lyons glanced back as Blancanales chose the prisoners for the snatch. The elder member of Able Team had specifically trained for this task: seeking out high-value targets for subsequent interrogation, part of the Rangers' role in the war on terror. Intelligence gathering was as natural to Blancanales as breathing. Picking the right prisoners would not be difficult.

Schwarz was about to pause to update the Farm's progress with the Heathens' computer systems. With Lyons mounting a rather substantive defense to the basement and especially the safe room, he felt he had time to check in with his fellow cyber wizards back at the Farm.

Blancanales spoke up. "Uh, sir, I'm going to have to ask you to power down your mobile device."

"What?" Schwarz asked. "The Farm's still digging into their computers."

Blancanales waved the electronics genius over to his side. That's when Schwarz's earmuffs picked up the sounds of distant splashing. Soft, there were easily several sets of feet sloshing through the sewer runoff.

"Someone else is coming in," Schwarz murmured.

"Get on the horn to Barb," Blancanales said. "This might be a death squad, or it might be law enforcement. If it's the first, then no problem, we just blow through them…"

"But if it's cops," Schwarz concluded, "they're just doing their jobs. But they won't feel the same about us."

With a single touch, Schwarz's combat tablet connected him to Barbara Price. She had a very concerned look on her face already.

"Guys, a combined ATF and FBI force have penned off the area," she announced. "We've been working so many angles, this slipped past our ears to the ground."

"ATF and FBI?" Lyons asked. The electronic earmuffs keyed all three members of Able Team together in a single communications network. What one heard via wireless, they all would hear, cutting down on debriefing time.

"An HRT team is heading through the sewers right toward us," Schwarz answered. "Subterranean infiltration was something most of those guys learned from us or Phoenix Force while we were training blacksuits between missions."

"Then we head up through the Heathens," Lyons returned. "We're here to find out why innocent lawmen were slaughtered. We're not adding to their body count, damn it."

"Even if we get through the bikers, we're still going to have a police perimeter walling in the Heathens' HQ," Blancanales said.

"Jack Grimaldi's firing up *Dragonslayer* for an aerial exfil," Price said. "We're going to keep him off radar for as long as possible, and the bird should be able to fend off small-arms fire from the police cordon."

"How much time do we have?" Lyons asked.

"Fifteen minutes," Price answered. "I got the signal from Jack that he's wheels-up ready."

Lyons grunted. "Thanks."

Able Team was in a bind. Even if they could get through the outlaw bikers within the time allotted, they would have opposition that they dared not harm. That would be at least ten minutes while they couldn't shoot back.

There would be no peace between this hammer and anvil, and Lyons intended to dig through the anvil to safety.

CHAPTER SEVEN

Able Team was faced with a textbook example of a tactical disadvantage: three men, the members of Able Team, with eight unconscious and bound prisoners in an underground safe room. There were two exits, both wide-open, but only one could be closed.

The easiest way out would be through the hole that had been cut into the wall by the high-velocity detonation cord and shaped charges. That way, however, would lead them straight into the guns of the FBI's elite Hostage Rescue Team, a counter-terrorist group made up of lawmen nearly as highly skilled as the warriors of Able Team. Since the HRT was heading through the sewers to punch into the building from beneath, the Able Team leader had little doubt there would be a tunnel branch that wasn't cordoned off or a manhole cover for blocks that wasn't manned by a police squad.

As the FBI agents were likely students who had received advanced training at Stony Man Farm as part of the blacksuit program, and as Able Team had come to this basement to capture murderers of other lawmen for interrogation, punching through the law's lines was out of the question.

The second easiest way out was to fight through an army of paranoid, edgy outlaw bikers who had taken the consciousless murderers into their clubhouse to save them from the police dragnet. The bikers would be nearly as skilled and dangerous as the HRT, and they were defending their own home ground. Fortunately the Heathens' membership was made up of unapologetic criminals, brutes who broke arms and legs, murdered and dealt methamphetamine and illicit guns to other criminals. Any guilt over killing these thugs would only amount in wasted ammunition.

Even if they could get to ground level, the clubhouse was surrounded by various police and law-enforcement agencies in an effort to contain the outlaws.

"Pol!" Lyons called Blancanales by his shortened nickname. "Pick two of those goons for the FBI and leave them with the other four. We're going out the roof and I don't want to overstuff *Dragonslayer* or spend too long loading prisoners aboard."

Blancanales nodded and then addressed the team's leader by his nickname. "Anything else, Ironman?"

"Choke the tunnels with smoke and tear gas," Lyons ordered. "They'll have masks, but the clouds will impair their visibility and slow them down. Gadgets…"

Schwarz responded to the name he'd almost literally been born to. "Wire the sewer to blow up, slowing them down?"

Lyons nodded. "Right. Then grab the tarp sled and follow me. Make sure you don't make it too hard."

Blancanales had already loaded CS rounds into the small grenade launcher beneath the stubby six-inch barrel of the Honey Badger subgun. CS was the official title for capsicum, the primary ingredient of tear gas. Made from some of the hottest pepper extracts in the world, even a small particle could inflame mucus membranes. Noses would stuff up and swell, impeding breathing, and eyes would feel as if they were exposed to open flame. Blancanales fired one, reloaded swiftly, then fired another, then switched to magnesium flares, which he planted at the base of each of the billowing clouds of burning smoke.

The HRT members would now be exposed to the intense brightness of a million candles' worth of light. And if they were like Able Team, they came through the sewers with light-amplification goggles. Anyone wearing those while the flares glowed in front of them would deal with headaches caused by their goggles blazing white in their vision. Peeling them off would expose them to the tear gas, at least their eyes, further inhibiting them.

Even with that slow-down, Schwarz swiftly assembled a web across the ceiling of the sewer tunnel in front of the entrance they had cut into this fortified basement. It would drop heavy rubble in front of the hole, while sending minimal shrapnel to the prisoners or the elite team approaching through the tunnel. Blancanales followed up with more CS-CN and two more magnesium flares. The advancing FBI agents were now stopped for the time being.

Able Team formed up behind Lyons, who was holding off the owners of the basement: the Heathens outlaw biker gang. Three men, their legs smashed by Lyons's SRM 1216 shotgun blasts, lay dead or wounded at the bottom of the steps.

"Pop the tunnel," Lyons ordered.

Schwarz thumbed the detonator and a rumble resounded behind them. The unconscious six murderers were covered with dust, but were otherwise unharmed. The men had been laid low by 12-gauge slugs made of neoprene, leaving them with blunt trauma bruises and likely broken ribs or jaws. Bound wrist and ankle with cable ties, they were perfectly packaged for the FBI force in the sewers, once they made their way through the tunnel toward them.

More delay for the soldiers on the same side as Able Team.

"Pol, discourage the bikers," Lyons ordered.

Blancanales stuffed a high-explosive 40 mm grenade into his Honey Badger's launcher, slid to prone and fired at the landing in the stairs leading to the basement. The HE shell didn't have much shrapnel, but the round was meant to create a wave of overpressure that would burst blood vessels and rip nerves. It went off in a thunderclap, shaking the basement around Able Team. The walls of the stairwell were pulverized into stone splinters that made up for the lack of steel wire fragments.

As soon as the grenade roared, Lyons was out the steel door and up the stairs. Schwarz let Blancanales through with his drag-bag of prisoners, then slammed the steel fire door shut. He then placed a bar across the front, further buying the three Stony Man commandos time to escape and minimizing chances of having to harm a fellow lawman. Then he rushed to keep pace with Blancanales.

Each spared a hand for the drag-bag, leaving the other free for the compact little Honey Badger. Knowing they would be limited to only one hand, Blancanales and Schwarz had secured their slings to provide better support and activated the laser sights on their weapons. Firing from the hip was a desperation act, made easier to aim with the lasers and recoil rendered more controllable by the tension of the nylon straps anchoring the weapons to their shoulders. Blancanales and Schwarz were up the stairs in Lyons's wake, hearing the bellow of the semiautomatic shotgun in the team leader's hands.

Carl Lyons was where he belonged, where he'd turned his nickname of Ironman into more than just a clever title. The moniker first came from his days as a Los Angeles

Police Department beat cop, where he'd never missed a shift of duty.

In the rough streets of New York and Los Angeles, in the lawless deserts of Mexico and the untamed Amazon, Lyons's title of Ironman was reforged, not as a cop who never let sickness or injury slow him down. He became a steely, no-holds-barred warrior. He was the living battering ram of the trio of Able warriors. He carried the weaponry that shattered ambushes and turned superior numbers of enemies into a wasteland of the dead and slaughtered. He was the bedrock that allowed the more cerebral skills of Schwarz and the more behavioral skills of Blancanales to step back and take in solutions as he broke assaults against his iron will.

Wearing Able Team's lightweight chain-mail, Kevlar and carbon-fiber body armor, Lyons lived up to the eponymous armored hero he was matched to, though the blond, burly ex-cop produced flashes of thunder to match that one's avenging ally. The four tubes of ammunition from the 1216 ran empty, finally. Twelve-gauge blasts had taken their toll on the defending Heathens, bursting rib cages open like rotten watermelons beneath a sledgehammer.

"I'm out!" Lyons called, letting the 1216 drop on its sling, immediately pulling his Smith & Wesson .45 up in one smooth movement. He pivoted and hit one of the biker goons with a pair of rapidly fired 230-grain hollowpoints, the big bullets smashing the rifle-armed thug center mass and hurling him into eternity.

As soon as Blancanales and Schwarz heard Lyons's announcement, they let go of the drag-bag, holding their Honey Badger PDWs with both hands and ripping off short bursts, .300 Blackout rounds ripping into another pair of bikers and hurling them to the ground with authoritative punch. This gave Lyons a moment to pull another of the quad-tubes for the SMR from his backpack. The process took two seconds, but in the midst of their enemy's lair, Lyons didn't need his friends without cover fire.

The brief respite that his teammates' rain of full-auto provided gave the Able Team leader his few seconds to reload, and the mighty shotgun was up and tracking for targets.

"Mobile!" Lyons announced.

With that, Schwarz and Blancanales went back to one-handing their stubby weapons, grabbing the drag-bag with their prisoners.

A dozen Heathens, their M-16s and shotguns dropped from where they'd stood their ground, were now corpses. Be it by 12 gauge from Lyons or .300 bullets from Blancanales and Schwarz, their bodies were mutilated, massive chunks ripped from flesh and bone by the impact of high-powered rounds. It was a brutal massacre, but Lyons was feeling the ache across his chest. The body armor kept him from getting riddled with enemy bullets, but the impact of incoming fire still felt like a flurry of crushing punches. His torso would be mottled purple, black and blue in the morning, but at least his torso would still be in one piece.

The same could not be said for the criminals who had harbored mass murderers. On their brief infiltration, both Lyons and Schwarz had made careful observations about the lack of "old ladies" present. There were prospects outside the building, standing wary guard, but only those who were either full patch or close to full patch members of the Heathens were inside the clubhouse—the Church, as outlaw bikers called it.

It was a certain enough sign that things were buckled down tight for illicit purposes. No chicks, only moderate drinking and lots of coffee in the Church's bar meant the Heathens were up for business. The place was on complete lockdown and only Lyons's and Schwarz's Reich Low Riders identification had allowed them past the doorstep.

As Lyons passed one overturned table, he saw a spill of crystals from a torn bag on the ground. It was next to one of the Heathens that Lyons had emptied three thunderbolt bursts of buckshot into before he would stop shooting and collapse. He didn't even need to touch the stuff to know that some of the bikers they battled were hopped up on methamphetamine. The crank they took could stave off sleep for days, even a whole week. Lyons also knew that madmen fueled by the lethal crystal endured handgun fire as if they were hurled grains of rice. Only the 1216, with its rapid fire and Lyons hitting him with one last shot to the head from a range of two feet had finally put the cranked-up biker down for the count.

"You bastards!" a voice gurgled from the ground.

It was another man on meth, because he sported a sopping wet T-shirt, blood pouring through half of a dozen bullet holes from abdomen to shoulder. His eyes were wild, glazed and unfocused, in direct contrast to the rage in his voice and the energy with how he scrambled to his feet. Lyons also recognized him as Rucks, the homophobic creep who'd challenged Schwarz's undercover role.

Lyons pivoted his shotgun toward the thug, but Rucks threw a wooden bar table up into the air, hurling it between the two men. Lyons's 12-gauge blasts cut into furniture, not biker as the Heathen threw himself to the better cover of the oaken bar.

"The faggot and the pretty boy!" Rucks bellowed at the top of his lungs as he disappeared for a moment. Lyons waved to the other two members of his team.

Schwarz let go of the drag-bag and broke to one side of the bar to flank Rucks, while Lyons stood his ground, waiting for the goon to come out fighting. The only reason Rucks went back behind the bar had to be to settle in for a renewed resistance to Able Team's rampage through the clubhouse. The bar provided a small-arms-resistant barrier and there was likely more firepower for the biker to continue his battle. Rucks's injuries, stitched up his side, would prove fatal if and when he bled to death in a few minutes' time, but the crystal meth kept him alive and alert through otherwise crippling pain.

At this point only the destruction of his brain would end the Heathen's threat. Against a psychopath amped-up on crank, Lyons might use all fourteen shots remaining in his shotgun.

"Surprise!" Rucks bellowed, popping up. Lyons saw the flare of an automatic weapon in the biker's hand. The muzzle-flash also was inches from the Able Team leader's chin, so close he could feel the stubble on his jaw crackle from the heat of escaping gases. Punched in the upper chest by a salvo of slugs, Lyons toppled to the ground, gasping in pain.

Concern seized Schwarz's chest as he watched Rucks fire the machine pistol mere inches from his friend's chest, but the logical, prepared part of the genius's mind was locked on task, another part reminding that worried bit that Lyons wore the Able Team body armor. Multiple sandwiched layers of Kevlar, chain-mail and carbon-fiber trauma plates would protect Lyons from almost anything. The vests had been tweaked by Stony Man armorer John Kissinger, keeping up with the latest in lightweight materials. The chain-mail and Kevlar mix had been enough to keep Able Team alive against AK-47s in Egypt and the Amazon rain forest. The newer carbon fibers and metals had only served to make the body armor lighter and more durable. As there was no blood on Lyons's face, he had not been penetrated by a bullet.

While Rucks's attention was focused on Lyons, Schwarz lunged toward the distracted biker. With one hand, Schwarz yanked on the biker's denim vest and bloody T-shirt. With the other, he stabbed viciously with the muzzle of the Honey Badger. The muzzle brake was toothed, akin to a breaching shotgun's, the teeth meant to grip locks so the gun fired directly into the lock mechanism. The muzzle brake teeth did far more than seize Rucks's ear; it tore through skin and cartilage, digging into the side of the man's head with a vicious grip.

Sure that the Honey Badger would not miss, Schwarz pulled the trigger, the biker's brains exploding from his skull as a flurry of .300 Blackout bullets obliterated both gray matter and bone. The other half of the corpse's skull was an ugly, emptied cavity, and the gunman collapsed in a nerveless heap.

Blancanales had released his prisoners and was kneeling by Lyons's side. He tilted the Able Team leader's head back and checked for an obstruction to his windpipe. No bullets had penetrated the high collar of Lyons's vest, and his throat only had some mild bruising. Lyons opened his steely blue eyes and focused on Blancanales, the team's medic.

"How's your breathing?" Blancanales asked.

"It smells like I'm in a biker bar," Lyons grunted.

Blancanales smirked, opening the vest and looking, probing along the man's collarbone. As soon as his fingers touched a bump on Lyons's clavicle, the big man winced and growled. "Fractured bone. Need me to tape the arm down?"

Lyons's lips were twisted in distaste for the pain.

"My fingers and hand are moving just fine. Put a quick-splint on."

Blancanales pulled one from his medic pack. At the core, the quick-splint was moldable metal mesh, with a non-toxic adhesive that sealed it to the skin and a swiftly drying and hardening polymer gel that became as hard as a rock when exposed to air. It hurt like hell to put it on a fractured bone, but once in place, it solidified and stayed there, preventing movement of the fractured bone.

Lyons growled once more, gritting against the seething pain against his clavicle, but Blancanales had the quick-splint in place. Already the polymer stiffened, holding the bone beneath against its molded contours. The fracture would not grow now that it was sealed in place.

As Lyons got to his feet, he saw Schwarz shooting the last of the biker corpses in the head, making certain no one else would follow Rucks's example and spring from the dead in a meth-fueled rage. Lyons and Blancanales heard the electronics whiz cursing under his breath about "zombie bikers."

"You're being redundant," Blancanales chided his friend. "You shot one of the bikers through a hole he already had in his head," he explained.

Schwarz looked down at the biker whom Lyons had blasted in the head with his shotgun.

"Hey, it could be worse," Lyons offered.

Schwarz tilted his head, his body still tense, wired from Lyons's near-death experience. "Worse than zombie Nazi bikers?"

Lyons nodded. "Zombie ninja Nazi bikers."

Schwarz sighed, shoulders loosening up. "Dude...not funny."

Schwarz and Blancanales helped the Able Team leader to his feet.

"Someone had to step up," Lyons returned. "You better now?"

Schwarz smirked. "For now. But the first throwing star that hits me, I'm blaming you. And if they kill me, yours is the first brain I'm eating."

Lyons rapped on his head. "You'll break your teeth."

"And for not much of a meal, either," Blancanales joked.

Lyons and the team, sharing some banter to take the edge off, now refocused their attention.

"We burned four and a half minutes clearing the first floor," Schwarz announced. "What are the numbers based on our prior visit?"

"A half dozen left," Lyons replied. "Then we clear through to the roof."

Schwarz checked his tablet. "Bear and the gang are ripping through the Heathens' system. They'll be done by the time we exfil."

"What kind of force is Jack going to use to keep heads down out there?" Blancanales asked.

"Jack's a soldier, not a maniac," Lyons returned. "I'm thinking signal flares, blanks and dummy rockets."

Schwarz spoke up. "Let me double check." He brought up a secure com to Grimaldi in *Dragonslayer*. He was nothing if not aware of the needs of modern intelligence in the twenty-first-century battlefield, so among the hardware he'd built into the mobile device was a powerful encrypted radio link, which allowed not only real-time conversation with the Farm, but also any other operational units in the field with them. Grimaldi, with the high-tech helicopter's systems already keyed in directly to receive instant data from the Farm, as well as to transmit data from the bird's sensors to home base, immediately acknowledged Schwarz's call.

"What's up, Gadgets?" Grimaldi asked over the radio.

"Ironman's a little concerned that you might have brought live ordnance to this little dust-up, G-Force," Schwarz said, using the Stony Man pilot's code name.

"No worries on that front," Grimaldi returned. "No way I'm bringing any of *Dragonslayer's* full heat to bear in an urban environment. I brought crowd control in the form of tear gas, smoke and diversion shells, as well as plastic training bullets for the lady's mini."

"No direct fire on the perimeter," Lyons told him. "Even with just plastic, at 6,000 rounds per minute, it will tear up even body armor."

"Nothing but tears to be shed, Ironman," Grimaldi promised. "And a few ringing ears."

"See you in ten," Lyons said.

Schwarz killed the call.

"Six guys, going by the numbers we counted. But it ain't going to be easy," Blancanales noted. "I checked Crunch's rap sheet. He's a meth user, as well as a dealer. Broke a cop's jaw and snapped another one's leg while on crank."

Lyons nodded. "I saw that, too. If he's going to hit up, it's going to be now."

Schwarz sneered. "Then let's give him a chance to go out in a blaze of glory."

Lyons took a moment, feeding shells into the partially spent shotgun's quad-tube magazine, then filling up the spent weapon. His grim pronouncement brought back memories of another murderous, racist biker who had caused the death of an ally of Able Team a few years back. A young Los Angeles assistant district attorney who had joined the trio on a hunt for an escaped murderer to Colombia had reunited with Able Team to battle another gang of thugs.

The prosecutor had given his life assisting Lyons and the men, as had other southern California lawmen. The rallying cry for Able Team to bring the violent thugs to justice was a callback to their pursuit in Colombia. "Prosecution to the max."

No Heathens would be taken alive by the FBI when Able was done, or Grimaldi would have no one to fly back to the Farm.

CHAPTER EIGHT

Alphonse MacCafferty, known to his brother Heathens as Crunch, felt the crank burning through his head, the world around him crawling with each moment. Crunch loved the tingle of a million spiders crawling on the inside of his skull, prickling his bare scalp from beneath. It meant that he was fueled for total war. And nothing would stop him.

There wasn't a single thing in the world that *could* stop him. Godlike strength surged through his veins, and he could hear colors and smell sounds. Maybe he'd taken too much, but damn those invaders, they were attacking the Heathens. If he lived and crashed too hard, then so be it. He'd be fried, but the goddamned pigs would not have done his brothers in without harsh payment.

His four remaining brothers were equally revved up, and he could see instances of their loss of fine motor control as fingers fumbled with shells being stuffed into revolver cylinders, cartridges bouncing off the floor. Crunch caught one of his slugs on the first bounce, his reflexes hyped to respond swifter than the blink of an eye.

Crunch had tweaked for years, and this time, he was in territory of the drug enhancement that he'd never even believed possible.

"No mere men can stand before us, brothers," Crunch said. Even his voice sounded different, the rumble of a hundred Heathens on their sleds, ripping down the highway. He smiled, relishing that trembling energy, feeding upon it. So this was what it meant to be reborn, to ascend to godhood. "They can send every pig at us for a thousand miles, and we'll destroy them."

"We lost too many brothers, boss," Gnarls, one of his lieutenants, stated. "We'll show them what that means. Those bastards will be their slaves in hell."

"Your lips to the gods' ears, Gnarls," Crunch agreed. He stuffed his Blackhawk into its holster and pulled out its brother. Where the one he always wore was a deep, rich, polished blue, the twin was hued in a matte satin silvery finish, and rather than well-worn rosewood grips, the "light sheep" was adorned with stag grips, white, pristine bone with deep, blackened scratches here and there.

Crunch gave the shiny revolver a flourishing twirl, then slid it in place in a rawhide leather chest sheath. If six rounds of .357 Magnum were the hammer of the gods, then twelve were befitting a king of the gods. Crunch would stand with Zeus and Odin, and when he was finally sent down to Hell, it would be as a Duke, not a prisoner.

He swept up a pair of shotguns, sawed-off Browning A-5 autoloaders, obviating the necessity of pumping during combat. Crunch wouldn't shoot one in each hand. He'd simply trade an emptied one for a full one, waiting for a chance to reload at leisure rather than fumble hulls into a magazine in the middle of a firefight.

Then Crunch heard an odd sound, one that bore familiarity, but he could not quite place it. He glanced around for the source of this odd new tone in his experience.

Gnarls finally solved the mystery after seconds that stretched like hours. "Crunch, your phone!"

"Who'd call at a time like this?" Crunch muttered, pulling it from his pocket. "What?"

"Was there something about low profile that you didn't understand, you walking rectal hemorrhage?"

It was his Arrangement contact, and the man didn't sound too happy. Crunch bristled. "Are you kidding me? Eight of your morons commit mass murder and then you expect them to hide in our basement?"

"That is why we gave you that basement!" came his liaison's response. "We gave you a bunker, on the promise that we could use it as a safe house for our operations."

Crunch felt pressure building inside his eyeballs. "You have to be shitting me. We built that ourselves, you—"

"Supplied money and construction materials," the Arrangement flunky interrupted. "Not to mention blueprints and the very idea of that safe room."

"Keep insulting me, Lester. Keep insulting me," Crunch responded. "Once these pigs are cold meat, you're next."

There was a sputter of reaction on the other end. "What did you call me?"

"Lester," Crunch repeated. "You think the Heathens were born last night? We've had you tracked for months, asshole!"

The silence on the other end was all that Crunch needed to know that the Heathens' investigation, research and supposition skills were as sharp as ever. Considering the need to vet prospects, as well as their identity theft enterprises, the Heathens were more than just beer-swilling, meth-abusing gearheads. Dirty denim and worn leather were just the clothes they were most comfortable in, but each of the Heathens could fit in with citizen society if necessary. One simply did not become an arms- and meth-dealing titan of underworld business without technical savvy.

"And if you're lucky, Lester, we might even get killed

by the assholes attacking us. When that happens, they'll get a good look at our files, including everything we have on your sorry ass," Crunch added. "One way or another, you're done, you miserable little douche nozzle!"

The line went dead, the drone of the line a baleful warble that tumbled in his brain.

There was a crack down below. It was the door to the stairs leading up to where he and his brothers had chosen to stand. Crunch looked at his cell phone and then grabbed a spool of duct tape, tearing off a length. With a hard slap, he made certain the device would be hung up and out of the way of any cross fire. It would be hard to mistake the little gadget, especially with two feet of silver bracing it to the wall. Whatever the outcome of battle, that phone would be there, complete with the last known incoming call from Lester P. Romaine, attorney-at-law.

"Good luck beating the rap on these guys," Crunch muttered. "They seem as interested in taking prisoners as we are."

Gnarls nodded. "No warnings. Just shotguns booming and head shots."

The reinforced door cracked again. The Heathens knew how to make a clubhouse.

"We gave you the blueprints…" Romaine had muttered.

"We've been making fortresses since the eighties," Crunch growled.

Gnarls held up his hand. "Ready, Sundance?"

Crunch nodded, high-fiving his friend. "Geronimo!"

The hard door down the stairwell finally surrendered.

Do-or-die time was now.

LYONS TOOK AN unprecedented third Shotokan kick against the armored door leading to the upper floors of the Heathens' clubhouse. Usually when the Ironman applied all of his weight and muscle with his years of precision and discipline in the martial art, even the sturdiest of barriers was broken. This door, however, had been reinforced by professionals, and Schwarz and Blancanales had added their power to taking the steel panel off its hinges. Nearly six hundred pounds of muscle and a combined sixty years of various martial arts disciplines were focused on the fire door, and finally the steel reinforced frame came off its jamb with the squeal and crackle of snapping metal.

"These boys don't mess around," Schwarz said. "Anyone else would have needed the kind of breaching charge that cut through the sewer wall."

"And that was neither small nor light," Blancanales added. "What's the play?"

"Blitz," Lyons growled. "Throw some boom up there. I'm not giving those tweakers a chance."

Blancanales fed a high-pressure flash-bang shell into the 40 mm tube, closed the breech and fired. The grenade hurtled into the ceiling of the stairwell, rebounding to the ground and clattering before it detonated. Flash powder produced more than sufficient brilliant light to leave eyes full of floating suns, obscuring any and all vision because the brightness was essentially akin to staring at the sun for more than a minute.

Not only would the Heathens bikers be blind, the several ounces of high explosive, wrapped only in cardboard to minimize the chance of lethal shrapnel, produced 175 decibels of thunder, louder even than standing only a few feet from an airplane turbine operating at maximum thrust. The threshold for pain and hearing damage was 135 decibels, and the scale of acoustics meant that each ten decibels was double the volume of the previous level, meaning that the bang of the flash-bang was sixteen times louder than necessary to induce even the beginning of permanent hearing damage.

In a way, it would have been kinder to simply smash Crunch and his allies in the ears with sledgehammers. Unfortunately for Crunch and the Heathens, Able Team had little intention of being gentle. They needed to get through the renegade bikers and to the roof, where Jack Grimaldi and *Dragonslayer* waited for rapid exfiltration back to Stony Man Farm. As soon as the air-shattering blast resounded, Lyons took the lead up the steps, vaulting four stairs at a time, his powerful leg muscles driving him up.

"Move on the bang," he had taught the hundreds of lawmen who had come through the blacksuit program. "You wait for the sound to finish, you give them time to recover. It's like in boxing. You don't throw one punch. You hit them, and then you hit them again as fast as you can, not giving them a chance to brace. The same goes for distraction devices. It cracks, and you get in there at the same time. That's why we wear eyes and ears, so we don't stop ourselves when we flash-bang a room."

And indeed, Lyons was wearing adaptive earmuffs that filtered out sound pressure and polarized goggles that prevented blindness, as long as he wasn't looking through night-vision goggles, like the FBI assault team back in the sewers. The wave of force pelted his cheeks, feeling akin to a stiff slap from an irate ex-girlfriend.

"You can't feel pain if you're dead," he reminded himself, plunging through the sonic blast rolling off Blancanales's grenade.

Lyons was alive; he could feel the trip hammer of his heart as he mounted the top of the stairs, catching sight of the assembled bikers, scattered and staggered by the explosive burst. He leveled the 1216 at the closest of the bikers and pulled the trigger twice. At a range of only ten feet, the double-tap of buckshot struck the Heathen in the upper chest. The copper-plated projectiles tore through meat, and the combined impact of nine of those pellets at once snapped ribs and collarbone in one mighty fist of hurtling death. The buckshot glanced off the intervening skeletal structure, their forward momentum turned violently at odd angles. First nine, then eighteen 9 mm tunnels opened up in mere moments. Long, deep wounds burrowed through lung tissue and heart muscle, bouncing off the rubbery aorta, the primary trunk line feeding the body oxygen.

All of these grisly injuries were exacerbated as the buckshot struck the inside of the rib cage, causing more ricochets; there were now thirty-six lines of destruction crisscrossing the internal organs of the biker. These wound channels all happened, multiplying in the space of tenths of a second, and no matter how much energy buzzed through the bloodstream of the meth-amped biker, he was now suffering from deflated lungs, perforated through and through.

With the collapsing air sacs in those lungs, there were brachial arteries, meant to draw fresh oxygen and add it to the bloodstream to keep the biker alive. The severed blood vessels, instead of supplying needed oxygen to his body, now flooded his thoracic cavity, increasing the pressure on the already cut and battered muscle of the heart. Lyons couldn't have stopped the outlaw's heart any more surely if he'd plunged his own hand through the man's chest and squeezed tight. Instead, a fist of blood wrapped around the man's life pump and smothered it.

Lyons didn't intend to take any chances, lifting the muzzle of the mighty 1216 and putting another blast through the biker's face. This stab of lead caved in the maxillofacial structure of the meth-fueled biker. Buckshot and splinters of bone spiraled and sawed through brain tissue, ending the Heathen's existence.

The Able Team leader turned toward a second of the bikers, knowing that he only had seconds to end these men before they gathered a semblance of consciousness. Even as he tried to acquire a new target, he scanned for Crunch's presence. There had only been three men present, and by all calculations, there should have been five. Crunch and one other had fallen back.

With preternatural speed, the biker he leveled the high-capacity shotgun toward lunged for him. Steely fingers clamped down on the barrel of the weapon and Lyons managed to pull the trigger. Buckshot roared from the muzzle of the cannon, catching the Heathen across both thighs. Heavy muscle and femur bones took the violent shock of the near-contact-range shotgun blast, but this time, the chemical fury of crank rushing through his opponent's bloodstream inured him to a wave of pain and physical overload that would have left a normal man writhing on the ground.

Lyons grimaced and leaned back, using weight and leverage to rip the weapon from the biker's grasp, but crank had granted the outlaw maniacal strength that dwarfed even the burly Able Team leader's. He stomped and pivoted, working to wrench the man off his feet, but the biker had a fifty-pound weight advantage, as well as mania that rendered him stubborn as a team of mules and nearly as strong.

Lyons released the shotgun. If he couldn't gain control of the weapon after two seconds of wrestling, he reverted to weapon-retention training. He flicked the safety to neutralize the 1216's ability to fire, then ripped the Smith & Wesson MP-45 from its holster, stepping back to create a buffer of distance. As soon as he landed on his back foot, the sights of the handgun were leveled at the center of his opponent's face. Lyons fired once, 230 grains of wide-mouthed jacketed hollowpoint bullet striking the Heathen between his eyes.

The back of the biker's skull erupted in a volcanic spew of bone and gore, and the outlaw collapsed instantly.

The crackle of Schwarz's Honey Badger submachine gun resounded over Lyons's right shoulder, the rumbling booms dampened by his electronic ears. With a glimpse from the corner of his eye, Lyons could see the frothy crimson spray of vaporized flesh and spurting blood issued by a dozen rifle-round impacts. The extended burst emptied into the cranked-out Heathen was more than normally needed, especially with the hard-punching .300 Blackout slugs. Once again, no chances taken.

"So glad that only a few of these bastards hit the meth," Schwarz said. "I don't think we brought enough ammo to take them all out."

"Sometimes it's just not a question of ammo," Blancanales said, hauling Able Team's prisoners up to the top of the stairs. The two unconscious men, secured in the drag-bag, would hopefully provide answers about those who were ultimately involved in the explosive incident of violence in Washington, D.C. The way things looked now, it was a global conspiracy, and one in which madmen sought to raise the tension between the United States and Japan.

A door exploded at the other end of the room, literally coming off of its jamb. It charged through the room, steel panels stopping and deflecting blasts of shotgun and PDW fire from Lyons and Schwarz. Blancanales fired from the hip, his laser sight pointed to the floor in a hope to intercept the feet of the madman behind the door. Even as Lyons was peppered in his body armor by shattered fragments of his own buckshot, more than a few splinters stabbing into his forearms and cutting through his BDU pants and into the flesh of his legs, the doorman barreled into Schwarz, slamming him off of his feet.

Gnarls, the man behind the door, was like a twelve-cylinder pickup and the door was his plow. Schwarz, however, was not a seven-foot snowdrift. He was slammed by the armored door panels and pushed along violently. Blancanales's laser-guided gunfire swept across Gnarls's feet and lower legs, but if the impact of Blackout slugs had any effect, the way Schwarz was launched off the door was no evidence. Gnarls still had the door in hand, holding it by a pair of U-clamps that would normally hold a crossbar to secure the doorway. The Heathen's strength allowed him to swing the slab of steel.

Blancanales backpedaled, but Gnarls, wild on crank, was swift enough to connect with the barrel and frame of the stubby submachine gun. Iron on iron wrenched the weapon from Blancanales's grasp, the reverberations of the blow numbing his fingers. With a deadened hand, Blancanales knew that swiftly drawing his side arm would be a clumsy, ineffective response. Rather than risk accidentally putting a bullet into Lyons, or allowing Gnarls to gain control of the handgun, Blancanales reached with his off hand, pulling out his ASP collapsible baton. The rod snapped open to three feet in length, all but the neoprene-coated handle gleaming, telescopic steel with a blunt, bone-cracking knob at the tip.

Gnarls was a six-and-a-half-foot tall bruiser, while Blancanales was merely five-eleven and weighed in at 175 pounds of lean, rangy muscle, compared to what appeared to be double that on the Heathens lieutenant. Giving up his entire body weight to an opponent would be almost suicide for any other man, but Rosario Blancanales was a master of *bo jutsu,* the way of the short fighting staff. The ASP baton that Blancanales carried extended to thirty-six inches, nearly the length of the walking stick he sometimes carried to appear unarmed. Made of alloy steel, it was extra long to make use of his adeptness with a fighting cane. Blancanales hoped that he would actually take back that advantage.

Gnarls let the door fall from his hands, sausagelike fingers curling into claws to clutch and rend the Puerto Rican–born Stony Man commando limb from limb. Blancanales brought the point of his baton up, its metal whistling through the air before crashing under Gnarls's chin. The biker's jawbone showed white through torn skin, but the furious engine of crystal meth burned like orange fire behind Gnarls's piglike eyes. A fist the size of a boxing glove shot out, clipping Blancanales on the shoulder, staggering him despite his attempt to roll with the blow.

Blancanales sliced down with the *bo* stand-in as if it were a machete, and once again, meat parted under the lashing speed of the metal slicing through the air and anything else in its path. A thick, hideous flap of forearm muscle and skin gyrated wildly, as if Gnarls had grown a tentacle off his arm. If Blancanales expected a reaction to the pain of carved flesh, he was disappointed as the berserker biker lashed out with his other paw. Hooked fingers clawed the uniform shirt sleeve on Blancanales's arm, red lines of liquid seeping to the surface where the Heathen's nails tore skin.

As fast as Blancanales could backpedal or sidestep, the beast in front of him was nearly as quick. Fueled by crank, Gnarls would not tire as quickly as Blancanales, even bleeding profusely from two savaged slashes. The defensive would mean that Blancanales and the biker

would nickel and dime each other to pieces. At half the
Heathen's weight, Blancanales had fewer pieces by far.
No, it was time for the offensive, and Blancanales lashed
forward, whipping his ASP in a figure eight in the air.
The first slicing arc took out Gnarls's right eye all the
way down to the corner of his mouth. On the back swing,
Blancanales was a step closer and the steel baton cracked
down at the biker's hairline, splitting skin even more,
leaving the end of the collapsible weapon bent askew.

As strong as Gnarls was, his bones did not share his
muscles' immunity to trauma as the methamphetamines
roared through his bloodstream. Skull imploded under
the vicious chop and the handle twisted free from Blancanales's grasp. At this point, thirty inches of steel projected from the center of Gnarls's forehead, making him
look like a stainless-steel unicorn. A flood tide of stringy,
destroyed brain matter and blood poured from the wicked
injury.

Blancanales grabbed the shaft of the baton with both
hands and twisted it upward, throwing all of his weight
against the length of the steel. Bone squelched against
metal as he plunged the fighting stick out the back of
the man's head.

Behind him, Carl Lyons was blindsided by Crunch
in the wake of Gnarls's freight-train passage. Alphonse
MacCafferty hit him; six-gun barrels first, fanning their
hammers with his thumbs as he crushed their triggers
all the way back. The storm of .357 Magnum rounds
stabbed and stung the Able Team leader, even through
his body armor, a half-dozen shots released at a range
of only inches. Air rushed from his lungs in a grunt of
extended agony.

Lyons wouldn't get a chance to inhale, to replenish
his lost oxygen, as Crunch pistol whipped him. The mur-

derous blow and front sight of MacCafferty's revolver opened up Lyons's cheek, whipping his head around and hurling him to the floor. The Heathens chapter president loomed over the fallen Able Team commander, wild eyes taking in the sight of his foe.

"Goddamned liar! Your ink isn't even real!" MacCafferty bellowed.

Lyons painfully sucked in a much needed breath, but didn't speak. Rather, he'd let the Ruger GP-100 do that, ripping it from its holster. Crunch jerked violently as 158-grain slugs smashed into his upper chest. These weren't jacketed lead, which rarely opened, even at their top velocity out of the six-inch barrel of the Magnum. These were nylon-polymer coated, so when they struck, all that speed caused the .357 inch-wide projectiles to flatten and deform into ugly flat flowers of polymer and lead, expanding into flesh-shredding blossoms fully three quarters of an inch across, all the while tearing through blood vessels, bone and nerve junctures.

Even under the abuse of six Magnum impacts, Crunch managed to stay on his feet, though one shoulder slumped as if it were about to melt off his torso. He raised the shiniest silver-white revolver Lyons had ever seen and pointed it right at the Able Team commando's unprotected face.

"Shot your wad. Revolvers only hold six!" Crunch sputtered, blood bubbling over his lips from a perforated windpipe.

Lyons adjusted his aim. "Not this one."

One last pull of the trigger and Alphonse MacCafferty's nose seemed to disappear into a sinkhole in the middle of his face. Smith & Wesson had developed their .357 Magnum revolvers to hold seven rounds in the cylinder. Brilliant Stony Man Farm gunsmith "Cowboy"

Kissinger had worked his magic, matching that capacity for the brawny Ruger's even heavier frame.

Crunch's name was a grisly description of the end of his existence as his skull burst under the tunneling force of Lyons's final bullet.

Blancanales and Schwarz came over to help their friend and leader back to his feet.

"You guys okay?" Lyons asked. Something wasn't quite right with his speech and he realized that the laceration across his face must have been deeper than he thought.

"Yeah, but the cops are knocking at all the doors," Schwarz answered. "Time to blow this pop stand."

Blancanales tore open a pack of gauze, covering Lyons's damaged cheek to control the bleeding and prevent further skin tear. "We've got a date on the roof. Try to look good, okay?"

Lyons nodded. Despite his injuries, he still took the lead. Not until Able Team and their prisoners were aboard the *Dragonslayer* would Lyons allow himself to swallow a handful of pain pills and close his eyes to concentrate on controlling the agony seething across him, literally head to toe. And as an added bonus, he managed to watch Schwarz grab a cell phone that had been taped to a wall. Likely by Crunch, a contingency for revenge.

Mission accomplished. Intel gathered. Murderers put down like the parasites they were.

Lyons couldn't feel a shred of relaxation at this accomplishment.

This war was far from over.

CHAPTER NINE

Dragonfin knifed through the icy waters of the Ross Sea, its engines snarling as the sleek catamaran hopped from wave peak to peak, almost literally flying. Just because the Japanese whaling fleet had been turned around and ordered to return to the home islands did not mean that whoever was at work sinking ships was done.

"Right now, the Australian navy has patrol craft searching for the attackers," Price informed them. "And considering that whoever is on the rampage is looking toward making the Japanese look bad…"

"They might take a few pot shots at the Aussies," David McCarter said. "Australia has *not* been a friend to Japan when it comes to whaling."

"No, it hasn't," Price agreed. "You three have had more than enough time to review the history of these so-called whale wars on the flight down."

"In between drooling over the cool new toy you gave them," McCarter noted.

Calvin James and Rafael Encizo sat in the twin pilot chairs of the high-speed watercraft. Right now, they skimmed the ocean surface at a "leisurely" 120 miles per hour, the resistance of the waves at an absolute minimum as they rocketed along. *Dragonfin* from the very start had been designed in the mold of great racing boats, and while the absolute world's best versions could top 300 miles per hour, the former cocaine smuggling rig had been built for endurance not pure velocity. As such, the twin-hulled craft, looking for all the world like a space fighter from a science-fiction movie, was meant to make long runs at incredible speeds, and keep the crew in relative comfort across the hours of travel.

Cocaine runs were easily 1,300 miles, depending on the launch point, so a little less thrust in exchange for a greater range as well as the ability to carry tons of payload was a necessary trade.

James heard McCarter's complaint and clucked his tongue. "Like you haven't been itching to put the Mk 19s through their paces."

"If the two of you rotters actually could locate our mystery marauder, I'd feel a lot better," McCarter said.

Encizo's swarthy face split into a wide smile. "Don't worry, David. *Fin* has as sensitive a nose as *Dragonslayer* and is twice as pretty."

"Grimaldi might take offense to that," McCarter mentioned.

The two men returned to guiding *Dragonfin,* keeping her engines in good trim, monitoring temperatures and fuel consumption as well as radar and infrared.

Encizo and James were experts in boat operation. One of Encizo's major jobs had been ocean salvage, but he'd also earned his boat pilot's miles while assisting the Drug Enforcement Agency. The Cuban expatriate had cut his teeth vying with cigarette boats that had been the choice of Colombian drug smugglers. James, a former Navy SEAL, had his own experience on RHIBs—rigid-hull inflatable boats that were lightning-fast craft and could deliver nearly a dozen armed commandos, as well as provide considerable cover fire in the form of multiple machine guns.

Dragonfin had been designed with their input and

since the boat had much more area for high-tech electronics, she possessed radar, sonar and infrared sensors, as well as computer-assisted targeting and individually controlled turrets. With a pair of 40 mm grenade-launching machine guns, four light machine guns and two heavy machine guns on board, she was deadly and powerful. The 40 mm cannon and the .50-caliber M-2 Brownings could deal with anything on the ocean with up to two inches of homogeneous steel-armor plating.

If necessary, the quartet of 7.62 mm M-60D light machine guns were meant for sweeping the decks of enemy soldiers or providing precision fire into areas where a .50 Ma Deuce or grenade would cause monumental collateral damage. All the weapons could be slaved to a single operator, enabling any one of the three men to pour sheets of withering firepower on a target, making any foe inside a kilometer the recipient of a wall of murderous lead.

The main weapon of this beast, however, added for the sake of anti-ship warfare, was the M-242 Bushmaster, a 25 mm cannon with an effective range of 9800 feet. The chain gun was capable of firing the Mk 210 HEIT—high explosive incendiary with tracer—shells designed for the navy. Anything without armor would be vaporized; it had been rated to even do damage to main battle tanks.

"You act as if we're not doing anything here." James spoke up. "We're keeping on course to shadow Australian naval craft investigating the area. The last thing we have on hand is a means of seeing stealth craft."

"So we keep close to the targets," McCarter concluded. "Yes, I know that.

"Barb, any idea what hit the factory ships?"

A new window opened up on McCarter's monitor with shots of the underwater wreckage. "Five missiles were fired at the first whaler, and it went down in waters where a nearby science crew had an underwater Remote Operated Vehicle to assist in the investigation. Only four of those missiles detonated. Judging by the blast patterns and the materials at impact, each warhead was approximately 350 pounds of high explosive."

McCarter scrolled through the pictures until he came to the bent, battered shape of an undetonated missile. It was dull, plain metal and had no colors or decals. However he recognized the general shape. "Chinese anti-shipping missile?"

"It corresponds, design-wise, with the Yingji-82," Price said.

"Still in use by the Chinese military, but hardly the kind of stuff exclusive to them," McCarter said. He frowned, scraping his chin with his thumbnail.

"Which is why you're in a rocket-ship and patrolling in support of our allies," Price said. "There's really not much of a way to narrow down all the potential users for the Yingji-82."

"Was the ROV able to see if the fifth missile was live in any way?" Encizo asked.

Price tapped on her tablet a couple of times, visible through their conference cam. "No definitive details on whether it was a dud or a faulty detonator. That was as close as they wanted their cameras to go. But I see your inference. This could have been a plant."

"If the Japanese government gets the feeling that China is somehow behind this, suddenly things get a hell of a lot stickier," James interjected.

"I can imagine a few war hawks in the U.S. government who'd love nothing more than an excuse to rattle a saber at China," McCarter mused. "And didn't you say something about Koreans?"

"T.J. and Gary encountered a group of North Korean

operatives in Tokyo. They may have been behind the murder of an American CIA NOC," Price clarified.

"Baby Butterball doesn't seem the sort of kid to be this tricky," Encizo offered.

Price nodded. "Even so, who would be able to appeal to both American white supremacist bikers and prison gangs and North Korean thugs?"

McCarter went to another monitor and pulled up a screen on the Yingji-82. "Ground-based launchers, decktop launchers, even fixed-wing aircraft."

He focused on a photo of a ship-mounted launcher, holding four of the deadly missiles fitted on a Pakistani naval craft. "Four cells. Five missiles hit. Only four exploded. It's a plant. It's a carrot for us to follow."

"Conserving ammunition for the other three cells in a second launcher?" Encizo asked.

"Why?" James countered. "Multicell launchers aren't all or nothing. They could refit the cell with a fresh missile."

"This is a 2700-ton frigate that has two quad cells," McCarter said. "And those back up an eight-cell SAM launcher, a 76 mm main cannon, torpedoes and antisubmarine rocket pods."

"Well, then it couldn't have been a frigate," Price said. "We didn't detect anything that large on satellite radar infrared."

"No, you'd need a fast-attack boat, something like the Albatross or Roussin," McCarter noted. He wasn't a naval expert, but he knew that most of the patrol boats in the Royal navy were just too small for a multicell missile launcher capable of wrecking the Japanese whaling craft, and there was little in terms of fighting craft between the 50-odd ton Archer-class maritime patrol and 1,700 ton River-class corvettes. Thankfully, for his British pride, McCarter knew the Roussin-class was at least of British design.

"What made you think fast-attack boats?" Price asked. Then she thought of outfitting a German navy craft with a Chinese-designed anti-ship missile. "Pakistan has Albatross-class ships license-built for their navy. And they've armed them with Yingji-82 cells."

"Yeah," McCarter replied. "The Yingji itself also fits nicely into the same envelope as many other anti-ship missiles, like the Exocet family."

Price nodded. "And if one country has access to license-build a ship…"

"Chances are the genie is out of the bottle on those designs," McCarter said. "A country like Pakistan has already showed how trustworthy it could be by housing the world's most wanted terrorist less than a mile from their version of West Point."

"Most of those license-built boats are ordered from Turkey, however," Encizo noted.

"Considering they made our NOC's murder look like a Thuggee assassination, we're never going to untangle this web," James grumbled.

"Don't be such a downer, Cal," McCarter said. "We haven't dropped a ball yet."

"Law of averages, man," James murmured.

"We've got faint shadows on a RAN frigate," Price announced. "Sending coordinates to your screens."

"Changing heading to intercept course. Permission to lay on the throttle?" James asked.

McCarter nodded. "Make her fly."

He pulled up the satellite image on his screen. It wasn't a single craft; there were two faint signatures, and this from some of the best downward-looking radar systems in the United States's intelligence service. The

Australian ship, an Armidale-class patrol boat named the *Frankhurst,* was moving at just under thirty miles per hour.

Even as he looked at the screen, an informatic popped up next to it. Twenty Royal Australian naval personnel were on board the craft. It was fitted with electronic countermeasures and a 25 mm Bushmaster cannon as its main weapon, a couple of M-2s riding on turrets on the deck. Against craft armed with missiles, it was going to be a slaughter.

The shadows were twelve miles from the *Frankhurst,* but going by McCarter's reckoning of the ship-killers being aboard fast-attack craft, that meant the Australians were almost within range of not only the Yingji missiles, but also the main 76 mm cannon that such a boat would be carrying.

"We're not much better armed than they are," McCarter mused.

"Don't be a downer," James returned. "We're low profile ourselves, and we've got more than sufficient punch to deal with a lot of things."

McCarter hoped that *Dragonfin* would match up to a 200-foot, 400-ton enemy ship as easily as James boasted.

The catamaran accelerated to its full 180 miles per hour and Phoenix Force peeled off to intercept an ambush on the Australian naval vessel *Frankhurst.*

Back at Stony Man Farm, Price sent them silent prayers of support, even as she sent the team real-time telemetry. *Dragonfin* had twenty miles of ocean to cross to catch up to the murderers.

Seven minutes to save more than twenty lives.

As much as Price's stomach churned, with the odds likely against them given the size of the ships that could carry such missile launchers, this was right up Phoenix

Force's alley. The Stony Man teams had all fought against impossible odds.

While the teams had achieved victories in most of their cases, there were more than a few allies who'd gone down that deadly alley with them, even members of each squad who had never returned.

Price prayed that this would not become one of those dead-end plunges.

THE PRESIDENT DIDN'T have a lot of time, but he managed to take a few minutes away from prying ears to be briefed on the current situation by Hal Brognola. Along with debates in constant flux, the international tensions rising around at least a group of Japanese businessmen going rogue and engaging in murder on American soil were making the White House a buzz of madness.

"Please tell me that you've got something that will keep us from going to war with Japan," the Man said to Brognola.

Brognola had earned his bulk the hard way and the wrinkles he sported showed the years for which he'd fought for this country, sitting on the front lines against criminal and foreign espionage conspiracies. His eyes held the haunted gaze of a man years older than his middle age, weighed down with the horrors of far too many innocents killed, their bodies left as wreckage for the sake of ideology and greed.

The President, before meeting with men like Brognola, had always assumed that anyone in charge of a covert agency was a man filled with personal ambition or the desire to gain influence and power. Yes, Brognola and his co-founder of the Sensitive Operations Group, Mack Bolan, had *sought* that influence, that clearance, that sanction in the form of the federal government, but the power was a means to an end.

The world of corruption that Brognola and the Farm fought against operated with far fewer reins than the agency had given itself. In government, the term discrimination often signaled an unfair bias, a prejudice against a particular group. For Stony Man Farm, however, discrimination was exactly how they determined what the real threats were, and how they proved capable of doing their job without inflicting needless harm and suffering on those not involved in the wrongdoing.

Brognola and his people "discriminated" between guilty and innocent. And when they made that determination, they applied their force with extreme prejudice. The SOG's track record had proved their effectiveness, their dedication to truth and justice. There were times when the President looked at these brave men and women and wished that he could put them in front of the bickering ninnies in Congress to show them what real teamwork, what real dedication to home and country, stood for. However, as with the rest of American lawmen and servicemen, the Stony Man team worked best when it was completely divorced from a political agenda.

Brognola finished scrolling on his tablet to refresh his memory from notes and turned to the Man.

"The good news, it seems like the Japanese government itself is innocent of wrongdoing," Brognola stated. "It's highly unlikely that they would hire white supremacist extremists to do their dirty work in the U.S. and then utilize North Korean intelligence operatives in Japan."

"North Korea?" the President asked. "Does this seem like an official operation? Something that little Kim would be interested in?"

Brognola shook his head. "Too much obfuscation.

North Korea isn't known for its intense subtlety. There's far more at work here. We've speculated and are tracking ships being built in Turkey, meant for the Pakistani naval forces."

"Ships? What kind?"

Brognola pulled up a picture on his tablet. "We're looking at German-designed, license-built, fast-attack boats, likely in the 400-ton range, to combine speed but also to provide enough bulk to be a good missile platform. These ships are likely to have a complement of roughly forty sailors to operate anti-shipping missile pods, as well as torpedoes and long-range heavy cannons."

"Long range?" the President asked.

"Ten miles in many cases," Brognola returned. "Three-inch shells. Some shells like the VULCANO 76 system can shoot even farther—twenty-four miles."

The President frowned. "Turkish or Pakistani naval craft?"

"It's one example of what we could be looking at. We've been double-checking other potential license-built, high-tech warships capable of carrying multicell missile pods," Brognola said. "I'm also not ruling out Q-ships or reverse-engineered warships produced by a more covert shipyard."

"Like the one your team took down in Maryland?" the President inquired. "Or the follow-up that supplied the ship and subs for the La Palma crisis?"

"Exactly," Brognola answered. "Building a 400-ton warship, or retrofitting an appropriate-size freighter or fishing boat for weapons and high speed, is not a small, quiet operation, but it has been done."

"Does the enemy ship have to be that big?" the President asked.

"We're looking as far down the scale as the Tiger

class, which is three-quarters the size and a little more than half the weight, but we're looking at worst-case scenario," Brognola said. "That size still doesn't go faster than forty miles an hour, so our crew on the seas can easily catch up."

"But something tells me your high-speed interceptor doesn't have the weight or firepower," the President responded.

"We've got a forty-foot, twin-hull ship that is the closest thing to a Buck Rogers star fighter. It's well armed for dealing with most problems, but if it comes to a stand-up slug fest, the fast-attack-size ships only have to hit it once, while the best weapons on board are four torpedoes and a 25 mm cannon," Brognola explained.

The President looked at the accordant list of similar-size ships, their speed and armament. "Could we scramble air support for them?"

"I'd prefer to minimize the number of people in the area shooting at each other," Brognola said. "As it is, we've sent our telemetry to the Royal Australian navy."

"Something is happening right now?"

Brognola nodded.

"Damn," came the response from the most powerful man in the Free World. "And we can't do much more without jeopardizing the secrecy of Stony Man?"

Brognola shook his head. "Our plan is to at least delay any attack on the Aussies. We slow them down, and then the bad guys pick up Australian aircraft on their radar and they head out and run for the hills."

"But in the meantime, we hope to get lucky and at least damage one of them?" the President asked.

"Phoenix is not in the habit of letting wounded enemies escape justice," Brognola answered. "And we definitely do not shoot to wound. It sounds ruthless…"

"How many hundreds are dead so far?"

"Murderous or non-murderous?" Brognola queried.

The President nodded. "They started with the ruthlessness. It's time to show these psychopaths what it feels like."

"That is our job."

Brognola watched the President take a few deep breaths, wash the bitterness from his mouth with a swig of bottled water then head to the White House press corps to discuss new legislation.

Brognola wished the Man luck, but not so hard as he wished his own warriors good fortune on the seas of battle.

CHAPTER TEN

"Sir, we have faint radar contacts aft," Lieutenant Haggarty announced on the bridge of the HMAS *Frankhurst,* the anxiety and surprise in his voice jarring Captain McKintridge. The *Frankhurst* had been dispatched as part of a larger strike force to aid in the search for those who had attacked Japanese whalers in the Ross Sea.

While the *Frankhurst* wasn't a missile boat like the one that had been speculated to have attacked the factory ships, it was still full of men trained and dedicated to protecting fisheries. At nearly thirty miles per hour at full speed, the Armidale-class could cover a lot of water. It also had an impressive range of well more than 3,000 nautical miles, meaning that it would be ideal for aiding in the search.

Her 25 mm Bushmaster and .50-caliber machine guns might prove of use, but the real "firepower" the *Frankhurst* would summon would be a squadron of RAAF F-18 Hornets dispatched as Combat Air Protection for the fleet as it hunted the marauders. One call and the Hornets would be on their way at Mach 1.8 before slowing to their low-altitude attack speed. Their 20 mm cannon and air-to-surface missiles would hammer any target they needed to.

"'Faint radar contacts'?" McKintridge asked, moving to the radar screen. "All hands, full speed ahead. Battle stations."

The bridge went to full alert and the thrum of the engines grew. McKintridge looked over the radar screen. "They're beyond the horizon. We can't get a better signal?"

"We shouldn't even be getting this kind of feed. They're too low profile, and our S and X bands shouldn't be picking them up," Haggarty responded. "We seem to be getting this data from downward-looking satellite tracking. As it is, we're tracking them at 40 knots and they're closing in on us from thirteen miles."

McKintridge grumbled. "Raise the RAAF. We've made contact and we need air cover."

"On it, sir."

McKintridge looked over the radar returns. "They look about 180 feet each."

An alert klaxon blared on the screen. "The Prism III has picked up incoming projectiles."

McKintridge frowned. "Evasive action!"

A thunderous explosion landed forty yards off starboard, the 76 mm shell landing awfully close for the captain's taste. He wasn't certain how much gun power was on each of the enemy craft, but they'd reached ten miles and come within yards of striking the *Frankhurst*. That kind of distance and the size of the column of froth thrown up by the shell's impact meant that he had very little intention of finding out what would happen if the bastards hit him. There were twenty men on board and McKintridge vowed to bring them home from this patrol.

"Where're those Hornets?" he asked Haggarty.

"Four hundred miles northwest," the lieutenant answered. "More shells incoming."

This time the double splash of shells striking the waves was fifteen yards off their aft. The shells were only about five yards apart from each other and had struck simultaneously. McKintridge swallowed. "They're both shooting."

As soon as he realized how close the enemy ships had homed in on the *Frankhurst*'s position, he gave an immediate order. "Full reverse until we slow to half! Helm to starboard immediately!"

The equivalent of hitting the parking brake for a power turn was an iffy proposition, but then, this was truly an emergency situation. Momentum pushed him up against a console as the 3,112 horsepower diesel engines thrust in reverse. The engine room alarms blared, mixing in with the Prism III's early warning about the incoming shells.

Off the port bow, another pair of shells impacted, slamming into the water they would have been in had they continued at full speed ahead.

"Full speed now!" McKintridge commanded. "Hard to port!"

He hoped the maneuvers would keep them ahead of enemy gunfire until the Hornets arrived. He also realized that there was an odd dissonance in this ambush. They'd been on the lookout for missile-armed craft, armed with weapons that had 250-mile ranges. Why risk coming within ten miles to use guns?

Because they're either not the same people who opened fire on the whalers or they want to look like they're not the same, McKintridge thought.

"The Hornets are reporting they have nothing on radar," Haggarty said. "They can't see a thing at the coordinates we've given them."

"No sight, no laser paint, no air-to-surface missiles," McKintridge murmured. He gave another course and speed correction, and the *Frankhurst* rocked as a 76 mm shell landed only yards off the hull. The pressure from the detonation, amplified by the density of the ocean, made it no surprise to the captain when he had reports of the hull nearest the explosion buckling.

We're taking on water, and our planes can't see to get a shot on the bastards trying to kill us, McKintridge thought. He looked upward. Anytime you feel like answering prayers, God…

A wash of foam splashed across the windshield of the bridge.

"One more shot and they've got us," McKintridge muttered. "I'm so sorry, men.

BY THE TIME *Dragonfin* had approached the two faint radar contacts given to them by Stony Man Farm, the first volley of high-velocity gunfire had taken off. They were six miles out from their targets and McCarter knew they had another seven miles before they were in range with their .50s and the mighty Bushmaster. That was even if the 25 mm chain gun had any hope of punching through the armor of the enemy ships.

Downward radar imagery from the satellites only provided rough estimates of the two craft that hounded the Australian patrol boat, but with their 190-foot length and their speed of 46 miles per hour in full attack mode, McCarter was certain that these were not converted fishers or freighters. That kind of speed at that particular bulk only came from professionally built, military-grade engines and screws.

"Cal, they're gonna blow those poor bastards apart," McCarter announced. "They're calling for help, but air support is minutes out."

"Six miles to firing range," Encizo announced. "We're three minutes from engagement."

"I've got the throttles wide-open," James said. "We couldn't go any faster if Gary and Carl were in the back pushing…"

McCarter frowned, then took a look at the angle that

he could elevate the cannon. "Barb, can you give me a GPS lock on where at least one of those bloody barges is sitting?"

"You're thinking of dropping some Hail Mary bombs on them," Price interpreted. "You'll be able to cut loose in another four miles, meaning two minutes instead of three."

"Every second counts when those poor bums are being shot at," McCarter returned.

"At the speed we're moving, and I'm squeezing another few knots out of the engines, we should be fairly stable," James offered. "So take your shot if you can figure the range."

McCarter nodded. "Already doing the math right now. Thanks for a great calculator function and weather reports so I can adjust for wind."

Encizo and James kept *Dragonfin* on course and McCarter caught a glance that they had accelerated to 192 miles an hour. Given his calculations and the new speed, they'd be in firing range in a minute and a half. Even so, he took a look at the satellite imagery of the HMAS *Frankhurst* and just how close the enemy's guns came to the Australian patrol boat. McCarter commended the captain and the helm, the hard reverse thrust and sharp turns had bought them precious moments, but that wouldn't last forever. All the horsepower in *Dragonfin*'s twin turbines would prove to be an ideal counter to the fast-attack ships, but the *Frankhurst* was a third slower than the pair of ocean predators closing in on her. Those guns would find their target soon enough.

Judging by the projectile velocity and range of the enemy's fire power, it was no doubt that the ships were armed with 127 mm Otobreda guns. They were de rigueur for navies from the United States to Pakistan. Japan's own fighting ships were armed with the Otobredas, so it wouldn't be too unusual for those cannons to tear into anyone. Even if the crimes weren't pinned on Japanese interests, Otobredas had been used by dozens of nations on multiple platforms. Tracking down the origins of the shells or the guns would be next to impossible.

Painful seconds hurtled past, McCarter constantly adjusting his aim by hundredths of a degree. On another screen, he watched as incoming fire drew closer and closer to the men he and his partners were speeding to protect. He watched as a shell splash sprayed, engulfing the *Frankhurst* in a cloud of foam, the shot missing by only feet.

She was already slowed, a near hit having struck the water and producing a pressure wave that buckled the hull. Encizo read off the data being fed to them via the Farm's surveillance of the Australians. The *Frankhurst* was taking on water, the engines losing efficiency as the mass of the ship increased with the sudden flood belowdecks and the cruel dent altering her normally streamlined hull.

McCarter kept his eye on the targeting. His jaw was clenched tight, as if the grinding of his molars could somehow increase the speed of *Dragonfin* or impel the shells from his gun to reach hundreds of yards farther with greater accuracy. He saw the threshold of the Bushmaster's extreme range clocking down closer to zero, and even before they hit that point, he triggered the mighty cannon.

The first four 25 x 137mm shells erupted from the muzzle of the heavy gun at 3,600 feet per second, soaring in a parabolic arc that, McCarter's calculations willing, would sail past the horizon and land more than four miles away. The gun was essentially part of the Mini-Typhoon weapons system and, as such, was equipped with fire-control radar, laser range-finding, forward-looking infrared and other enhanced electronics. Even with all of that technology aiming and directing the cannon, it was still a matter of human marksmanship.

The volley of shells, ripping along at 1,203 yards per second, would take a little more than six seconds to reach his target. In that time his enemies could alter their course, a shell could strike a bird in flight, an errant gust of wind could knock them off course...

Any small factor such as that, and suddenly the twenty Australian sailors would be doomed. If McCarter could hone or alter the course of his fire by isometrically tightening every muscle in his body, then so much the better. The enemy didn't have to worry about hitting with their shots. The Otobreda guns had a huge store of 76 mm shells and didn't have to worry about the slower Armidale-class ship racing out of their ten-mile range.

Six seconds that McCarter held his breath, waiting for his shots to strike. Even with the wait, he triggered two more four-round bursts at 200 rounds per minute.

Hit! Hit! Hit! The chanted thought wouldn't do anything more to telekinetically manipulate the accuracy of his opening salvo, but it had to do something.

"Radar is picking up impacts!" Encizo announced. "The Bushy might not rip their ship apart, but it's torn whatever stealth cover they have. The one you smacked is now blatant on radar and its shadow is breaking its original course."

McCarter took the input from Encizo's sensor readings, feeding them into his calculations to hit the other target. Even as he did so, Encizo gestured that the next eight shots he'd hammered out had also struck their target.

"Olympic pistol marksman," McCarter mused. "Fundamentals of hitting a target, any size, any weapon."

"Gold medal performance," James said. "But they're turning right on us."

"Missile launches!" Encizo added. "They've got us targeted. Guns also discharging."

McCarter hit the chaff trigger and thousands of flakes of foil burst from a dispensing canister in a streamlined bump atop the sleek *Dragonfin*. At his station, Encizo was quickly working the scrambler equipment, sending out false radar positives and beams of "white noise" radiation to confuse the incoming missiles. Looking out of his cockpit, McCarter could see splashes striking the water behind the fast-moving catamaran.

Even if they managed to put the missiles off their tracks, those 76 mm shells would take them out with a single hit. McCarter pushed that thought out of his mind. Encizo and James were milking and massaging all the performance they could out of *Dragonfin*'s systems to avoid being hit by the enemy's gun or missiles. All of this would have been for nothing, however, without return fire. Sooner or later, if the Briton didn't keep their attention focused on Phoenix Force, the marauders would realize they were under attack by one ship, and the two fast-attack boats would split their efforts, guaranteeing the destruction and demise of the Australian patrol boat.

McCarter sighted on the other craft and held down the trigger. The ten-round burst erupted, and already he was feeling off about his chances on that salvo. *Dragonfin* had four torpedoes, but going up against warships that could aim beyond the horizon, he didn't think they could get through any countermeasures the marauders would have.

Not if they had the technology to slam targets from miles and miles away, such as their missiles and guns.

Surely the conspirators would have equipped their murder craft with defenses. Only the unguided nature of the Bushmaster rounds and McCarter's marksmanship skills allowed him to hit.

"Three miles and closing," Encizo announced. "We've broken their missile lock, but their radar is sweeping."

"Cal, we'll need to get in close," McCarter said. "I want to punch them with one of our torps."

For the sake of weight, *Dragonfin* was armed with four Mark 54 Lightweight Hybrid Torpedoes, each of them a little more than 600 pounds and able to generate the equivalent of 238 pounds of TNT. That kind of energy would prove quite powerful, but McCarter, like many of the U.S. Navy's experts, was less than thrilled with the concept of the repackaged guidance systems. However, if the MAKO LHT did hit, that warhead would shatter even the sternest of hulls.

"I've got the RAAF Hornets closing in on one of the ships. Registering missile launches from both," Encizo said. "Here's where we see if the ships have CIWS for antimissile defense."

"What about the other?" McCarter asked.

"We're inside a mile and a half," Encizo returned. He looked up and all three men scanned the horizon, hoping to catch a glimpse of the enemy ship with their naked eyes. It was one thing to get the craft on FLIR or radar, but they also wanted confirmation; they had a need to actually *see* the damned enemy ship.

Encizo returned to monitoring the radar. "One missile down. They've got CIWS. Second missile hit. Ship's limping."

"Barb, if you've got *anything* coming off those fighters…" McCarter ventured.

Back at the Farm, Price had already anticipated the

request. "We've been tracking guidance signals on the missiles. No TV guidance, though. They're hitting the ships with HARMs."

"High-speed anti-radiation missiles homing in on their radars," McCarter said. "The same radar that allowed them to nearly sink the *Frankhurst*. Any news on her?"

"Still up and cutting the waves," Encizo returned. "Hornets are firing again. Not letting the other ship go."

"No sympathy for those bastards," James added. "There! She's got some good stealth paint, but I can make her out from her gun."

McCarter's lips pulled tight. "Rafe, hit them with everything we can to scramble their sensors. I want to put this torpedo down their throats!"

"One haze of static dropped on their eyes," Encizo replied. "Barb, maybe a little assist from home?"

"We've got our satellites pumping them with false data as we speak," Price said.

"All right," McCarter cajoled as he slaved the Brownings and the Bushmaster together at the gunner's console. "Rafe, you have fire control on the Mako."

"Sizing him up," Encizo returned. "That does look a bit like a Houbei catamaran, but it sure as hell is bigger. It's also got a third hull, making it a trimaran."

McCarter sneered. "Here I was hoping it was just happy to see us. Looks about 400 tons, easily double the *Houbei*."

"Not license-built, but close enough to fool people at a distance," James noted. The catamaran swerved, the Chicago badass taking evasive maneuvers as the super-Houbei's arsenal turned toward killing *Dragonfin*. Where missiles and the 76 mm main gun had failed, perhaps their heavy machine guns would work.

McCarter cut loose with the combined fifties and the

25 mm, sweeping the enemy ship even as their gunners sought to track and destroy the nearly 200-mile-per-hour boat. In thirty seconds they zoomed within a hundred yards and James whipped *Dragonfin* into a tight orbit around the enemy ship. With the raking fire of the automatic weapons, the decks of the ship were peppered with detonations and sparks from heavy slug impacts. McCarter clicked on the Mk 19s and suddenly the Bushmaster's thunderous impacts were joined by the kind of mayhem that only 40 mm grenades could bring to bear. Even so, the armor of the super-Houbei lookalike held well.

Unfortunately the heavy machine gun positions on the deck were not as sturdy and well-armored as the hull. McCarter targeted one of the units—a dual DShK turret from the quick glance—and he obliterated the position. Grenades and cannon shells shredded the weapon and the men operating it, a flurry of devastation that caused the bigger, slower craft to cut course hard.

The Otobreda swiveled in its attempt to track the lightning-quick catamaran, and 76 mm shells boomed so close that McCarter could feel the air compress around them.

"Cal, give me an angle on this son of a bitch," Encizo called.

McCarter held on to his chair tightly as *Dragonfin* whipped around, making a turn so tight that he almost wished he'd been wearing a G-suit. As soon as the catamaran was remotely facing the enemy ship, Encizo cut loose with the acoustic-guided torpedo.

The CIWS—close-in weapon system—blazed away, 20 mm rounds smacking the waves in their wake. The guns, whose radar was calibrated to shoot down supersonic anti-ship missiles, had trouble dealing with a slower but more laterally maneuverable ship that was producing bursts of radio static. The CIWS wanted something like an Exocet or a Yingji missile, producing its own radar impulses, not the now relatively passive catamaran.

The acoustic homing systems on the Mark 54 torpedo didn't even register on the radar-guided guns. And at 46 miles per hour, on an angled intercept course with the marauders' ship, it cut completely past the beleaguered senses of the swiftly racing 400-ton trimaran. Roughly 97 pounds of high explosive erupted like the crack of doom, an intense wave of pressure folding back entire sections of the hull like tinfoil.

Mortally wounded, the enemy ship slowed from its breakneck pace of forty miles per hour. McCarter sighted in on the missile cells with *Dragonfin's* guns and hammered the launcher with everything. Heavy-caliber bullets, 25 mm cannon and 40 mm grenades smashed into the killer pod. Fuel in the stored missiles ignited as the sheet of dragon fire ripped into the weapon.

A grisly blossom of fire crisscrossed with carbonized air washed over the hapless marauder, adding further to the mayhem on board. Crew members of the fast-attack craft had either been reduced to standing hunks of charcoal or had thrown themselves into the ocean between Australia and Antarctica. Encizo decided to send them something to warm themselves in the form of withering scythes of M-60D automatic fire.

A slurry of 7.62 mm NATO rounds sliced into the men, slashing them to ribbons to spare them the slow, numbing agony of death by hypothermia in the chilling waters. Blood frothed from Encizo's raking bursts. McCarter, on the other hand, continued to hammer the deck and superstructure of the warship with explosive rounds.

James didn't seem concerned with the thudding impacts of bodies against the catamaran's hulls.

Six tons of *Dragonfin* sank its figurative talons, breathing withering metal and fire on the super-Houbei. Smoke and flame roiled off the decks, especially the horrible, gaping wound in the starboard hull of the ship. McCarter decided to pour salt into the wound in the form of .50 BMG and 40 mm grenade rounds that hosed through the gaping hole in the side of the boat.

"David, we're giving you a fifteen-minute window to investigate the ship," Price offered. "The Hornets are chasing down a false craft, while Search and Rescue are checking up on the damaged patrol boat."

McCarter took a look at the map. The *Frankhurst* was miles away, as was the other ship, obliterated from the surface of the ocean by the wrath of Australian F-18s.

Investigating the ship meant going aboard and going through the dead. On a ship that was now taking on water, sinking, with flames and possibly angry survivors on board.

Even so, the 200-ton warship would have information on board regarding this conspiracy.

McCarter motioned for James to get closer to the wounded ship and then reached for his combat vest. Time to get close and deadly.

CHAPTER ELEVEN

James steered *Dragonfin* to the side of the ship as Mc-
Carter and Encizo, on the roof of the craft, moved easily
between the turrets mounted on the nacelles. Both men
had grapnel hooks and lines, multiple sets to the railing
of the other ship.

With deft tosses, they managed to snag the crippled,
burning, fast-attack craft with their hooks and quickly
tied off to moorings James deployed hydraulically. The
rodes in this case were nylon rope, strong and moisture
resistant, as well as being inflexible. The last thing that
any of the men involved needed was for elastic leads to
yank them around, rubber-banding them against the un-
damaged port hull of the larger, heavier ship.

With those lines secured, James would stay on board
the catamaran, using the M-60Ds in their mounts to cover
his partners as they climbed aboard. When it came time
to leave, James could either wait for his partners to untie
the rodes from their moorings or simply retract them. As
they descended, the hydraulics had enough strength to
stretch the rodes tight so the closing lids of the moorings
could slice them.

McCarter crawled up the rope, hand-over-hand, hanging beneath and glad for the knots that served as hand-
holds.

Encizo's climb was even faster. Scaling rigging was
something Encizo had done since he was a child. Few

things developed musculature like a life at sea; either rowing, climbing, even dealing with rodes made of steel cable or chain. He was over the railing and standing guard, scanning with his Heckler & Koch UMP-45 shouldered and ready. "Need a hand back there?"

McCarter bit off a grunt of effort as he tugged himself up the last few feet of rope. The last thing he needed was to be seen as slowing down. Granted, McCarter was in fantastic physical condition, even with a Player's cigarette habit and the occasional pint at the pub, but the men of Phoenix Force were the world's best. With that rank, there was the occasional competitive ribbing between them. Encizo had a few years on McCarter, so when it came to climbing, the Cuban always felt a need to ride the Briton. "Sod off, old man."

Hands on the railing, McCarter twisted lithely, planted his feet against the side of the ship and then kicked off to vault onto the deck. As he did so, he had his FNX-45 pistol out, thumb resting on the safety, ready to deactivate it and open fire if necessary. He'd gone with the FNX pistol because it was the most functionally and ergonomically similar firearm to his beloved classic Browning Hi-Power. It also took the same ammunition as James's and Encizo's HK 45Cs and UMP submachine guns. As they'd be spending most of their time in *Dragonfin*, the three of them had opted to go for the big .45 ACPs for use in close quarters. The Phoenix Force leader also wanted to end the incessant ribbing about him being so hidebound about carrying the most perfect personal handgun in the world. Locked and cocked, the FNX-45 carried just like the Browning and shared both a company and design heritage. That it was carrying fifteen fat-jacketed hollow-points plus one in the barrel was simply icing on the cake.

"Maybe if you cut back on the cigarettes," Encizo offered, noting the faint signs of exertion on his friend.

McCarter rolled his eyes. "Maybe you should cut back on the catamarans—"

Encizo cut him off. "Movement right." Both men moved away from the railing, seeking the cover of a hatchway.

"The bridge," McCarter motioned.

Dragonfin's M-60D turrets suddenly roared to life. Whatever had caused the movement had attracted Calvin James's attention and he applied a smear of 7.62 mm NATO medicine topically to the source. Whoever sought to come after the Phoenix pair was either well dissuaded or turned to a greasy smear. James had their back, so McCarter and Encizo made their way through the superstructure.

Already, clues as to what was behind all this were readily apparent. Signs were written in Kanji, something that McCarter made certain to take a good look at. One of the things that would make this recon much easier was the high-quality digital camera he wore on his helmet. In recent years, both soldiers and athletes had taken to utilizing portable, easily mounted miniature cameras to record their work.

The technical minds at the Farm had been working on something similar for a while. Able Team's Hermann Schwarz had field-tested telephoto lenses and directional microphones on rifles for the purpose of surveillance and real-time intel.

While most of the sporting cameras were incredibly light—2.6 ounces normally, double that with a protective housing—they were relatively large and stuck out, likely to snag. Schwarz had worked to maintain the same hour-plus of battery life on maximum image settings—

with more than two hours on other settings—but fit into a sleek, flat, streamlined design that wouldn't stick out farther than the operator's ear. The result was not only two ounces less than a well-armored polycarbonate shell, and low-profile, minimal-snag wires connecting it to a power source that could run for ten hours even utilizing night-vision and illuminators, his design could hold a terrabyte of information, as well as hook up with Phoenix Force and team communicators in real time.

"Getting this, Barb?" McCarter asked. "Looks Chinese."

He couldn't see the mission controller's face but he could "feel" her wheels spinning as thoughts went through her head. "Computer Kanji translation confirms. Mandarin Chinese."

"And yet it looks like a German design," Encizo offered. "Possible knockoff?"

McCarter scoffed. "T.J. grabbed a P-228 off a Korean assassin that was manufactured, sans license, in China. Of course this was a knockoff."

"A lot looks unfinished, like this was a prototype," Encizo noted.

"That's because the People's Liberation Army navy went with the Houbei-class trimarans for both its fast-attack capabilities *and* stealth profile," Price returned.

"Trimarans," Encizo murmured.

"Now is not the time to take your boner pills, old man," McCarter chided. "We need to focus."

Encizo chuckled at the brotherly insult. "All right, slowpoke."

In the distance behind them, fresh gunfire sounded.

"Cal? Trouble?" McCarter asked.

James sounded nonchalant even as the unmistakable rumble of the M-60s resounded in response. "No. Just the same assholes who tried to sneak up on you in the smoke before. They think they can hurt *Dragonfin* with an SMG."

"Any look at their faces?" McCarter asked.

"No, but the turret camera is being fed to the Farm," James replied.

"Barb?"

Price sounded distracted. She must have pulled the footage and was isolating the best frames for identification of the enemy force. "I'm handling this bit myself because the rest of the team is still tied up with sorting out the data from Japan and the Heathens."

"No rush," McCarter returned. He transitioned to the UMP-45 from his pistol, holstering it. He and Encizo were moving through the superstructure, watching their corners, sweeping for anyone who seemed to be a threat. Thankfully, the submachine gun was only 30 inches long with its stock extended. An integral suppressor extending the barrel by only three inches. Though he was wearing electronic hearing protection, the suppressor would also tamp down the muzzle flame in case they ended up in a flammable environment, such as the middle of a fuel leak. "You might end up with personnel footage from our end."

Despite the sound of alarms blaring on the ship, the distant crackle of gunfire and the groaning of stressed metal as the ship shifted on the swell of waves, McCarter could hear the loading of weapons ahead of him. The Mk 54 had torn this warship a brand-new hole and it was crying out in agony as the very ocean beneath her stretched her out as if on a torture rack. This ship was a battleground now, and there were men up ahead who had attempted to murder a crew of Australian navy sailors and had been implicit in the slaughter of Japanese crews.

Mercy had not been one of the virtues of this band of pirates. And mercy would not be something McCarter would spare for them. "Bang 'em, Rafe."

Encizo plucked the pins on two distraction devices, winding up with his brawny arm and hurling both canisters in a single lob. The flash-bangs bounced off the wall and around the corner where they'd heard their enemy waiting. As soon as the grenades were thrown, McCarter was on the move, racing to the turn in the hallway, UMP ready to spit out lead and fire in a deadly scythe. The bangers went off simultaneously, each producing 175dB of sound pressure. McCarter had his hearing protection on, yet even with that he could feel the wave roll through his skull like a headache.

The men around the corner, likely not armed commandos kitted out for war, were unprotected. Their eardrums took the full brunt of the blast. Chances were they wouldn't have normal hearing function for the rest of their lives if it wasn't for McCarter slicing around the corner and cutting loose at 600 rounds per minute. His first shots obliterated the facial structure of the closest of the enemy sailors; big .45-caliber slugs caving in the front of his skull and belching out a gout of obliterated brain matter in the back.

McCarter wanted information as to who these bastards were, so he lowered his aim, taking the next man with a five-round burst to the upper chest, 230-grain hollow-points smashing his breastbone and tumbling through into lung tissue. Two were down instantly, and compared to the volcanic eruption of noise, the other three men, still deafened and blinded by 6 million candelas of bright light, weren't even aware of the fox-faced slayer in their midst.

McCarter scanned the group for an instant and picked

out the most ranking member of them, judging by their uniform. He could already see that there was a mix of uniform types, as well as two different nationalities among the dazed, blinded and deafened gunmen in front of him. McCarter stabbed out with a front kick, catching the highest-ranking man just under his sternum and blowing the air from his lungs with a savage kick.

With him hurled to the deck, the other two were clear of any impediments to shooting them down. He touched the throat of the first man with the muzzle of his UMP-45 and pulled the trigger. McCarter all but cut the Asian's head off with the contact shot. The other felt the hot, sticky spray of death splash across his face and he began shooting wildly in a panic. Unfortunately for the gunman, McCarter was already standing parallel to him. The Phoenix vet ran a line of auto-fire up and down the man's back, unzipping his torso to the point where entrails burbled and burst from the perforated flesh. Intestines spilled to the deck and the guy collapsed to his knees.

Enzizo was there an instant later, plucking the pistol from lifeless fingers. "Korean version of the Makarov."

"What took you so long, slowpoke?" McCarter taunted.

"I was still midthrow when you took off," Enzizo returned.

McCarter shrugged. "Excuses from an old man as he slows down."

Enzizo grinned. "Touché, douche."

McCarter nodded. "Grab him and secure him."

The Cuban bent and hauled the stunned survivor of the defense team. The prisoner was Chinese. McCarter had spent enough time operating in Hong Kong to have a familiarity with the language. The sailor would be a useful prisoner given time.

McCarter did a short recon up toward the bridge. Smoke was beginning to fill the air and the crackle of flames was growing closer. He knew the ship was dying quickly and that the fifteen-minute window before the Australian Hornets homed in on this particular trimaran was a far too generous estimate of the craft's sturdiness.

"Cal, does the ship look to be in as bad a condition as we think it is in here?"

"We messed her up pretty good," James answered from his point of view on *Dragonfin*. "I'd say you've got another four or five minutes at best."

"Damn," McCarter grumbled. "I'm almost at the bridge. Rafe, head back with our prisoner. He might slow you down getting back to the ship."

Even around the corner and through thickly billowing smoke, the Briton could feel Encizo's distaste for such an order. The Cuban Phoenix pro was loyal to the rest of the team, and he, Manning and McCarter had an especially tight bond since they were the three sole surviving founders of the Force. Even so, McCarter was his field commander. Disobeying an order, one that could deny Stony Man intelligence gained through interrogation, would make this journey onto the knockoff warship a futile gesture. All that came from Encizo was a muffled grunt as he heaved their prisoner across his shoulders in a fireman's carry and went on his way.

There was a time for joking with each other and there was a time to do what was right for the greater good. Information about these mass murderers was far more important than helping to mop up the crew of this death ship.

This trimaran was of a scale larger than the Houbei-class, and from what he'd seen, was more than capable of housing a complement of forty men. There were plenty of charred bodies in the ocean, but there was no telling if there were more men stationed aboard, perhaps as a security force or less as the enemy's forces was spread thin. Not every world-wide conspiracy could field more than eighty men to run a pair of fighting ships. Not if they seemed to be drawing from wildly disparate sources of manpower such as racist biker gangs or communist spies.

Reaching the bridge, McCarter felt the icy chill of winds off the Antarctic waters cutting through shattered windows. Looking around, he noted great levels of destruction caused by .50 BMG and 25 mm cannon rounds that had sliced through the superstructure. A body was slumped over one of the helm consoles, back perforated in dozens of places by shrapnel produced by an exploding shell. Other bodies were strewed across the floor.

McCarter moved to one of the closest consoles. He saw that the screen was cracked, yet still managed to display the image of the shipping routes the trimaran had followed. He scanned it, the camera on his helmet looking parallel to his point of view. He looked slightly off the display panel to give the people back at the Farm something better to look at. He scanned further, looking for any connection ports to plug in to the electronics to see if he could pull some of their navigation data.

And once again the follies of distraction in a combat situation rose up to bite McCarter on the ass. It didn't happen often, but as he narrowed his situational awareness after assuming that everyone on the bridge was dead, a powerful impact clubbed him between the shoulders, staggering him to his knees. Even as McCarter lost the strength in his legs, he knew it was time to retreat from the source of pain that nearly paralyzed him. Tingles of misfiring nerves ripped along his back like shorting wires, but that didn't stop the Briton from lurching to his left, catching himself with that hand and tucking into a shoulder roll.

McCarter's acrobatic tumble came not a second too soon as the crash of a follow-up chop to the consoles told him that he'd barely escaped a finishing blow. From the ground, braced on one arm, the British battler lashed back with his long, lean leg, cracking his attacker across the shins and toppling him against the helm. While the man recovered from a handful of broken monitor shards and his loss of balance, McCarter rolled again, his legs wrapped around his opponent's ankles. The leverage of his leg scissors yanked the man backward, and his hands pawed hopelessly at the air, hoping for some rung or hook to latch on to to keep from falling. Instead, he toppled back into a railing, the metal striking him across both shoulder blades with a numbing smack.

Doubly upset and off his pins, McCarter's ambusher would spend more time and effort getting back to his feet, leaving the Briton free to get up first. The Phoenix Force commander was still fit and agile, and he was quickly to his hands, kicking his feet flat to the floor and rising in a single fluid movement. As he did so, he whirled to face his opponent, catching sight of a Korean officer. While the man's eyes were surrounded by the crow's footmarks of age, his jaw was still strong and square, and the brown orbs flashed with a fire of intelligence and fury.

McCarter was facing a warrior, and by the looks of his uniform, he was the captain of this vessel. It would be a big score, if he could capture this man. That meant a minimum of lethal force. Judging by the wreckage of his opponent's two karate chops, both of McCarter's wits and the console panel, this would be a horrific fight.

If I fought fairly, McCarter added silently to that assessment. Even as the Korean started to struggle back to his feet, the Phoenix Force commander whipped out, ramming his toe into the crease between the man's groin and right leg. Once more deprived of the strength in one leg, the captain lurched, reaching to recover his balance. With merciless speed and efficiency, McCarter rushed in, interposing the dome of his forehead to the Korean's face. There was a crack, and the helmet on his forehead shifted under the impact. McCarter's combat goggles took a spurt of misty blood as his opponent rebounded off the head butt.

The Briton reached out, snagging the captain by the lapels of his coat and yanking him close. This time, he lifted his knee high, pumping it hard into the Korean's sternum. Fetid breath exploded from emptied lungs. His foe, bleeding profusely from a dislocated nose mashed even flatter than normal by McCarter's meeting of his mind to the Korean's face, had little focus in those formerly rage-lit eyes. The Phoenix commander raised both forearms, scissoring the man's neck between his two clenched fists. The knots of bone and muscle rammed right under both sides of the captain's jaw with fearsome violence and purpose.

The twin impacts against thick trunks of nerves and blood vessels widened the Korean's eyes, but McCarter kept his fists jammed there in an improvised choke hold. The captain feebly struck at McCarter's ribs, but with his brain deprived of blood and nerves pinched, any force bled from those blows and the chops was further dampened by the rigidity of the Briton's load-bearing vest.

"Just let the sleep come, mate," McCarter murmured, continuing to apply pressure, keeping the man pinned against the helm. He wasn't certain if the captain could understand English; that would prove to be a minor problem. He also knew that these two prisoners would need to be wound up pretty tightly and stuffed into areas formerly intended for storing cocaine pallets.

The bridge lurched, jarring McCarter from his roost of control against the Korean's neck. The Briton struggled to keep his balance, his booted, deep-treaded soles scrambling for purchase. As *Dragonfin* had perforated the cabin, blasting out glass and structure, frost was quickly forming, making his footing treacherous. Dressed in a black, close-fitting immersion survival suit that made the Ross Sea's ambient temperature bearable in the cabin of the Stony Man speed craft, he hadn't quite noticed the frigid air until its whistling icy bite made all the metal surfaces around him ice up. The captain slithered to the floor in a boneless, unconscious heap, but the deck beneath them lurched farther and farther.

McCarter found himself skidding on the ever-inclining floor, headed toward a hole in the superstructure.

CHAPTER TWELVE

In the brief moments before gravity and the rise of the tossing warship deck broke him loose from his perch upon the icy bridge floor, David McCarter knew that exiting the superstructure would land him in the path of a several-hundred-ton ship, the bone-chilling Ross Sea acting as anvil for the fast-attack craft's hammer. He wasn't the only one at risk; a North Korean naval officer tumbled toward that same deadly stretch of ocean through the hole in the superstructure. While McCarter was clad head-to-toe in multiple layers of 8 mm neoprene and Gore-Tex fluoropolymers, designed for survival in freezing water, the Korean captain's uniform had no such properties. Unconscious, the marauder captain would take the intel with him when he dies.

McCarter dug in his heels, letting momentum push him to both feet, then kicked himself toward the tumbling, unconscious prisoner. It was a desperate maneuver, but the Phoenix Force commander needed to know where the attack craft had come from and how many there were. Two ships were good enough to account for the damage done to the Japanese whaling fleet, but when the factory ships turned back toward their home islands, these attackers should have followed them.

Chances were there were more ship killers out there.

McCarter scooped up the unconscious captain and drove himself into the wall where an explosive shell had ripped a hole in the superstructure. The wall was perfectly horizontal now as a floor, and the Briton found himself serving as cushion for his unconscious prisoner. He watched as water, seemingly pushed down by the hole for several feet, burbled up and into the wrecked bridge.

So much for recovering navigational data from the consoles, McCarter thought as the super-Houbei-style warship continued its writhing spiral in the waves. He scrambled to the ceiling of the bridge, seeing what shattered glass remained in the window frames suddenly burst inward, forced in by the swamping pressure of the Ross Sea.

In a heartbeat, McCarter was ankle-deep in ice-cold water the flood rumbling and crushing inward. In another instant McCarter and prisoner were waist-deep in turgid water that felt as if it were made of frost-forged knives, even through the immersion suit.

The sudden cold jarred the Korean sailor to consciousness. He looked confused as McCarter carried him, anchored to his feet with one arm across the Briton's shoulders. "You fight me," the Briton warned, "you'll die slow and frozen."

The bridge continued to churn and the force of cold water had them both up to their necks, legs kicking to reach the pocket of air at the inverted cabin. The physics of water movement pushed them sideways, driving them toward the surface, which was in constant flux thanks to the tumble of the cabin. McCarter grimaced, expending a lot of strength in keeping the spin cycle of the ship's superstructure from ripping his prisoner from his grasp. The man kept fighting alongside McCarter, both kicking for their lives.

Somewhere in this topsy-turvy nightmare, the Briton became aware that metal screeched and moaned, howling at the abuse of centrifugal force and water resistance. The bridge was now plunged into darkness, but at least the smoke was no longer present, so the pocket of air wasn't contaminated.

Suddenly a surge of water pounded down upon both men from above. Even with his eyes covered in protective goggles, McCarter clenched them shut under the nearly breathtaking pressure that assailed him. The downward current shoved him backward, but he finally stopped against some surface, which only made the forces splashing down upon him feel worse. There was nothing to give behind him, and the Ross Sea squeezed down on him like a python. He fought to keep the breath from bubbling out of his nostrils and lips, knowing there would be no replenishing the lost oxygen.

McCarter, once uncaring for the condition of the crew members of this warship, now felt a pang of concern for his prisoner. Maybe it was an instant of compassion, and maybe it was just the fact that this guy had information he needed, information that could not be shared once they both drowned. Either way, he opened his eyes, then fumbled on his helmet to find the LED switch. In an instant, the all smothering darkness disappeared in a brilliant blaze of blue-white as his headlamp came on.

The Asian marauder flinched, the powerful LED giving McCarter significant illumination in the inky waters. Surrounded by the Swiss-cheese remains of the bridge, they were currently in a very dark place. Buoyed by the cold waters, he no longer had a sense of gravity or motion. There was very little in way of even momentum. Out of desperation, McCarter allowed a few bubbles to burst from his numbed, frigid lips and watched which way they went.

Air bubbles would always travel toward the surface,

just like droplets would always succumb to the pull of gravity. Right now, he and his prisoner were upside down. McCarter braced himself, kicking to follow the stream of bubbles, hopefully to the surface. He was the only one capable of powerful kicks, the Korean having gone limp in his grasp.

McCarter kicked and pawed at the water with his free arm, knowing that each exertion came close to sending bubbles of precious air from his lungs. His jaw felt like a pincushion as the icy water brought down the temperature of his sole exposed bit of face. He could imagine the formation of spiky, cell-bursting ice crystals inside the moisture of his epidermis.

A powerful beam of light blazed into McCarter's eyes, then a second, and two sets of hands wrapped around his outstretched wrist. The combined strength of James and Encizo proved more than up to the task of yanking McCarter from the submerged superstructure of the ship. As he was tugged into open water, he could see the hull of the damaged ship above them.

A regulator was pushed between McCarter's lips and in an instant the Briton drank in life-giving air after expelling a gout of built-up carbon dioxide. Hands had pressed another regulator into the mouth of his Korean prisoner.

Thank the gods of war we've got two expert scuba divers on this team, McCarter thought. Suddenly all of his strength was no longer needed. Two powerful swimmers hauled him toward *Dragonfin,* the speedboat so small and slender in comparison to the badly damaged warship. Within a few moments his head was above the surface and Encizo was tugging off his goggles and checking his eyes.

James dragged the other man onto the ship, pulling him atop the top deck of the sleek craft. James had been

Phoenix Force's medic since his initiation into the team. Hopefully those skills would come in handy with resuscitating the nearly frozen, nearly drowned North Korean captain of the attack vessel.

"You okay, boss?" Encizo asked.

McCarter's eyes were full of tears from the slash of cold air across the surface of the sea and the sting of saltwater. He blinked hard, clearing his vision. "Never gonna complain about you being too slow, Rafe."

The Cuban chuckled. "Let's go… I love swimming, but this dip is a little too chilly!"

Encizo released McCarter and the two men swam for *Dragonfin,* each under his own power.

LESTER P. ROMAINE had rarely been seen without his long dark hair perfectly combed, swept back from his forehead in a leonine mane centered on a nub of a widow's peak. Romaine had been blessed with good genes; male-pattern baldness would never be a problem in his lifetime. He'd also been nearly religious about keeping his teeth in perfect condition. He was a lawyer without peer, and after multiple big cases, he was almost a household name, so that perfect hair and smile were all worth the money he spent keeping them immaculate.

Now, however, after the burlap bag had been torn from his head, strands of hair, made greasy from perspiration, hung over his eyes. He could swear that one of his front teeth had been loosened by the punch that had put him down for the count. Romaine tasted the coppery flush of blood in his mouth. Despite now being able to see around him, he didn't have much to see. He was sitting in the center of a yellow-orange cone of light from a naked, filthy bulb. He saw that, of course, when he wasn't blinking away irritation from fibers that had left his cheeks and neck raw, and had shed into his eyes, leaving them red-rimmed and runny with tears.

"Who are you? Why are you doing this?"

A rumbling, dissonant voice stretched and distorted in his ears, yet he could still make out the words spoken. "This ain't court. We ask the questions here."

"What?" Romaine asked. "You can't do this—"

A big hand, looking the size of a frying pan, slashed out of the shadows and crashed into his cheek, causing the lawyer's eyes to cross under the impact. The strike was one of fury; this wasn't some kind of interrogation.

"You screwed my brothers," the voice responded. "Crunch didn't like what you did to the Heathens. You led that death squad to us. You spilled the blood of my people..."

"Death squad? No, they were doing work for all of us..."

Romaine squirmed. Whatever bound his wrists felt as though it had been dipped in glue and then rolled in crushed glass. He saw someone ignite a blow torch outside of the circle of dingy light.

"Not the guys who hid in our basement, Greasy," came a growl of response. "The guys who came *after* them!"

Romaine looked up, eyes agog with shock. "Death squad?"

"What did you think was going to happen?" asked another distorted voice from over his right shoulder. "You make the Zionists' puppet president look bad, they're gonna come down hard on you."

"Zion... What?" Romaine asked. Panic sliced through his bowels like an Arctic tide, and he struggled against his bindings. Fingers laced through his long hair, knotted and pulled. It felt as if the man was trying to take his scalp off without benefit of knife or tomahawk.

One of the founding principles of Stony Man Farm had been dedication of the protection of human rights for all, even prisoners. Torture was something utilized only as a last resort, a desperate last-minute shot in the most extreme of cases, and even then, only against heinous opponents whose tactics had resulted in torture and murder of innocents.

Lester P. Romaine was a lawyer and, by all appearances, a flamboyant counselor who helped his clients evade murder convictions. He was an officer of the court; part of the system that Stony Man supported as much as possible and only went into action upon when dangers and threats burst outside the boundaries of normal law enforcement. If anyone should have had the expectation of receiving treatment as a "soldier of the same side" it would have been Romaine.

But evidence loomed and grew about this man's involvement in a heinous act of terror. Those policemen who Romaine was bound by oath, law and ethics to assist in the pursuit of justice had been murdered by armed killers directed by his voice. Able Team and their two prisoners had boarded *Dragonslayer* and flown immediately to Romaine's law office in nearby Baltimore after identifying him as the last person to contact Crunch.

With blood spots still damp on their combat gear, muzzles still hot from the blazing gun battle that had left dozens of the Heathens and their heavily armed prospects dead, they'd dropped to the roof of the ten-story building. Looking as though they'd stepped from the front lines of some futuristic war, they'd barged into Romaine's office, bellowing and firing blanks into the ceiling to cow clerks and secretaries, frightening them out of the way.

The three warriors had kicked down his private office door, advanced and flipped over his desk. Carl Lyons had punched Romaine into unconsciousness with a single strike to the face, loosening his front teeth.

Torture was a last resort and only used on the worst of traitors and murderers.

Romaine had hired gunmen to slaughter other men who were viewed by the law as officers of the court—police officers and federal agents. He'd betrayed his oath, but even that was not quite enough for Lyons, Schwarz and Blancanales to engage in full-on physical trauma.

That didn't mean that Able Team was going to hand him over to the police. They could still engage in psychological games to make Romaine believe he was in peril of being executed.

"It wasn't my idea!" Romaine shouted. "They only had me hide those idiots!"

The jet of the blowtorch went from a long writhing tongue of flame to a sharp neon-blue pencil of light that illuminated one captor's welder-mask hidden face. The steel shell flickered and altered its shape in the darkness, reflecting in far more detail the fluctuations in the superhot jet issuing forth from the spigot. The glass panel in the center of the mask was a black, emotionless void despite the pair of eyes that Romaine knew was on the other side.

"Who asked you to help?" the figure in the welder's mask asked as he strode closer.

Romaine looked from the faceless horror to the gleaming lance of fire he wielded and murmured, "The Arrangement."

"And yet publicly they call for you to be hoisted on a cross and burned," the welder said, now five feet from Romaine.

The heat bleeding off the torch was horrendous. Romaine's clothes sloughed from his skin as sweat burst from every pore. He shifted his hips, trying to wriggle free, but he was too firmly held. His slacks and underwear, already drenched with sweat, grew warm as his bladder emptied.

"Smokescreen," Romaine whispered, his throat dry and seemingly filled with sandpaper. "Smokescreen."

The welder tilted his head and then looked down at Romaine's lap. "The Arrangement would have left *us,* the Heathens, out to dry?"

"I don't know. I don't care," Romaine said. "I know Crunch said…"

"Crunch told us to come for you if anything happened to him," the welder replied. "So we want our pound of flesh, Iago. Where shall we cut it from?"

Romaine tried to look left and right, but those fingers were still knotted in his long wavy hair. "Cut it from the Arrangement, man! Cut it from those bastards! They set this up!"

The welder's mask moved closer to the end of Romaine's hooked nose. The lawyer could see his brown eyes reflected in the ebony glass. The hiss and growl of the torch was so close, and his pant leg was searingly hot against his left shin. "Really? How do we know where to get them? How do we know you're even telling the truth?"

Romaine whimpered. "Because…man…I don't wanna die. Not like this."

"You got to pay." The voice came from over his left shoulder and was accompanied by a talonlike squeeze that threatened to crush the joint. "But you might just convince us to make it quick."

Romaine tried to nod. Each tremor of his head felt as if he were tearing scalp from the top of his skull. He was surprised he didn't feel blood pouring down over his eyes and forehead, the agony was so intense.

"I have a private phone, meant for direct communication to inform or be informed of dead drops," Romaine said. "I keep it off most of the time, so it can't be spied upon."

"And they call you through that? What makes you think they don't take even better precautions?" the man in the welder's mask asked.

"I don't know," Romaine answered. "But I have my own insurance…in case they tried to betray me."

"Insurance?" the welder asked. "We're not looking for a settlement…"

"No. Insurance to protect my ass," Romaine replied. "Or at least guarantee me a bullet to the brain."

"You'd give that up for a painless death?" Lyons asked from behind the welder's mask.

Romaine tried to nod, then coughed out a "Yes" because Blancanales's grip on his hair was just too tight. "If I'm gonna die, then I'll die quick. You just have to promise me that you'll destroy the Arrangement."

"You've got enough to destroy them?" Schwarz asked, his throat-mounted voice distorter—invisible under the collar of his BDU tunic—and a black knit ski mask disguising his features.

Romaine looked out of the corner of his eye. He was surrounded by nightmares, killer entities that promised no mercy with words dripping with the grave and full of unearthly tremors. "Yes. I have it in a safe-deposit box."

Blancanales released the lawyer's hair. The clawlike grasps on his shoulders faded. A knife slid between his wrists and his hands were freed.

"Where?" Lyons asked, extinguishing the torch. He pulled a 1911 from his holster and dramatically racked the slide.

Romaine gave up the bank where his information was

stored. "It's in electronic format. In an external hard drive."

"Kneel," Lyons ordered, his voice disguised by the welder's mask.

Romaine did so. His heart spiked its rate, fear flushing through him. *This will come quickly. I won't suffer. I'll die without pain.*

The sound of a .45 boomed behind him, but there was no impact of a bullet. Rather, it was a tranquilizer dart that stabbed into his shoulder from behind. The effect was swift and, for an instant, Romaine had thought he had died.

When he awoke, however, it was to an FBI high-risk arrest team, their guns leveled at him as they shouted for him to keep his hands where they could see them.

CHAPTER THIRTEEN

Min-seo Geum came clean that she'd known that "Veronica Moone" was a CIA non-official cover, and that she herself was a member of South Korea's National Intelligence Service, also in NOC as a fellow teacher. The two had first become friends and coworkers. Both had kept in touch, eventually developing a very close relationship... She was numb and still trying to process Moone's death.

Geum assumed that the two men—Gary Manning and T. J. Hawkins—were CIA operatives, most likely some form of wet works or black ops team. She said as much, but neither member of Phoenix Force had been inclined to disabuse her of that notion.

She also seemed nervous to give the truth about her affection for the deceased woman, worried that the two stone-cold killers might decide to eliminate her, especially if she'd somehow been trying to pump Moone for information.

"Don't worry about us." Manning consoled her. "We honestly don't care. She gathered intel and we vetted that she didn't give up any secrets."

That much was true, Hawkins admitted to himself. Moone had been a good agent, and what notes she'd gathered had showed that Geum had been of phenomenal assistance in picking up snippets of information. They had both been working at a school to educate members of an electronics firm in better English speaking and writing. Through their combined investigations, they'd discovered some very unusual happenings at the electronics company.

In her off time Moone had looked into the books and had flagged multiple inventory discrepancies, as well as pulled together various obituaries of members of the electronics firm who'd died in unusual accidents. The Farm was digging into all of this information back home, but Manning, Hawkins and Geum were working together on the patterns of activity.

Even as Manning and Geum looked over the notes, drawing up clues on a whiteboard, Hawkins took a few moments to open the gear cases left in the safe house. They had come in low-profile, which meant they hadn't had the ability to sweep their usual Pelican gun cases past customs. There was still a possibility that Japan did have some form of involvement with the ship sinkings; a form of very public self-victimization to polarize the world to its point of view for some reason.

The Diplomatic Security Service, however, had been informed of the arrival of the two Stony Man operatives and aside from this safe house, had left some care packages for the Phoenix Force members.

As soon as they'd returned to the safe house, the first thing Manning had done after securing their prisoners and the perimeter, was open one of the cases. He'd been pleased to find a Smith & Wesson M-19 in .357 Magnum. After all, he was a woodsman with an appreciation for hunting cartridges. The Canadian had quickly donned a shoulder holster for the sleek six-gun.

The DSS had also provided a quartet of Glock 19s, which had left a spare pistol for Geum. The Glock 19 was a worldwide standard of reliability and accuracy. Holding sixteen shots, yet not being much larger than seven inches in length, it was both big enough to deal with most fights, yet small enough to disappear even on Geum's five-foot frame.

Phoenix Force had utilized 9 mm Glock 34 automatics before and had developed a respect for the line. Simple to use with no safety catches to inadvertently activate, yet with a trigger system that would not inadvertently misfire if dropped, as well as the brute strength to survive being run over by an 18-wheeler, there was a reason why Glocks were so widespread as to be an alternate approved pistol for the DSS.

For long arms, the DSS had provided four Close Quarters Battle Receivers with two extra uppers with longer barrels. The CQBR was officially known as the Mk 18 Mod 0 in its carbine format. For its close-quarters role, the carbines were normally equipped with 10.3-inch barrels and flash hiders. With the stock retracted, it only took up 26 inches of space and yet had far more punch than most pistol-caliber submachine guns as it was chambered for the same cartridge as the M-4 and M-16. Manning was pleased that the extra "uppers" were 18 inches, which were suited to the altered specifications of the CQBR. With those barrels, the Mk 18 could be used as a marksman's rifle. The Canadian's experience and skill as a marksman would have been legendary in any other age; his long-range accuracy had allowed him to stop hundreds of killers with a single pull of the trigger.

Geum readily understood the function of the pistol and the accompanying rifle, even though she didn't carry one in the course of her work in Japan. She'd been trained on firearms—especially the Korean-issue M-4 carbine—back home. The Glock also fit her well enough.

Like it or not, the young woman had found herself on the front lines of this war against a conspiracy that had dug its fingers into Japan's manufacturing scene. Someone, either outside or inside the electronics firm, was obviously putting together the kind of materials necessary for assembling a warship. It would take some thorough research by the Farm to see if any one company could complete the task of assembling communications, targeting and electronic warfare suites for the ships that McCarter, James and Encizo finally encountered.

Two of the craft were down, but, given their notes, already Hawkins was aware there was just too much tech gone missing to have all gone down with the two destroyed ships.

"You sure?" Manning asked.

"I'm the com guy on this team, and I'm looking at what's been put together. There's enough to account for the two sunken warships and a home base to communicate with," Hawkins replied. "But there're components for at least one more ship."

Manning nodded. Geum figured out the math necessary in longhand on a legal pad, and was done at about the same instant as confirmation from Aaron Kurtzman back at the Farm.

"Three warships. Two are down," Kurtzman announced over the speaker. "However, right now, we've got a description of the enemy ship distributed to friendly navies and air forces to search for them."

"They would have been recognizable as combat ships," Hawkins said. "This gear, however, can be calibrated to return any Identify Friend or Foe signal as friendly if they need to. Or shelter themselves from electronic notice."

Hawkins glowered at the inventories of equipment laid out on the table, then turned back to examine the whiteboard. "Do you have anything else, Min-seo?"

Geum shook her head, brushing long black hair from

her eyes as it wafted into her face. "Nothing in regard to the kind of electronics related to the ships. But Veronica took notes about this, though I can't see how a kid's sick days could have anything to do with this case."

Manning and Hawkins looked closer. "Bear, do you have anything on this kid or his family?"

Kurtzman looked up the notes. "This'll take a few minutes of cross-referencing. I gotta see where his family and such were working. As it is, according to the records I'm looking at, there doesn't seem to be any relation to the child in her notes and the firms she was teaching."

"Keep on it," Manning offered.

"You've got something in mind?" Geum asked.

"We're going to take a look at the electronics firm," Manning said. "Infiltration time."

"How hard of an infiltration?" Hawkins asked.

Manning frowned. "We go in soft, but take enough in case it goes hard."

Hawkins and Geum shared a glance. This meant going in under the assumption that something was crooked inside the firm's complex.

In the meantime the two prisoners they had taken were to be kept detained. Their fingerprints and faces had been transmitted to the Farm, as well as high-definition photographs of their personal identification. While the faces and fingerprints could be tracked by intelligence agencies, the IDs might provide other clues. The cards and other paperwork were obviously forgeries, but with good scans of each, little cues and details might betray the actual forger, or identify the equipment or level of technology of the maker of the fakes.

Right now, it was going to take boots on the ground to see what was amiss at the plant.

"I'll get the car ready," Hawkins offered. "Min-seo...?"

"I'll look in on the prisoners one last time," Geum answered.

"And I'll call in DSS to pick them up," Manning added. "We don't have the time or space to keep them, and they'll be much better equipped and trained to interrogate them."

With that proclamation, the three people set to their tasks in grim silence.

CHARLIE MOTT WAS glad that the relatively small catamaran McCarter, James and Encizo crewed was fast enough to attempt this moving pickup over the Ross Sea. The Globemaster wasn't the most agile or nimble of craft, but it was capable of a remarkable stunt, skimming inches above a runway, its four F117-PW-100 turbofans each pumping out 40,000 pounds of thrust and then releasing pallets of supplies or vehicles via parachute.

Because the massive Globemaster III needed 7,600 feet of runway to launch at maximum takeoff weight, and one of these ships destroyed its landing gear while alighting on a 3800 foot airstrip, C-17 pilots had learned to use drag chutes to "poop" out cargo aboard pallets onto the runways, maintaining flight speed so as not to have to deal with takeoff. Right now, however, Mott and Phoenix Force were going to attempt the opposite. The goal was to have *Dragonfin* catch up with the Globemaster and accelerate up the lowered tail ramp via momentum.

Mott had done the C-17 drop-off maneuver before, but this would be his first effort at a pickup. It would take timing and all of Phoenix's skills to bring the catamaran home safely. Once that was done, Mott would close the ramp and head toward Japan to rendezvous with Manning and Hawkins. Hopefully, the high-speed boat would then be in a position to find the last of the marauding craft. Stony Man Farm's cybernetics crew was utilizing every resource they could tap into to find the last ship that was definitely out there.

As a stopgap, Mott knew that Hawkins and Manning had decided to infiltrate Goisama Technologies, the electronics firm that Veronica Moone had been investigating. Hopefully, the murder meant that she'd been close to finding out exactly where the conspiracy was operating from and their infiltration might provide clues about the location of the last warship.

Stony Man Farm had also uncovered information about the disappearance of a trio of hulls from the Turkish shipyards building for Pakistan. The hulls were an upgrade from Pakistan's usual Gepard-class fast-attack boats, but splitting the hulls up to become a trimaran would give less profile and resistance in the water while providing more surface contact for stability.

The hulls had apparently gone missing during an earthquake, which made NATO officials somewhat secure in the feeling that the sudden "act of god" had somehow scuttled the craft. Sunken hulks had been located to give proof of their fate, but having only been seen through sonar and remote operative vehicle, the truth could have been easily obfuscated. The conspiracy had proved quite good at muddying the waters to the point of increasing global tensions between the United States and Japan.

Kurtzman and his cyber crew continued searching, but the information gave Phoenix Force confirmation about the number of warships that had to be destroyed.

Speaking of muddying the waters, the Stony Man pilot looked down to see the streak of wake left behind by the racing catamaran charging along to make its appointment with the Globemaster.

Mott homed in on where *Dragonfin* was heading and pushed the yoke down, lowering the mighty cargo jet until the wave caps lapped at the belly of the nearly 300-ton aircraft. He eased up on the throttle, decelerating the plane until it skimmed along at just under 200 miles per hour.

"In position, catch up," Mott announced over their secure communications line.

"We dropped some weight, so we'll be there," James said from the *Fin's* controls.

Mott bit his tongue, resisting the urge to make a joke about the lightning-fast catamaran literally plunging into the rear end of the plane. He hit the controls for the loading ramp, hydraulic motors swinging the hatch downward. Now his attention was focused like a laser, keeping the Globemaster level and at constant speed. Too slow, it was possible that the engines could stall out or *Dragonfin* could damage itself by hitting the ramp too hard. Too fast, he'd waste fuel circling for another pickup because James and Encizo couldn't catch up with him.

Hold Steady was his mantra. Mott's sweat was soaked up by the band of his battered old baseball cap, and he could feel the muscles popping in his forearms as he maintained control and course on the mighty jet. He was currently sitting atop more than 160,000 pounds of thrust from the four engines and he had to keep the throttle perfect to ensure *Dragonfin* slipped aboard the transport ship. From there, it was a swing toward Japan at 530 miles per hour.

"Brace yourself, Charlie," McCarter warned over the radio. "And be glad we're coming in wet."

Mott fought the urge to laugh. His lips tightened to

keep him still and steady and, by extension, doing the same for the plane.

There was a bump and Mott could feel the tail of the C-17 waggle as the weight of *Dragonfin* landed on the ramp then skidded farther into the cargo hold. He could almost follow the progress of the catamaran as it slid further into the ship as the center of gravity altered with the increase of only a fraction of the plane's weight. He could hear the thuds as the men of Phoenix Force quickly put down mooring ropes to secure *Dragonfin* to the inside of the Globemaster.

"How much longer?" Mott asked.

"Tying it down," Encizo said with a grunt.

"Secure here!" James announced.

"Hold on. Charlie…"

Mott pulled back on the yoke, pushing the four-engine jet higher into the air. He opened the throttle on all four turbofans and, riding up on a column of 80 tons of concentrated thrust, shouted, "Hang on!"

There were no smart remarks this time, just grunts relayed over Mott's headset. He hoped he hadn't taken off too soon, but there was no way to look behind him now.

"Close the ramp!" McCarter called over the headset. "We're clear."

Realizing the C-17 moved a bit more sluggishly from the added bulk of the catamaran, Mott hit the controls, then tilted the Globemaster toward its intended course.

"Welcome aboard Air Stony. I'm your captain, Charlie Mott, and today we'll be flying toward the Japanese archipelago. We'll be cruising at an average altitude of 20,000 feet at 530 miles an hour. Our in-flight movie will be *Midnight of the Sparkly Vampires,* starring people too untalented for prime-time television."

"Ugh, can you drop us out, please?" Encizo asked.

"Never mind that, Rafe," McCarter returned, asking Mott, "What's our ETA?"

"Fifteen hours," Mott advised. "If you want to spell me up here..."

"We have a mid-flight fuel stop?" McCarter asked.

There was a fit of coughing over the com sets.

"Yeah. We've got an appointment with a tanker over the Solomons," Mott said. "Don't worry, guys, I won't let David play around with midair refueling."

"And what's wrong with me as a pilot? I'm right brilliant," McCarter complained.

James interrupted McCarter's whine. "Listen, I know you're good. Good as Jack or Charlie. So good that you can pull whatever pilot pranks you want and we'll still be fine. We just don't want to let you anywhere near the temptation to make Rafe or me sick."

"That right?" McCarter asked.

Encizo butted in. "He's right."

"Enough of that," James mentioned. "We've got prisoners to deal with. Now that we're on the C-17, we have room for a proper medical examination and interrogation."

Back on the floor of the cargo hold, Encizo emerged with the two men. Both were bound with nylon cable ties and duct tape had been wrapped around their eyes. Their mouths were also gagged with swatches of the tape, so neither of them could communicate with each other and come up with a story to confuse interrogation.

First to be interviewed would be the Chinese sailor, if only because McCarter's time in Hong Kong allowed him to communicate freely. The Korean, if he understood English or Chinese, would be spoken with second. There was a little worry about using scopolamine as a truth serum on the Korean captain as he'd only just survived a dip in the chilling Antarctic waters of the Ross Sea. He'd already been through CPR and his health wasn't the best right now.

Scopolamine would lessen the man's tendency to lie, but it did so at the risk of cardiac stress, which would compound with nearly drowning or freezing while trapped within the severed superstructure of an over-turning ship. The other prisoner had undergone much less abuse, and James had conducted a quick exam to ensure the Chinese man was in good health. James would con-firm everything with a quick run through an EKG that they kept on hand to monitor body stress levels during interrogation naturally.

They spent three hours with the Chinese prisoner, James watching his EKG while McCarter went back and forth, asking questions over and over again while looking for discrepancies in his story. Pretty soon, things began appearing based upon the officer's tale.

Han Kyeuk Soo had been a part of the Chinese mili-tary that was itching for utilizing North Korea as their cat's paw when a wave of worldwide drone attacks set nearly the whole globe into a state of war. McCarter was familiar with the situation, as Phoenix Force and the rest of Stony Man Farm had scrambled in an effort to prevent an apocalyptic world conflict. One of their allies had been, thankfully, an old North Korean ambassador who'd been aided by a young officer who had earned the trust and friendship of Mack Bolan in an even earlier crisis.

Now, it was apparent that most of the naval officers who'd survived being ousted over that debacle had sought protection with North Korea and absorbed into a program that was masterminded from across the Pacific Ocean. Those who hadn't left the country and had been in favor of starting the war that Stony Man ended had either been executed or "re-educated."

Either way, McCarter was glad to have the knowledge that the Chinese government wasn't involved in this conspiracy. While Japan had committed a multitude of sins across several centuries, of which their attempted conquest of Southeast Asia and the Pacific islands during World War II were only the most recent, even China would not risk the possibility of World War III in taking revenge on the nation. They had enough at stake with their claims for Taiwan, and China was smart enough not to risk blindly storming into a war for the splinter island nation.

North Korea, however, troubled McCarter. This wasn't a scheme started in Pyongyang, but it obviously had either a blind eye or grudging approval from the Democratic People's Republic of Korea. Someone was playing fast and loose with the nation, infusing money for this operation, and all out of spite to cause pain and suffering all around.

Whoever was truly behind this was inviting worldwide chaos.

With warships across the Pacific and death squads at his beck and call in the United States and Japan, he truly was a menace.

CHAPTER FOURTEEN

The campus for Goisama Technologies, Ltd., was a sprawl of two acres dotted with office buildings, three factories and scores of delivery trucks ready to move whatever products within the warehouses on the scene. KTL was nearly a self-contained city, complete with parks, restaurants, even its own old-fashioned radio tower, something likely to not just be a relic from the age of tubes and antennae, but subtly updated to be a Wi-Fi connection hot spot.

Indeed, the wireless traffic around the compound was busy, even this late in the evening. Half the compound was dark, though there were also apartment buildings and schools, Min-seo Geum pointed out, for the workers and their families. There was an evening shift operating in two of the factories, and pallets being shuttled between production and storage.

T. J. Hawkins and Gary Manning were in Geum's personal car. A Toyota compact, Hawkins was sitting in the seat next to the young teacher-cum-spy and Manning was folded in the back, concealed beneath a blanket.

Hawkins was dressed in a suit, basic black, with a white shirt and a simple red tie. The Texan wore smeared-on makeup to darken his skin to match Geum's complexion, as well as hair color for his eyebrows and his trimly cut locks. Horn-rimmed glasses, sculpted putty to resemble encephalitic folds and dark contact lenses completed the transformation into Geum's "cousin from America."

Hawkins even allowed his voice a little bit of twang, allowing that he'd grown up in a Texas city, having been born there after his parents immigrated to Austin, Texas, from South Korea before his birth.

The gate guard looked over the two in the car.

"My cousin Jeff," Geum offered.

The printer that the members of Phoenix Force had brought with them had spewed out the passport and paperwork to identify Hawkins as "Jeff Geum."

"Came to see the school where Minnie been teachin' at," Hawkins offered, putting just enough Texas into the voice. The guard raised an eyebrow at that.

"You sound like a cowboy," the guard said, looking at the paperwork. "Oh, Texas. Bang, bang?"

"Yeah," Hawkins said, sounding bored. "Bang, bang."

The guard chuckled at Hawkins's annoyance. "So not on the prairie?"

"Nah," Hawkins replied. "I'm a schoolteacher, too. I've been on a horse once in my life and my ass still hurts today."

"This is Hideo." Geum introduced the guard. "He's a very good student."

"No wonder you know English so well," Hawkins said. He leaned over and shook the guard's hand.

"What do you teach?" Hideo asked.

"I'm a high school history teacher," Hawkins replied. "Got into it after I got out of the army."

Hideo smiled. "Cool. Is she going to have you join the basketball tournament they're holding at the gym tonight?"

"Trust me, I'm as far from Lin-sane as you can get," Hawkins answered with a chuckle. "I ain't a ringer."

"Too bad," Hideo said. "Might have tempted me to put some money on the game."

Hawkins shrugged. "Yeah. Too bad."

"Well, the school's open for the game, so a tour won't be too hard. Just give me a call if you two want to visit a restricted area," Hideo responded.

"If," Hawkins said, wrinkling his nose. "You know how much people shove broken electronics under my nose because I'm Korean?"

Hideo laughed. "Just don't get me in trouble, okay, Min?"

Geum smiled. "I won't."

With that, they left the gate.

Hawkins tilted his head back. "You all right there, blanket man?"

"Perfect," Manning said, muffled.

"Sure?"

"I've spent days lying in cow shit to get a shot. This back seat is comfy *and* I've got a blanket," Manning confirmed. "Don't worry about me being cramped."

"Good news," Hawkins returned, settling into the shotgun seat.

"I want to check something on Veronica's notes," Geum said. "Maybe the absences she noted are some kind of code."

"That makes sense," Manning said from behind. "There seem to be plenty of things going on at this facility. According to what I've read so far, Goisama was founded about ten years after World War II."

Hawkins noticed another bit of tension show up in Geum's tightened shoulders.

"What's wrong?" he asked the Korean agent.

"Goisama was one of the governors of Korea before the war," Geum answered. "His is one of many names that went down in infamy. He shut down all but one Korean-language newspaper, rolled back reforms of the governorship and sent thousands of Korean soldiers to die in battles across China and the Pacific Islands."

Hawkins didn't need to be told about the history of the Japanese and the Koreans. Indeed, for fifty years, from 1895 to 1945, Korea was nothing more than a conquered state, ruled with disdain from 1910 on. Korea had been one nation then, not split along the 38th Parallel on the basis of political ideals. And the Empire of Japan began a thirty-five-year program to smother Korean customs and traditions. Seven thousand people who had resisted this clamp-down had been killed by occupation forces. That was last century, Hawkins realized, but in Japan, in China and the Koreas, memories were long. Sins against ancestors were remembered and harbored, grudges nurtured and given free rein to make use of the female populace as "comfort women."

Hawkins frowned. No, seventy years was *not* going to erase the horror of generations of women being raped and used for pleasure, then disposed of. With this name, the name associated with one of the most desperate eras for both Japan and Korea, when tens of thousands of Koreans were forcibly conscripted into the army and thrown at the allies in the Pacific, it was no wonder that this place would prove to be a linchpin of some sort.

Whether it was a North Korean renegade's plan of destroying the family that had caused his land such horror and loss or whether it was perhaps one of Goisama's ancestors feeling that those who were under his rule were responsible for his punishment. Goisama had died imprisoned by the U.S. government. The loss of face for such treatment would have been something to crush the spirit of an otherwise upstanding citizen.

Geum brought them to the school building where Moone had worked and the three of them exited the vehicle, getting inside quickly. It was unlikely that Moone would have kept anything in her teacher's desk, but they would have to try.

Hawkins opened the lock to the classroom and while Manning stood guard, he and Geum took a row of drawers and went through them, looking over paperwork with pocket flashlights. Once those were cleared, they felt around for false bottoms or other hiding areas that Moone might have utilized. Even working with all of their efficiency, scanning as quickly as they dared so as not to miss a single bit of potential data, the effort still took fifteen minutes.

"Attendance folder," Manning pointed out.

Hawkins glanced around, then noted a group of binders atop a cabinet. One of them, marked in English, read Attendance.

"Sharp eyes," Hawkins muttered, getting up to take a look inside. He set it on the desktop and both he and Geum looked over the pages.

"The student she named as being missing was present on the days she mentioned, at least according to this binder," Geum noted.

Hawkins took a look at the child's name, then the numbers. He flipped the pages to the back, then to the front, looking for annotations. "This might actually be some book code."

He quickly took a small pad of paper and jotted down the child's initials and the dates mentioned. "Does that look familiar?"

"She could be using either days or months," Geum said. "What's the sixteenth month?"

Hawkins winced. "No. In the U.S., civilians usually

use month, day, year. Not like overseas where it's day, month, year."

He quickly reversed the numbers and Geum's eyes flashed with realization. "That's a warehouse that has been under construction seemingly forever."

"Define 'forever,'" Hawkins said.

"I started teaching here four years ago and they're still working on it," Geum responded. "And when I got here, it seemed mostly finished structurally. But there's always workmen around, they keep bringing in cement and hauling away trash…"

Geum winced. "They bring in as much matériel as anything. Nothing seems to be done…"

"But there's still need for bags of cement, rolls of insulation and junk going back out," Hawkins concluded. "It's a shortcut. While there's going to be ledger accounts of electronics being sent out for delivery, nothing about the construction would be on the books here."

"No," Manning replied. "And I'll bet if someone were to take a look for the construction company, if someone tried to look up the name, it'd be a dummy firm. A slight difference in spelling, which would give an investigator the runaround."

Manning secured the door, then brought a pair of compact, low-light binoculars up to his face. He could see the warehouse the murdered CIA agent had mentioned. "There're two security guards patrolling outside."

"That doesn't seem too unusual," Hawkins said.

Manning handed him the glasses. "Take a closer look," the Canadian told him.

Hawkins focused on one of the men. For some reason, the man was wearing a jacket that was just a bit too warm for the weather. Then he realized that he was looking at the shell of a coat as the man turned slightly.

The guard seemed lopsided; something large was tucked against the left side of his body as the breeze whipped the nylon shell of the jacket against his back. "Concealing a machine pistol?"

"Even professional security isn't supposed to be armed in Japan," Manning observed. "And why the hell would they conceal anything larger than a handgun if that were the case?"

Geum looked out the window. "You must have some pretty good eyes."

Hawkins handed her the glasses. "No. That gadget has good eyes."

Geum brought the small set of binoculars to her eyes, then lowered them, looking at Hawkins. "How the hell did you get that much zoom *and* night-vision with resolution like that?"

Manning took the glasses back. "Ancient Chinese secret."

Geum tilted her head, confused for a moment, then smirked. "This isn't store-bought."

"We've got a *very* creative friend," Manning told her, then looked at his partner. "So, two men with machine pistols. No idea who else would be in that warehouse, either. And this *could* just be circumstantial evidence. He might just have a laptop under his jacket."

"We're forgetting one thing," Hawkins noted. "There're a few dates that don't correspond with that building but do correspond with activity related to this case."

"The attacks on the factory ships?"

"The sinking of the first ship and then another burst of activity, likely, on the date when the shootings occurred in Washington, D.C.," Hawkins answered.

"Command center," Manning mused. "Where they've centralized their communications, likely."

Hawkins nodded. "Let's pay them a visit, while things are dark enough we won't be noticed and the basketball tournament will keep them distracted and away from any action."

"I'll set things up when we get to the car," Manning said. "Let me get some more intel on that spot from the Farm."

Hawkins and Geum carefully quietly returned the paperwork to its proper position in the binder, which they then placed back on top of the cabinet. Because they had worn latex gloves, they didn't have to worry about leaving behind fingerprints.

Once outside, they found Manning, working in the trunk. The Glocks had their barrels replaced with ones with extra length and threaded ends designed to accept suppressors. These were locked into place, ready for quiet action. The same went for their compact Mk 18 SMGs, suppressors extending a mere six inches past where the stubby barrels would normally end. Utilizing more than 70-grain loads, the Mk 18s would provide plenty of punch without having a full-length barrel or maximum velocity. Even so, Manning could see the potential hazard of having to put more than one burst into an opponent.

Also, despite the suppressors, the sound of the gunshots would still travel, potentially alerting legitimate security officers in the area. The last thing that Manning and Hawkins wanted to do was to engage honest men only doing their day-to-day job in a gunfight.

Those at the warehouse were exempted simply because they possessed illicit firepower, and Veronica Moone's observations put them surrounding a very suspicious building. Once the two men of Phoenix and their ally were properly equipped, they got back into Geum's car. Once more, they let the South Korean agent do the driving.

Hawkins took a look at his PDA as the Farm uploaded satellite imagery of the factory complex, focusing on the oddly abandoned warehouse. Thermal scans showed a vastly different setup from the blueprints that had been shared with the local zoning commission, adding weight to their suspicions about the building. Something beneath the building spread out somewhat, meaning there was either underground tunnels, or an actual set of lower levels in a building that, according to zoning regulations, wasn't allowed a basement.

Things were growing more concrete.

"Keep the car ready to go," Hawkins reminded Geum. "Anyone but us comes running out of that warehouse, and has a gun, defend the car. If the proper authorities show up…"

"Put her in gear and take off," Geum replied. "I'll try to circle back if I lose them."

"We'll do our best to handle this quietly," Manning said. "If things go well, one of us will come up."

"There might be a smorgasbord of intel that we'll need help going through," Hawkins replied.

"We went over this four times," Geum said. "I know how to support an intelligence op. The only reason I'm not going in with you right now is vehicle security and unit integrity. You two know each others' moves better than I could learn in the short time we've been teamed up."

"Thanks for understanding," Hawkins returned.

The Canadian and the Texan left the Toyota as Geum reached the lot closest to the warehouse without attracting the attention of the two sentries on patrol. Once more, the pair halted and brought out the high-tech binoculars to scan the guards at a closer angle.

At a quarter of the previous range, the high-definition night vision and zoom allowed them to get an even better look at their quarry. An attempt to take one or the other out, even with a silenced pistol shot would only end up alerting the other. At 80 to 90 decibels, even a suppressed Glock would still be as loud as a shout. The main purpose for their weapons' suppressors was to prevent their hearing from being blown to hell in close-quarters combat in a confined space. It would also give them a slight bit of secrecy from farther out by security, though going full-auto would definitely bring a response from Goisama's legitimate security guards.

Getting a closer gander at the sentries, both Phoenix commandos noted they were wearing hearing protection in the form of small electronic earbuds, as well as having donned night-vision goggles.

"Think that gear in their ears will improve their hearing?" Hawkins murmured.

Manning shrugged. "This is a Japanese electronics firm. It's possible that their 'ears' are as advanced as the ones Gadgets and I put together."

Hawkins nodded. "I'll circle wide and see if I can get to the second guard while you close with the first. Our hands-free will let us coordinate and try to put them down at the same time, limiting our exposure."

Manning remained still and stoic, keeping his gaze locked upon the closest of the sentries. "Try to make it as bloodless as possible."

Hawkins gave silent assent to that suggestion, and with that, the two brothers in blood separated.

Manning moved with the grace and silence of a sea-soned woodsman, keeping toward the shadows and always leaving some form of obstruction between him and his target. His approach was one of stealth, always making certain that he did nothing to attract the attention of the sentry. His long legs allowed him to eat up the ground with fewer strides and he took care to time his footsteps with the guard's, even though the soles of his boots were designed to produce minimal sound. It only took a few minutes for the Canadian to get within pouncing range of the target. The fortunate thing about his opponent's use of night-vision goggles was that the man was limited to a smaller tunnel of clear sight; Manning remained in the sentry's peripheral vision. Stealth was of the essence here, because even the slightest sound could cause the other guard to spot Hawkins and possibly kill him.

Manning clicked his tongue to code that he was in position. Even breathing too hard could potentially alert his prey, so subvocalization over the hands-free microphone would be too risky. The vibrations conducted through the Canadian's throat to the microphone taped there.

Hawkins gave the code that he, too, was in place.

With that, Phoenix Force moved in on the two guards.

Manning was four feet from his target before the man turned, perhaps catching sight of the brawny Canadian's shadow or simply hearing the rush of air and silent scuffs of his soles on the ground. Either way, Manning lashed out with a solid right hook that landed just under the left ear of the guard. Soft tissue cushioned the big man's knuckles from cracking against the back of his target's mandible and the punch lifted the sentry off of his feet.

In the space of a heartbeat, the man landed, but was in a wild scramble, momentum carrying him along to the ground. Manning continued his lunge after the falling guard. He reached out and grabbed the sentry's wrist, keeping him standing, but it was hardly an act of kindness. The Canadian's yank snapped the man's shoulder straight, and his head still continued rolling on his shoulders with the momentum initiated by Manning's punch. The G-forces at the end of that "whip" were staggering to the point where the night-vision goggles slid off his face, twisting until the strap was around his eyes.

Blinded by the very gear meant to allow him clear vision in the darkness, the guard let out a groan of pain, his free hand drunkenly pawing for something under his jacket. Manning pulled harder, raising his palm to greet the sentry's ribs underneath his left arm. Sure enough, the Phoenix pro felt a machine pistol in a shoulder harness. All that metal and polycarbonate, wrapped in its holster, amplified the force of Manning's palm strike against the guard's ribs.

Fetid breath exploded from his lungs in a long, wet rasp. When Manning released his foe's wrist, the man's legs folded beneath him in an instant. Breathless, brain scrambled by being launched and stopped by incredible forces, he bent again at the waist, left arm flopping almost bonelessly to the ground next to him. The guard's right hand clutched the shirt over his breastbone, squeaks of effort signaling the breath trying to return to his emptied lungs.

Manning straightened his hand into a rigid blade, then chopped down swiftly into the guard's deltoid muscles. That shock finally jolted the battered man into unconsciousness and the Canadian was satisfied that his enemy hadn't suffered any permanent damage. Quickly, he took off the goggles and got a closer look at the stranger's face. A quick flare of illumination from his filtered flashlight showed Manning a set of Asian features. His experience told him that this was a Vietnamese face, not Japanese.

"T.J.?" Manning called out softly on his hands-free microphone.

"My guy's down," Hawkins answered. "He looks Chinese."

"Vietnamese," Manning returned. "Someone's been hiring people who wouldn't mind seeing Japan screwed over."

"And equipping them pretty well," Hawkins replied. "Heckler and Koch MP-7 machine pistols. High-tech, expensive ammunition, but can be worn almost invisibly in a shoulder holster with a well-tailored jacket."

"Same here," Manning said, examining his unconscious foe. "But the NVDs are Japanese design. The MP-7 is JASDF Special Forces issue."

Hawkins continued patting down his fallen enemy. "USP handgun. Also common for their SF teams. Why would…?"

"We can figure that out later," Manning offered. "Farm, you pick all this up?"

Price interjected into the pair's radio chatter. "We did. Thumbprint them with your PDAs and let's take a look at who these two really are."

Manning pulled his device, turned on the scanner mode and pressed the unconscious man's thumb to the screen. In a moment, the thumbprint was picked up and transmitted to the Farm. Manning pocketed his PDA, then hauled his unconscious foe deeper toward the shadows. He used the sentry's own belt to bind his ankles together. The straps from his shoulder harness and his wadded-up tie made a good gag, as well as further securing the guard's arms. Using a spare bit, he tethered ankles to bound wrists. It wasn't comfortable, but the Canadian didn't want to deal with him as an opponent later on, nor did he want to execute a helpless man.

The sentry's firearms were added to the trunk of Geum's Toyota for safe storage. Hawkins offloaded his prisoner's gear, as well.

Now it was time to see what was underneath the warehouse.

CHAPTER FIFTEEN

The midmorning sun blazed through the windshield of the Able Team van as they drove north from Maryland toward New York City. The notes that Romaine had given them contained conclusive data that the Arrangement not only had bought and paid for a trained death squad straight out of Ezekiel, Oklahoma, but had also hired even more of the brutal, racist mercenaries to make a statement.

Ezekiel, Oklahoma, had been founded after the Vietnam War by a man who was the antithesis of everything Stony Man Farm stood for. Rather than battling against corruption, cruelty and bigotry, the Confederacy of Armed Warriors believed that the downfall of America and the world was due to tolerance of so-called impure religions such as Judaism, Islam, even Christian sects such as Lutherans, Catholics or Mormons. The CAW had set itself up as a church and, as such, had been granted certain rights and legal protections, all of which were assisted by their offshoot, the Arrangement. To the CAW, the world was currently in the end times, an era of tribulation spurred on by God's punishment for the erosion of human faith and the mixing of races.

Able Team was familiar with the two organizations, having dealt with multiple incarnations of their direct-action arm, the Aryan Right Coalition. From plots to contaminate metropolitan water supplies with radioactive waste to taking over the meth trade in Las Vegas, the ARC had risen like a phoenix from the ashes of conflict.

"You'd think that the CAW would learn after all of these years," Schwarz said, riding shotgun and looking over his tablet, scrolling through the notes on the thumb drive plugged into one of its USB ports. "Maybe the ARC is just the island of 'let's get rid of them *and* give Able Team free target practice and guilt-free opponents.'"

"That'd only work if they knew about Able Team," Lyons replied. "No, the Arrangement knows what works in getting their short-term goals—murder, mayhem, striking fear into their targets with terror attempts. The CAW has a fall guy to decry when they get caught, but they still profit from meth sales and bank robberies."

"Too bad it's taken this long for us to find a concrete enough link to them," Blancanales said, driving. "I can't wait for a shot at their head."

"First things first. The ARC has a strike force ready to move on the Japanese delegation in their hotel," Lyons countered. "We can't allow these animals to hurt anyone else. Not when we've got information on where they are about to hit next."

"Barb's dispatched the information and local FBI HRT and others are on alert for the attack," Schwarz told him. "And Jack's on his way to pick us up. We'll be at the lot in a minute."

"Blacksuits are going to drive our baby back home?" Blancanales asked.

"She's got a team for that. No worries," Schwarz answered.

Lyons had gear bags already arrayed on the floor of the van. He'd restocked the ammunition in spent magazines all around, placing them in vests. New munitions replaced those expended in prior combat. Any magazines that had been dented were set aside for recycling and replaced with ones that had no defects that would cause a misfeed or failure to fire.

This time their job was not to garner prisoners, so the M-26 MASS units had been set aside. Able Team was coming straight out to exterminate the death squad before it could engage in an attack on the Japanese diplomatic mission as it readied to meet with the United Nations.

Making use of satellite imagery and local law-enforcement traffic cameras, Stony Man Farm had confirmed that the death squad was in their headquarters, ready to deploy. There was little chance that Able Team would be able to drive to the city in time, but a helicopter pickup would make things go considerably faster.

Barbara Price, thanks to her liaison clearances, had managed to inform local police to stay away. With luck, Able Team would catch them in their building, a rundown garage in Long Island City, New York, a few miles east of the United Nations headquarters building and the nearby diplomatic missions in Murray Hill. If not, then Grimaldi would intercept them on the road with *Dragonslayer* and the team would attempt a take-down and contain the gunfight as much as possible.

Both courses of action were intended to have only one outcome.

Complete wipeout.

This time, these would-be mass murderers would get no escape, would no longer prove to be a threat to the public at large. There would be no less of a threat than shot dead.

Blancanales pulled the van to the edge of an empty lot and all three members of the team could see the small dragonfly shape of the combat helicopter in the distance. They were a few moments early, but Lyons was out the back, hauling along the duffels with weapons and extra gear. Schwarz and Blancanales secured their load-bearing vests as they hopped down from their respective seats.

Lyons tossed each one of them their gear packs. "Saddle up, gentlemen. Time to take out the garbage."

MANNING WAS ON point as the two members of Phoenix Force stalked into the warehouse. The burly Canadian had the Mk 18 at his shoulder, sights at eye level, and both eyes wide-open as they looked for the doorway to the lower level of the building. Hawkins, behind him, only took brief pauses to scan the darkness through night-vision binoculars, not wanting to lose his sensitivity in the dark by looking at the illuminated screen too often. The guards with their goggles worn constantly in place had fallen victim to the tunnel vision of those devices' narrow angle of sight.

There was still light seeping through the windows from outside, but the shadows inside the half-complete warehouse could still be discerned. Without the NVGs, both men had their ears peeled for sounds of enemy movement, as well. Using their natural eyesight not only gave them better peripheral vision—especially since peripheral vision was actually more acute in darkness than standard binocular sight—but it also allowed them to rely more on all of their senses.

Manning's foot touched the edge of a trapdoor and he halted Hawkins. A quick glimpse through the binoculars showed that it was not secured, but it definitely was a hatch into the ground, big enough for both men to climb through. Hawkins took over, shouldering his combat submachine gun as Manning opened the trapdoor. Even as it cracked open, light spilled out from under the hatch. There was a ladder leading down into a corridor.

Hawkins took his finger away from the trigger guard and aimed upward, allowing Manning to safely descend the rungs of the ladder. An instant later the Texan was down, closing the trapdoor above them. He threw a thick steel bolt, locking the hatch from the inside.

Manning stood to his full six feet in height and Hawkins noted that there was sufficient room for both of them to walk through the tunnel without stooping. The hallway also was lit, obviating the need for night vision. Even so, neither Phoenix commando stood still. As they moved, they walked in a semi crouch, making themselves smaller targets. Hawkins took the left wall, while Manning was on the right, both men making sure to not cross each other with the barrels of their automatic weapons.

Even as they moved, they listened carefully for signs of habitation in these underground tunnels. The lights were on, meaning that someone was down here, but so far it didn't seem as if there was a lot of activity. Maybe the enemy was secure in the knowledge that they had enough manpower to hold off an assault, or failing that, alert them to an incoming attack.

Underestimating the awareness of their enemies was not a habit that the members of Phoenix Force wanted to develop. Hawkins and Manning both scanned the floor and the walls for signs of electric eyes or other sensors that could give away their positions. But so far, there were no alarms going off, and they didn't hear the rush of feet as guards raced to intercept them.

So far, so good, Hawkins thought. But that doesn't mean we won't run into half a dozen men perched and ready to shoot us as we turn a corner.

Manning, as always, showed how prepared he was as he fished a small hand mirror from a pocket on his vest as they neared an intersection. Nothing seemed to be up ahead, but the cross corridor could hide anything. Using the mirror, he scanned around corners, looking for signs of enemy guards. Once more, nothing had shown up in their path. Manning nodded and Hawkins moved up, looking both ways.

"Too quiet," Hawkins said softly.

Manning nodded. "But we're far enough in, maybe we can start making some noise."

"Ears are in place," Hawkins confirmed to his friend.

Manning drew the Combat Magnum from its shoulder holster and took aim at a light fixture halfway down the hall. The confined quarters of the corridor would do wonders for amplifying the sound of the .357's report. A smooth pull of the trigger and the fixture ruptured. Even through the filters of his hearing protection, Hawkins could feel the wave of volume rippling off the powerful revolver.

Manning immediately lowered the handgun, plucked the spent cartridge from its spot in the cylinder and fed it a new one.

Sure enough, the crack of the Magnum did get a response in the distance. The electronic hearing protection picked up the sudden clatter of feet rushing down a hallway. Thanks to the two different microphones, one over each ear, Hawkins turned to the corridor where the sounds originated from. After a brief flurry of initial running, the guards on hand thought the better of racing out into the open.

"They didn't panic," Manning mused softly, just loud enough for Hawkins's communicator to pick up. "They know what they're doing."

"Hired guns," Hawkins agreed. "And they're smart enough to realize we popped off that shot to get a reaction out of them."

Manning checked a turn-off at ninety degrees to the corridor where they'd heard the enemy scramble in response. "They might want to come at us from another angle. Hold down this intersection, I'll see if this hall lets me flank them."

"Just make sure you don't make too big an explosion when you want to knock a hole," Hawkins warned.

"No. We don't need security or police coming down on us," Manning replied.

With that, Hawkins knelt, using the corner of the two intersecting hallways as concealment. The walls were drywall, so cover wasn't really an option. He'd been in enough gunfights and had done enough shooting through various building materials to know what stopped bullets and what only kept an enemy gunman from seeing you.

He set out a pocket mirror with a folding portrait-frame-style stand and stayed back from the corner, viewing everything in the hallway. Hawkins caught sight of shadows moving, but nothing that would give him a good shot. Drywall wouldn't protect him, but it also didn't let him know if he were putting rounds on target or simply wasting ammunition and giving away his position.

Rather than deal with that, the Texan pulled a flash-bang grenade from his harness. The concussion blaster would distract and impede the enemy for long enough that they might not notice Manning stalking behind them. He and the Canadian had not brought along fragmentation grenades in the hope of capturing enemy electronics. With control of whatever communications setup the conspirators possessed, they had a good opportunity to locate the last of the marauding ships, especially if it was on its way to a mission of destruction.

Things were such that the firepower of these super-Houbeis could spark a war, or potentially cause billions of dollars' worth of destruction. Japan, as an island nation, had plenty of power centers and fuel storage areas along its miles and miles of coastline. Well-aimed missiles could turn a nuclear power plant into a radioactive geyser of fallout, or ignite millions of gallons of stored petroleum or natural gas. Likewise, the fast-attack craft could spark a war by blowing up Korean or Chinese vessels.

International tensions were at their worst, and this conspiracy was more than a lit match; it was a road flare balanced precariously over a vat full of accelerant, ready to set nations ablaze.

"Make it loud." Manning's voice came through Hawkins's communicator and T.J. whipped the canister munition hard. It rebounded off the far wall from his corner, bouncing and rebounding from the force of his throw. The fuse wound down during the zigzag course before the flash-bang erupted in a bellow and flare of light.

Now it was Manning's turn to act.

GARY MANNING MADE his way around to circumvent the resistance that he and Hawkins had anticipated. Heading down the corridor, he found an open door that lead into a kitchenette. There was a sink and counter setup, complete with a two-pot coffee machine with warmer trays on top.

It looked almost identical to Kurtzman's counter setup back at Stony Man Farm, right down to the mess of cups and the half-empty coffeepots. Manning pushed into the area, listening for signs of movement. He came to a halt, crouched out of sight of the doorway. Again, going low, he took a look to see if the protectors of this underground base were already working to flank the intersection.

He caught a glimpse of running feet; one gunman racing toward the coffee room. A lone flanker, thinking ahead of the others. Manning had given Hawkins the order to "Make it loud" and his response was the clatter of the rebounding flash-bang. That broke the stride of the lone runner for long enough to keep him from noticing Manning as he stood to his full height, muscular arm stuck out like an iron bar. The guard whirled, sensing the obstacle at the last moment, but it was too late for him. The Canadian's forearm lashed across his throat, knocking the conspirator's feet from underneath him.

In an instant the man, a Vietnamese by his complexion and features, was flat on his back. Manning grabbed handfuls of his uniform shirt and hauled him into the coffee nook as if he were a rag doll. The guard tried to scream, but the thunderbolt detonation of the flash-bang grenade drowned out his cry of horror. With a savage twist, Manning put the Vietnamese's head through a set of cupboard doors with a particle-board shattering crash. That in itself would not have done much to damage the man, but the Canadian then yanked upward powerfully. The countertop was made of much sturdier material and a crack appeared in the surface as a parallel, sickening crunch signaled the snapping of his neck.

The man was instantly done, and Manning swept his Mk 18 to his shoulder, swinging around the corner to see the remaining sentries staggered but recovering their senses. The Canadian was reminded of the need to act immediately upon the detonation of a distraction device. Before Manning could shoot one of the closest of the gunmen, another of the sentries jerked violently, Hawkins ripping into him on full auto. Stunned and caught flatfooted, the underground guards whirled at the sight of their friend falling and the sound of the Texan's submachine gun.

The Canadian punched out a 3-round burst that tore

into the head on his target, slamming the man back into the rest of his allies. Now, the defenders of this hidden headquarters realized that they were being flanked. Flurries of 5.56 mm NATO lead zipped up and down the hallway, seeking out flesh and bone, leaving destruction in their wake. Manning didn't relish the thought of gunning down opponents when they were at their most vulnerable, but he and Hawkins were outnumbered by trained gunmen who knew what they were doing. Even now, the half-blind sentries started returning fire.

Manning threw himself backward, bullets punching through drywall as he ducked, folding over to avoid the return fire. They had more than simple handguns; they each had one of the MP-7 machine pistols. While the 4.6 mm bullets weren't particularly fast or heavy, they were still as deadly as a stream of .22 Magnum autofire, meaning that the Canadian didn't want to be in the way when they were flying his way. From his kneeling position, Manning figured the angle at which his opponents were shooting and aimed back through the wall at them.

The suppressed 5.56 mm NATO mini-carbine had a much larger powder charge than the MP-7, and its bullets were fully twice as heavy as the tiny HK proprietary rounds. When Manning fired, he blew through the wall, tearing a ragged gap in it. On the other side, he caught a flicker of movement as an enemy gunman stumbled backward under the assault. Seventy-two-grain slugs tore through flesh, already slightly deformed by cutting through the drywall between them, so when they made contact with human flesh, they cartwheeled through muscle and blood vessels. The whirling saws of peeled copper and spread lead made ugly, horrible channels through his target's torso, leaving his lungs deflating rapidly while severed brachial arteries filled up his chest cavity.

In moments the hired gun would be dead. Manning shifted his position swiftly once he caught sight of his hits, once more barely escaping a line of impacts that shattered the floor tiles. The Canadian reached into his pack and pulled out a small disc-shaped object. It was actually three ounces of high-explosive RDX with an electronic trigger in the center. Manning was an explosives expert who'd designed dozens of different munitions for various tasks. Here, the Phoenix discus was something that he could hurl and rebound off walls with incredible dexterity.

It was akin to the flying weapon of one of Manning's childhood heroes, except that man's thrown weapon was a shield of impenetrable wonder-alloy. Manning hurled the disc with a flip of his wrist, watching the object curve through the doorway, bounce off of the far wall and sail out of sight. The electronic trigger fired after a few moments of travel, producing a shock wave that carved the battered wall of the kitchenette across the middle at waist height. Through clouds of kicked-up dust, Manning could see the corridor was empty of movement, though he could hear the moans of the injured.

As he moved back into the hallway, he saw that the gunmen were down, put out of action with far more authority than the flash-bang grenade. Manning scooped up and pocketed the leftover ring, looking to see who was still in fighting condition. A guard tried to sit up, but the Canadian kicked him hard across the jaw, putting him down for the count.

Hawkins ripped off another burst at another figure out of sight of Manning and then approached to ensure that the gunman would not threaten them anymore.

"We're clear," Hawkins said, looking around. Manning peered down the hallway where the men had come from.

"That doesn't mean we won't have trouble in there," Manning returned.

Hawkins reloaded. "That's why we brought more than one magazine."

The Canadian nodded in silent assent to his partner's grim statement. They'd come this far. They wouldn't relax until they had secured this facility, and even then, there was the likelihood that someone else might come to the rescue of this group of mercenaries.

It was unlikely that taking over this headquarters would prove to be the end of this conflict.

CHAPTER SIXTEEN

Dragonslayer hurtled over the streets of Long Island City, New York, two thousand feet up, on course for a battle with a group of gunmen who'd been assembled to attack a Japanese delegation trying to calm the rising international tension.

Carl Lyons, Hermann Schwarz and Rosario Blancanales were loaded for bear, wearing their body armor, festooned with pouches of ammunition, explosives and other supplies. They were armed to the teeth with Honey Badger-style Personal Defense Weapons.

Schwarz and Blancanales were going to deal with opponents at full-auto. The compact little PDWs had replaced the smaller .223 Remington rounds with fatter and heavier projectiles that didn't require extreme velocity like the normal M-16 rifle bullet. At 1,000 feet per second at the muzzle, the 220-grain bullets had all the momentum of a .45, with even more energy and penetration, focusing 500 foot-pounds of energy per impact. If they switched to supersonic Blackout ammunition, the punch of the stubby rifle would be nearly triple the energy, but with less mass and potential penetration.

Lyons was packing his SRM Arms 1216 shotgun, deriving its name from 12-gauge 16 shots in an ingenious rotating set of magazine tubes. Slimmer and sleeker than his prior Atchisson 12-gauge, carrying more ammo in less space, it had already proved itself as a reliable combat weapon in a cartridge that was the gold standard of man stopping. Even so, its range with buckshot was a "mere" 190 feet, meaning that anyone at an extreme reach would have to be dealt with by another firearm, either his partners' PDWs or Lyons's own customized Ruger GP-100 in .357 Magnum. Upgraded to a seven-shot cylinder and with a six-inch barrel, the Ruger was a sturdy, powerful weapon, and Lyons was undaunted by its relative mass in exchange for a 200-yard reach.

At 180 miles an hour *Dragonslayer* was also laden with firepower and multiple sensor systems. At its stick was Jack Grimaldi, the ace Stony Man pilot. Actually, to call Grimaldi an "ace" was a misnomer. Aces were combat pilots who had five kills in aerial combat against other aircraft. The man nicknamed "G-Force" had passed that milestone years ago, and there was little sign of his amazing skills fading. As *Dragonslayer* had been built from the ground up around him and his reflexes, the helicopter was a living extension of his body. He could maneuver the swift craft through narrow city streets if he had to, and he had done so on multiple occasions.

"They're still in place," Schwarz said, watching a screen set up in the passenger cabin. Right now, the images were coming from an unmanned aerial drone, sweeping the garage belonging to the Aryan Right Coalition with Forward Looking Infrared. "But they're loading their van according to FLIR."

"I do not want to chase these pricks through Brooklyn," Lyons said. "Too much of a chance of bystanders getting hurt."

Blancanales put a pistol-gripped M-203 grenade launcher into a sheath on the back of his load-bearing vest. "I've got an engine-buster just in case they try to burst through the doors."

Lyons nodded. Already, Grimaldi had engaged stealth mode on *Dragonslayer* and dropped from their original altitude. As per their plan, Blancanales was going to be the "door" to the street, keeping any and everyone inside the garage. He would fast-rope down by himself, with cover from his two partners in the open side door of the transport helicopter. Once he was down, Grimaldi would swing over to the roof and deposit Lyons and Schwarz.

Schwarz already had a breaching web, designed by Gary Manning of Phoenix Force, ready to spread on the roof of the structure. Made up of detonation cord and "corner charges," it would burn through brick and cinder block if necessary. If the roof was further reinforced, the FLIR and radar scans by the Predator drone hadn't picked it up.

Once the fast-cutting det cord sliced a hole for the two men, there'd be a brief moment of shooting fish in a barrel, the drop of smoke grenades and flash bangs to cover their roping to ground level. Blancanales would then either act as perimeter guard or be called in to close off the killing box.

"Thirty seconds," Grimaldi called out to Blancanales.

The eldest member of Able Team hooked his rig to the rappel line via carabiner. Blancanales wore gloves to protect his palms as he gripped the rope, and clicked on a second carabiner to control the speed of his descent. They wouldn't have long. Even with silenced rotor-slap and muffled engines, *Dragonslayer* still kicked up a wind; it was a big aircraft, its rotors having a sixty-foot diameter alone. There was only so much "stealth" with such a flying beast.

Lyons and Schwarz bracketed their friend, ready to cover him as he dropped.

Grimaldi swung the helicopter around.

Blancanales kicked off, holding the rope at two parts. His padded gloves absorbed much of the heat of friction from his drop, and the carabiners gave him leverage to decelerate his fall as he neared the ground. With a whine of the carabiners applying braking pressure on the line, Blancanales was feet on the ground. Flicks of his thumbs disengaged the hooks from the ropes and he stepped back.

Dragonslayer picked up altitude and swung toward the roof of the garage, even as Blancanales pulled down his M-203, extending its stock and shouldering it. The Able commando kept both eyes open, checking windows and doorways while he left the muzzle of the grenade launcher locked on the garage door the drone's FLIR had placed one of the hit team's trucks behind. The sectional doors were made of plates of sheet metal as befitting a professional car repair business, and it was likely that the gunmen might have put some extra plating in the event of an attack.

Once again, however, the FLIR and radar scans hadn't showed anything thick enough to stop Blancanales's armor-piercing grenade. He had brought along a bandolier of MEI Mercury 40 mm shells, HEDP—high explosive dual purpose—rounds that could blast through more than three and a half inches of steel using a detonation that spit a jet of molten plasma out behind it. While his shot might not damage the enemy vehicles through the door, it definitely would make things extremely hot and dangerous inside the garage. Blancanales had seen the sizzling bolts of explosive liquefied metal easily burn deadly tunnels through the entire thickness of a man's torso, and windshield glass would not do anything to protect a driver behind the wheel.

As such, for now, Blancanales had his M-203 leveled

so that an angled shot would punch through the garage doors, and the anti-personnel jet of molten metal would riddle the cab of the truck with offshoot fragments. If anyone appeared in a nearby doorway or window, the Able Team vet would take a different tack. An enemy in a window would catch the grenade in the wall beneath the sill, taking the lance of liquid death head-on. One in a door would simply catch the grenade in the chest, his fragile body absorbing the force of 86 grams of high explosive while becoming ground zero for that brutal cone of death.

Blancanales concentrated to avoid the distraction of *Dragonslayer* swinging over to the roof of the building. Lyons and Schwarz hopped down only a few feet from the door of the copter. Now it was his turn to cover them. As he was situated in the street, he had the cover of a parked sedan, but he'd been in more than enough gun battles to know that even a car's trunk would not provide much in terms of stopping a fusillade of enemy bullets.

"Any movement?" Lyons asked over his hands-free communicator.

"None," Blancanales confirmed.

"Target beta," Lyons ordered. "In three."

Blancanales counted down, knowing that even as this conversation and countdown progressed, Schwarz was setting up the breacher web.

On zero, he squeezed the trigger of his M-203, punching the Mercury into a second sectional door at chest level. The grenade struck and detonated, producing a cloud of twisting smoke on this side of the door panel, while on the other, the charge vomited its blazing hot destructive plasma. As the HEDP detonated, a secondary blast echoed above, smoke puffing up from the roof of the garage.

Screams filled the air and guns suddenly blazed to life. Blancanales could make out the roar of Lyons's 12-gauge, its deep-throated booms punctuating the chatter of submachine guns and rifles. The front windows of the garage were alive with gunmen suddenly. Blancanales coolly, calmly, opened the grenade launcher, the shell dropping free, and stuffed a second one in place. He turned on one of the windows with an angry killer behind it.

The death squad and their support reacted swiftly, rushing to their perimeter to seek out their attackers. They were canny enough to hold their fire, even as one of the riflemen smashed out his window with the barrel of his weapon. Blancanales fired another HEDP into the wall below the gunner's window and in an instant the man was whipped out of sight. The stench of burning pork billowed through the broken glass as wails of agony ripped out of the now vacant portal.

Blancanales reloaded, feeding in a standard fragmentation round and sailing it through the opening. It was ruthless, as he had no doubt that the gunmen would be rushing to their wounded partner's aid. Considering that these men, and their ilk, were willing to murder citizens and policemen, the Able Team warrior put his misgivings over the bloodthirsty tactics aside.

The third grenade roared inside the garage, and that was Lyons and Schwarz's cue to drop from the ceiling. Blancanales plucked a smoker from his bandolier and fired it through the same window. There was no telling how much devastation occurred within from his assault, but it was now time to set aside the launcher and go for precision shots from his PDW.

Just the same, he loaded one last HEDP round into the M-203. Just in case the Aryan Right Coalition thugs decided to try to take this fight on the road.

ONE MOMENT THE roof between Lyons and Schwarz was relatively solid and then, with a press of the detonator, was a six-foot-wide hole, looking down on a scene of madness and confusion. Aryan Right Coalition gunmen behind one of the garage doors were on the ground in various states of injury; one of them wailing weakly as he only had one lung, his right arm and much of the right side of his rib cage having been shorn away by a scythe of liquid death from Blancanales's opening shot.

Lyons put the man out of his misery with a fist-size cluster of buckshot that smashed through his skull. As much as he would have been unconcerned about the suffering of mass murderers such as the ARC recruited, this was going to be a clean sweep, and the man was still a human being, despite his complete disregard for the rights of those not sharing his skin color or psychotic beliefs. Lyons brought the SRM blaster around to another gunman, who brought his weapon up to bear on the hole blasted in the ceiling.

The Able Team leader fired first; a dozen pellets ripping down into the quivering flesh of the racist thug. The swarm of shot snapped the gunner's collarbone before burrowing down through his aorta, severing it completely. The ARC killer was pinned to the ground as surely as if he were a piece of paper stapled to a tabletop.

Across from him, Schwarz had another angle on the group below. He unleashed short bursts from the .300-caliber PDW, sizzling subsonic rounds into the gathered forces below. There were no jokes from the man called Gadgets now. They had been going through this maze of murderers and thugs, picking up more and more information on them and their maniacal plans. Certainly, other parts of Schwarz's magnificent, multitasking brain were applying brainpower to other projects, but for now, his body was a finely honed killing machine, stopping to fire another burst into an enemy gunman only when his initial whipsaw of slugs failed to anchor a foe.

Blancanales's fragmentation grenade sailed through a window vacated by the jet of antipersonnel plasma from an armor-piercing grenade, and that fragger was the signal for the two Able Team warriors to let go of their slung weapons and pick up their rappelling lines. With a single kick, the two men descended into the garage. The fragmentation bomb had raised enough mayhem and put down enough of the enemy to make it relatively safe for them to descend.

Another shell, this one vomiting chemical smoke, came into the garage, but Lyons and Schwarz were both prepared. Hitting the concrete floor of the repair shop, they unhooked from the ropes and swiftly scooped up their weapons from where they hung on their slings.

Lyons went left while Schwarz turned right. Lyons twisted the quad tube, having gone through two of the four-shot magazines of the 1216 cannon, hammering blasts into the ARC killers. He scanned through the billowing smoke, navigating the garage floor with deft speed and preparedness. On the flight over, they had gone over both radar and FLIR imagery that peered through walls and relayed the floor plans of the building the Farm had hacked from the zoning commissioner's files. As Lyons and Schwarz moved in two different directions, they were assured that anyone walking around would be an opponent, even if seen only as a misty shadow through the chemical fog.

An ARC hired gun staggered out of the wisps of smoke, ugly burns having ravaged one side of his chest and leg. He stunk of overcooked meat and was half blind. Lyons fired from a range of three feet and the burst of buckshot dug a cavern through the center of his face, emptying his skull of gray matter and blood in a brutal excavation. The still-smoking victim crashed to the ground.

The shotgun was a big, loud, vibrant weapon. The muzzle-flash that Lyons put out ending the misery of the burning gunman had attracted attention, bullets slamming into his body armor and making him stagger off balance. He whirled and emptied the last three shots in the tube in the direction where he saw and heard the enemy gunfire. One machine pistol erupted from a dying gunman's death grip, auto-fire tracing an arc of flashes until it pointed straight up to the ceiling as its owner toppled backward.

There was a grunt from a second target, even as Lyons turned the tube to put a fresh magazine under the feed. The foe was too far back in the smoke to be seen clearly. Something had hit, though, be it only a glancing blow from a spreading pattern of shot, or more likely a rebound of pellets splashing off a nearby wall. Either way, Lyons found his opponent when the man cut loose with his rifle. In the enclosed space of the building, the sheer pressure and power of the assault rifle's muzzle blast was even more noticeable than Lyons's own shotgun.

The Able Team leader was glad that the unit's body armor was rated for up to 7.62 mm NATO, but even so, the bullets that struck him were bound to leave wide, ugly bruises on his chest. Lyons fired two booming response shots into the enemy gunman and this time the grunt turned into a wet, explosive rasp of escaping breath followed immediately by the thud of wet meat on the cold concrete floor.

Lyons moved closer to check on the state of this particular killer when the garage door started rolling upward to the ceiling. The engine of the truck ground into gear as the driver decided to make a run for it. Lyons wasn't surprised at this possibility. He could see the truck, a Peterbilt, judging by its shape and long front hood. Behind it was a flatbed trailer, the front half of which having been equipped with rails for the men who would ride back there. The back half was sans railing and covered with tarpaulin. Already Lyons could guess by the shape of the object and its length, it was likely a pair of pods for the Yingji-82 anti-ship missiles or some other form of artillery.

The notes that Able Team had uncovered revealed that the Aryan Right Coalition was planning to take the truck to Hunters Point and fire into the city. The Yingji-82 missile had the accuracy to hit something as precise as the Waldorf Astoria, which was close enough to the Consulate General of Japan to house the delegation. No matter what was fired, however, innocent people would be killed, either on American soil or the "Japanese territory." If the missiles struck the United Nations building, the fallout would prove even more chaotic.

The Peterbilt could not get away. If even two men were in the truck, that would be enough to aim and fire the missile or missiles. The truck lurched forward, halfway out of the garage in the space of instants.

Blancanales was ready to close the door on the ARC vehicle. The unmistakable impact of the Mercury grenade against the grille of the truck preceded the agonized death throes of the vehicle's engine. The sheer force and pressure of the liquefied copper in the armor-piercing shell slashed through the mechanisms that allowed the truck to roll forward.

Blancanales let the M-203 hang down and brought up his .300 Blackout machine pistol. The truck wouldn't move, but whoever was in the cab still could pose a threat. The Honey Badger in Blancanales's hands smashed the windshield to splinters and cubes of shattered safety glass. Lyons rushed up to the running board of the truck and looked inside to the bloodied mess of what used to be two ARC gunmen.

"Drone says we've cleared the building," Schwarz announced.

"No survivors?" Lyons asked.

"Everyone else in this hell hole is dropping to room temperature…even the truck," Schwarz answered.

Lyons stepped down from the running board and stepped out of the slaughterhouse.

"Jack, land at the intersection. Let the FBI pick up bodies and intel."

"Be there in a few seconds," Grimaldi responded.

One more group of maniacs united to kill under the banner of the Aryan Right Coalition was now reduced to chopped and butchered meat. Still, the name of this cursed group had arisen from the ashes of utter destruction to run afoul of Able Team once more.

"We can't cure this disease," Lyons grumbled. "Just the symptoms."

CHAPTER SEVENTEEN

Min-seo Geum turned off her car's engine, then grabbed the briefcase that contained Phoenix Force's communications link to their home headquarters. Geum only knew the two men as Gary and T.J., and they only spoke with "Barb back home." As tempted as she would have been to open the case or to simply make off with it to give to her bosses back in Seoul, the Korean agent had come to like and trust the two men.

Neither of the Americans—they both were white, European men with only T.J. betraying a hint of a regional accent—had showed any concern over the fact that she had been a lover of the dead CIA operative. While she'd score political points in Seoul, especially the National Intelligence Service, by uncovering an otherwise unknown operations team from the U.S.A., the truth was that they didn't care.

Geum had been a friend and she'd been helpful. They treated her as an equal, at least as far as planning and thinking was involved. She translated Korean for the operators and together all three of them worked with respect. They hadn't considered her an equal in regard to making a commando assault inside an underground lair, but Geum didn't begrudge them that. This wasn't a case of either nationalism, sexism or any other ism.

The two men were partners and had likely trained together, honing their in-field communications and their coordinated tactics until they were a well-oiled machine. Geum had seen other commandos like them in the NIS, and had done *some* training beside them. The Korean woman had been sent to train until she could get marksmanship and self-defense right.

Combat veterans like those who'd guided her and the two Phoenix Force warriors trained until they couldn't get it wrong even under the worst conditions. Geum could hit a three-by-five-inch note card with five or six shots out of a magazine in the space of a few seconds, but she was slower and much less certain than real gunmen. She knew her limitations, and while they trusted her with a handgun and automatic weapons, when it came time to unleash lethal force against an entrenched foe, Geum was happy to let the two of them have the risk.

Jogging along with the briefcase, she entered the half-finished warehouse that served as cover for the conspiracy's command center and electronics smuggling. Hawkins was at the trapdoor, flashing his pocket light to make things easier for the woman. She carried the briefcase to him and held it out.

"Hang on to it," Hawkins told her.

Geum nodded as he held the trapdoor for her. She descended the ladder into the underground area. The smell of gunpowder and spilled blood hung in the air, the desperate last issuances of dead mercenaries flavoring this stink with feces and urine. She paused and waited for Hawkins to join her.

"This way," he said.

Geum followed him, glad for the weapons they'd supplied her with. It had only been a few minutes since the two warriors had disappeared into the warehouse, but she saw sprays of blood on the wall of a corridor after two turns. The scent of spilled coffee added to the odors assaulting her nostrils, but that wafted in from up ahead. She saw drag marks, smears of gore from where someone had tugged lifeless forms out of sight.

She looked down at the blood trails and took a deep breath.

"Was it bad?" she asked.

Hawkins shook his head. "No. We out-thought them. We cheated, essentially."

Geum glanced to the Texan with some surprise.

"This isn't the so-called Wild West. There's no cowboy code," Hawkins explained. "We stacked the odds in our favor with flash-bangs and other explosives, and put the gunmen down."

Geum nodded. "The odds were against the two of you."

"Aren't they always?" Hawkins asked rhetorically as they continued down a corridor that opened up into a command center with consoles festooned with monitors. Maps were pinned on the walls and there was one wall full of computer hardware stacked on shelves. Dozens of blinking red-and-green lights signaled that the machinery was still in full operation.

Hawkins pointed to a flat spot next to a workstation and Geum set down the Stony Man briefcase. She stepped back as the Texan carefully went through the locking mechanisms and protocols. That was another reason why Geum had decided to hold on to the briefcase and keep it with her two new American allies.

If she delivered this piece of hardware to South Korean NIS, there was no guarantee that the operatives opening it up wouldn't have their arms blown off by booby traps inside the suitcase.

The lid opened and the monitor inside the top flared to life.

Whoever these people were, and whoever designed the briefcase for them, knew a thing or two about high technology and computers. The only devices that she'd seen spring to life so quickly were PCs with solid-state flash drives. That this particular device was to be carried into the field by these two commandos meant that "solid state" was the least of it. They were in instant communication with their support team in the United States, at least as near as California, but likely as far away as Langley, Quantico or Fort Meade.

They were terse with their communications, but from the way they spoke, this was an intimate, close-knit crew. They obviously had been together a long time, developing genuine friendships and camaraderie. They were a family, and Geum realized that was why she had fallen in so hard with Veronica Moone.

Geum and Moone had developed a friendship, a trust that went far deeper and warmer than simple same-sex lust. Such a thing wasn't rare, Geum knew from her friends in the small Korean and Japanese gay and lesbian communities, but among spies it was almost unheard of. Even after they'd stopped being lovers, they'd remained friends. They'd trusted each other.

If Geum hadn't been late engaging in a meeting with her supervisor, she might have been at Moone's home when the murderers had arrived. Instead, she'd arrived just minutes before the two Americans had arrived. Pure luck and circumstance had kept her alive for a few moments to act as a human shield, a distraction for the actual North Korean killers.

It was that training, that professionalism on the part of T.J. that had saved her life, keeping her from folding over a bullet of a blade when she was shoved toward him. He and Gary had showed concern for her, not just for the rough handling, but for the loss of Moone and the impact it would have on her.

No judgment over her confession of their relationship. Just support.

"How are you holding up, Min?" Barb asked. Geum looked at the speaker, a beautiful honey-blonde with clear, bright blue eyes.

Geum nodded. "Pretty well."

In the meantime, Hawkins and Manning were plugging in wires from the briefcase to the computer console. Geum's strengths weren't in information technology, but this was twenty-first-century Japan, so she understood firewire and USB 2.0 ports. The briefcase would be an intermediary, allowing their people "back home" to penetrate into the systems of the conspiracy.

"Min-seo, if you're willing, take the earpiece that Gary will offer you," Price said.

Geum looked at the small one-piece ear set that the brawny Canadian held out for her. She accepted the device and put it on her ear.

"This is a secure device, so you don't have to worry about speaking freely," Price told her. "You can even walk away from the boys so you can be in complete privacy."

Geum looked at T.J. and Gary.

"Don't worry, we've enough to keep us busy for a spell," Hawkins told her with his easy drawl.

Geum smiled and walked into the hall. "How much range does this have?"

"More than you'll need," Price answered. "Now, I'm not going to ask you to do anything against your ethics."

"I didn't think that you would," Geum responded.

"No?" Price asked.

"Your people strike me as being good and honest,

using only as much force as necessary," Geum said. "Just the way you've been working with each other."

"You've got great observational skills," Price complimented. "I was wondering if you'd prefer to use them to assist us from time to time."

"Observations of stuff that could turn into a national or international incident?" Geum asked.

"Precisely. It would not interfere with your work for the National Intelligence Service, but it could also end up helping them out," the blonde mission controller stated.

"That could be seen as treason by my employers," Geum said, but she didn't have conviction in her words. This idea of helping out this group, as an extra ear to the ground, akin to the Baker Street Irregulars she read about in Sherlock Holmes stories to improve her English, it was tempting. From the way they operated together, it seemed that the bulk of their intelligence came through such rumor sources if they weren't outright tapping into the files of other agencies, following on the threads that no one else picked up.

"You can probably guess that our operation isn't large, nor is it very official," Price stated. "If anything, we act independent of conventional channels. It allows us the means to cut off problems before they get too large."

"This situation seems large enough of its own accord," Geum said. "This crisis has spread to the United States, to Washington, D.C."

"Yes, it has, but while other agencies are tripping over themselves, we've slipped between the cracks and found solutions to some mysteries and are working to find others," Price explained. "You can keep that communicator. It will sync with local cell lines, which will then go through a series of filters until it gets to us."

"So, if someone else were to capture it, they wouldn't know who it was talking to?" Geum mused.

"Correct," Price said. "That's as much for your protection as it is for ours. It won't be picked up on your normal cell service, and the cut-outs we put it through would filter out all but you personally."

"I just need my code word," Geum stated.

"One you likely haven't shared with your bosses back in Seoul," Price hinted.

"Veronica," Geum whispered breathlessly.

"It'll remind you of why you're with us. We're fighting for the same cause," Price added. "And that's to keep good people from being murdered."

Geum didn't have to think about it for more than a moment. "All right."

She could almost sense the smile of relief on the other side of this faceless communication. "Thank you. If we can, we'll throw things in your direction that can help you out."

"Thank *you*," Geum emphasized.

Now she was even more certain of the small size of the organization that T.J. and Gary worked for, if they were this quick at making a decision that could potentially jeopardize the operational security of the agency, it was a tightly knit team. She didn't know what kind of resources they had, but judging by the electronics and the firepower, they either had friends and plenty of contacts, or often supplemented their income for supplies by raiding the coffers of their enemies. The briefcase appeared slick and sophisticated, but it also had an air of being handmade.

And now, Geum was one more resource for these people, people who scoured the world for cold-hearted murderers and fought them with their own tactics and tools.

The Korean agent felt at home.

T. J. HAWKINS looked over the charts and maps on the screen. Kurtzman and the cybernetics crew at the Farm had gone a long way toward giving this command center a more sensible layout. He was better able to identify its place in the world, but he still wondered where the last of those trimaran missile boats was located and why it hadn't showed up on the radar.

One thing he was grateful for was the alert that the Long Island City operation had suddenly gone into blackout, confirming that Able Team had survived their clash there and that the fangs had been pulled in North America.

Indeed, he pulled up a news feed from New York City, and was watching.

"The Department of Homeland Security announced the end of a potential reign of terror on the East Coast as federal and local law enforcement rushed to the scene of a series of explosions in Long Island City earlier this morning," the news anchor said. "Members of a renegade, extremist group known as the Aryan Right Coalition had fallen victim to their attempts at improvised bomb-making as bombs burst in their hideout on the edge of town."

The scene switched to footage from news helicopters that hovered over the scene. Smoke wisped lazily into the midafternoon sky as a fleet of vehicles surrounded the garage. The flickers of police lights on Mars bars speckled the area with red-and-blue flashes, like strewed pieces of hard candy reflecting the light of a bright sun.

"Police report at least twenty men had been in the

building, along with a truck loaded with high explosives. According to sources, the explosives were handmade."

Hawkins knew that source had been lying out of its ass. Barbara Price had even gone so far as to inform Hawkins and Manning that they had indeed found Yingji-82 anti-shipping missiles on the site. However, downgrading the presence from actual guided missiles to improvised explosives would cause much less of a stir among the populace.

"Firearms found on the scene and recovered by the BATFE have been linked to the shootings in Washington, D.C., where a number of protesters and law-enforcement officers were wounded and or killed only a few days ago."

Again, the truth was being stretched, especially since Able Team had personally captured and incapacitated the killers from that attack. However, placing the blame on the Aryan Right Coalition would go a long way for Stony Man Farm to both alleviate concerns over a pack of heavily armed maniacs on the loose, as well as reinforcing Japan's innocence and victimization by this conspiracy. With the ARC's violent, bloody history, they were hardly the type of men who would be the first choice of a Japanese corporation, let alone seem to want to work for a foreign government.

This news report would be one of many, guided and edited by Barbara Price and the rest of the home crew, along with the rest of federal law enforcement, to attempt to diffuse tensions.

"Police are still on the lookout for possible accomplices to the ARC, but for now, they state that the possibility of Japanese-hired mercenaries loosed on the East Coast has been dismissed."

Hawkins killed the screen with the video and surfed over to one of the bigger conspiracy theory BBS sites that abounded. While regular internet forums were likely to garner more attention, those sites were nothing more than poorly researched white noise.

No, if the truly paranoid "conspiritards" were going to have something approaching a legitimate theory, they would be present in the BBS realms.

Hawkins scrolled through the postings, scanning for that which would catch his attention. While he was sure that Kurtzman and the others would be meticulous about covering their tracks, there was always something that would upset the apple cart.

So far, every posting he checked was a dead end, simply more static farted out into the electronic ether. For everyone bringing up their doubts, there were enough answers from those who bought the Stony Man explanation.

"Why wouldn't they?" Hawkins murmured aloud. "We are telling most of the truth."

"Truth about what?" Geum asked.

Hawkins looked up from his screen. "The truth about this conspiracy. We're likely to have gotten Japan off the hook for anything they did in the U.S. That still isn't going to make things better for the ones who attacked the whaling ships…"

"I've got movement on the ocean charts." Manning spoke up.

"We see it, too," Kurtzman announced. "Someone is tracking a dozen different cargo ships heading to a dozen different locations on the East China Sea."

"Which ports?" Geum asked. The worry in the air was a palpable, physical thing and Hawkins could see the Korean woman tense up.

"Three ports in South Korea. Two in the North. Five more along China, and now we've got four ships going to Japan," Manning relayed. "Bear…is this real?"

"I've got the team checking actual shipping in the area," Kurtzman answered. "And now we've got ships targeted all the way west as far as Thailand's coast and as far south as Luzon, Philippines."

Manning's jaw tightened as he looked at the scrambled dots filling up the screen, scores of courses for billions of tons of freight lit up and crisscrossing. Pretty soon, the on-screen maps were filled with such sheets of colored threads that it looked like a knitted afghan.

"They know we're on to them," Manning pronounced.

"Undoubtedly. They're throwing everything up on this system to blind us," Kurtzman agreed. "By the time we sort all of these things out, the conspiracy would have hit any number of ships and disappeared."

"You have no sign of the other attack boat?" Manning asked.

"No. No signals, no communication links. They've sterilized this site," Kurtzman said.

Manning and Hawkins exchanged glances. Hawkins took it upon himself to say it out loud, but from the look on Geum's face, she was already aware of the danger. "They know we're down here. This place has been compromised."

Geum's eyes grew wide. "But where is the response going to come from?"

Manning pulled the wires from the briefcase computer, leaving the cords behind, snapping the case shut. "We're leaving now."

Price's voice came over Geum's earpiece. "Gary, everyone, the crew is busy fending off a cybernetic attack. The headquarters was booby-trapped with all manner of logic bombs and viruses."

Geum felt a gut-punch of surprise that she was in on the "party line" even as Hawkins shooed her along into the hallway. Price's warning was broadcast to all three, meaning that they, for now, were all one team. The Korean girl clutched the frame of her Mk 18 sub-carbine close to her. She reached down and thumbed the selector from safe to semi-auto. While she was experienced with firing the larger M-4 and M-16 variants used in the South Korean military, she didn't want to be overwhelmed by the muzzle blast and recoil of those same rounds exploding from this short of a barrel. Even so, at close range, the 5.56 mm NATO round would possess more than enough stopping power per pull of the trigger than the Glock 19 in its holster.

"Barb, any news from above?" Manning asked.

There was only an answer of static. The Farm's transmission had been blocked, either due to the crew members having to deal with a rampant virus tearing its way through their systems, or that someone was on the way and had brought along a jammer to isolate the three of them down in this lost command center.

Manning's supposition settled on the latter as, ahead at the trapdoor, a shotgun blast cut through the hatch and the crossbar holding it shut. The Canadian grabbed Geum and Hawkins by their shoulders and dragged them behind him. He let go of Hawkins and fished in his vest's pouch for another of his Phoenix discs.

Even as he did so, a canister landed and bounced down the hallway toward him.

He threw the disc bomb hard and fast, then whirled, wrapping his arms around his allies in the hope of absorbing the brunt of the enemy's bomb blast.

The two explosions hammered Manning's mind like a one-two punch from a giant.

CHAPTER EIGHTEEN

T. J. Hawkins felt Manning's bulk slam against him and Min-seo Geum as the flash-bang grenade detonated in the hallway behind him. The big Canadian's instincts had proved, once more, infallible as he'd plucked them out of the path of danger and shielded them with his body. Even with their combination of hearing protection and hands-free communication, the overpressure of the banger's detonation was more than sufficient to leave Hawkins a little cross-eyed.

Manning was on one knee, looking the worse for wear, when he noticed the detonator core of the grenade had launched and rebounded, tearing away a huge patch of his shirt. The Canadian's body armor had likely saved him from broken ribs and lacerated back muscles, but the impact had still dropped him to his knees.

Hawkins motioned for Geum to stay with Manning, then pulled his Mk 18 to his shoulder, aiming toward the opened trapdoor. He'd seen Manning hurl one of his plastic explosive discs toward the doorway, and hoped that it was the second blast he'd felt after the flash-bang detonated. If it was, then the flying bomb burst had bought them vital seconds that he could use to cover them. He glanced back over his shoulder, seeing Geum guiding the battered Manning to cover, then returned his attention to the one way in or out of this deathtrap.

At least he hoped that it was the only way. If there was

a back route their enemy knew about that Phoenix Force hadn't discovered yet…

"Min, can you hear me?" Hawkins asked softly.

"Yes," Geum responded. She was close enough to hear him, despite the jammer that cut out their communications. The hearing amplification of their earpieces helped with that.

"Keep an eye on our six," Hawkins told her. "This might not be the only exit."

The girl didn't say anything, but she clutched her Mk 18 tightly and took up a position of cover just around the corner.

The two explosions raised plenty of noise, but there was no guarantee that the Goisama security team would have heard it. The incomplete walls looked as if they might have been insulated for sound, and any noise that escaped would actually be channeled away from the front gate or other occupied buildings on the electronics firm's campus.

Something tapped against Hawkins's calf and the Texan looked down to see Manning holding out two more of the disc bombs. He reached down with his off hand and took the Canadian's inventions. Manning made certain that all of the team had familiarity with his munitions, how to activate them and how to best deploy them. Hawkins had been, during high school, a fan of Ultimate Frisbee so he'd gotten quite good with throwing the disc as a young adult. But that had been years ago, on the other side of a distinguished military career.

Even so, the basics came back to him. He pocketed one of them, then activated the detonator on the other, pinning it against his chest as he kept his PDW in the other hand. Primed, Hawkins let the Mk 18 drop on its sling and then flicked the disc into a rebound where, hopefully, it would bounce off the far side of the trapdoor opening and sail into open air. The Texan felt old muscle memory roll through his biceps, elbow, forearm and wrist, and the disc bomb sailed, gliding gracefully on the force of his throw. Sure enough, the stiff outer ring took the impact against the wall and snapped back with lightning speed. The simple truth was that steel bounced better than rubber, unless it was solid rubber like a so-called Super Ball, which resisted deformation.

An instant after that bounce, he saw, heard and felt the gush of force and shock waves pouring through the open floor hatch.

With the blast, Hawkins plunged through the hall toward the ladder, leaping halfway up the rungs leading out into the warehouse to cut down on his vulnerability during climbing. With a kick, he was up and on the warehouse floor where stunned and staggered mercenaries were strewed. Hawkins took a couple of steps to quickly recover his balance after bounding up into the warehouse, scanning around for signs of fight from his downed foes.

One man recovered quickly enough to catch Hawkins off guard, raising his pistol and putting three rapid shots into the Phoenix pro's center of mass. Luckily, Hawkins had his body armor on, as well, so despite the hammering he took, he was able to pivot and throw himself out of the way of subsequent shots. The stunned gunman aimed higher to hit the Texan in the head, but by the time he even thought of it, Hawkins was three feet away from where he'd been shot at, and crouched below the angle of the mercenary's raised pistol.

The Mk 18 snarled, suppressed 5.56 mm NATO slugs drilling into the gunman. The first few hits from the burst seemed to have no effect, but as Hawkins allowed the recoil to lift the muzzle, the last bullets from the salvo smashed the Asian assassin in the throat and jaw.

Struck from a range of only a few feet, the bullets violently upset and tumbled as they struck fluid mass and bone. A baseball-size crater was torn from the mercenary's neck and throat in a spray of misty blood, while the last shot broke his mandible wide-open, making the tattered halves of the jaw splay out like the grisly maw of some alien predator. Either way, the man was down and gurgling.

"Body armor," Hawkins noted, hoping that his hands-free still allowed him contact with Manning and Geum over this short range. If not, he hoped that Manning would have time to recover, or Geum would be smart enough to go for head shots if her body hits failed to stop a back-door assault.

The slugs that struck him right under the sternum left an ugly knot in Hawkins's stomach, but he couldn't let his discomfort distract him from finishing the job on the attack team. The Texan mentally counted the moments since the disc bomb had detonated, and had reached four seconds, one of which had been burned up by taking and returning fire. The other gunmen scrambled, either lurching to their feet or scrambling on all fours to get out of Hawkins's line of sight.

Their movement gave the Texan something to track and to act against. He was behind a pillar within a moment, listening to bullets rattle and clang against the two-foot-wide I-beam holding up an unfinished section of ceiling. Hawkins dropped to a kneeling position, swung around the side of the steel post and fired in the direction of the gunshots. The man took several hits, but he staggered out of sight, coughing and wheezing from the impacts of 5.56 mm NATO rounds against his armor.

Yeah, there's a reason why I preferred the full-length M-16, Hawkins mused. The ten-inch barrel might have been swift and handy in enclosed spaces and ideal for bailing into or out of vehicles, but the full-length M-16 A-4 simply had a much higher muzzle velocity, squeezing every ounce of performance out of what, in essence, was just a .22-caliber bullet atop a significant powder charge. Against the body armor these gunmen wore, Hawkins just didn't have enough penetration.

But it's a poor craftsman who blames his tools, Hawkins answered himself. While one target had faded from view, another started to swing into view. The Texan swiveled like a turret and fired, aiming for the mercenary's face. At 2,900 feet per second, the NATO rounds met the Asian gunman's face and tore through it as if his skull were made of rice paper. The dying attacker slumped backward, his rifle spitting bullets into the night sky.

I hope to hell that Hideo and his buddies hear the gunfire and stay out of this rumble, the Phoenix pro thought. Hawkins didn't relish the idea of rent-a-cops entering into a battle between Stony Man commandos and a death squad, both sides equipped with full-auto firearms. Hawkins didn't know if Hideo had access to any form of firepower, but it was likely going to be a 9 mm SIG-Sauer P-220, not a bad gun, but sorely lacking if he were to get into a gunfight with a submachine gun. The MP-7s that these gunmen seemed to be wielding had an effective range of 650 feet, meaning they could riddle the security officers a dozen times over before they were in handgun or shotgun range.

Another of the killers lurched into view even as gunfire roared from a far corner of the warehouse. Hawkins swung to that target and fired, even as he heard the buzzing zips of 4.6 mm rounds slicing the air where he'd been kneeling only a moment before. Standing at his full height, the Texan hammered a burst of 5.56 mm NATO into the gunman. Once more, either body armor or tactical movement had made Hawkins's gunfire ineffective except to force his enemy back into hiding.

The Phoenix warrior kept on the move, reaching a stack of drywall still wrapped in plastic sheeting. A few inches of the material might not have been enough to stop either of the PDWs deployed by Phoenix Force or the mercenaries, but the pallet was ten feet by six feet. Shooting lengthwise through a stack would be highly improbable for the tiny bullets they were utilizing.

Hawkins was getting tired of trading pot shots with entrenched opponents and withdrew the last of the discs Manning had given him. He primed the trigger and let it fly toward the area of the last muzzle-flash. Once more, a childhood of Frisbee throwing paid off as the crash of the disc's explosion sent a severed arm spiraling through the air.

If I hadn't played Ultimate Frisbee before, I'm sure as hell playing it now! the Texan thought as he continued to move around the flanks of the gunmen. There were at least three left, though one or two could have been injured in the initial blast from either Manning's or Hawkins's bomb tosses.

A Korean man whose features were raw and smeared with blood staggered in front of Hawkins, one eye wild as the tatters of eyelids and cheek hung from his skull. That bright white orb was a shock at such close range, buying the Texan's opponent more than enough time to jab the MP-7 up against his sternum.

Hawkins pivoted, whirling away. While the armored vest he wore had been sufficient to stop pistol-caliber rounds, the 4.6 mm HK bullets were intended to cut through Kevlar helmets and military-grade body armor. Had the Phoenix expert not been so swift in his reaction to the attack, the subsequent snarl of the machine pistol would have signaled his end as bullets cored through his vital organs. The Korean grimaced as Hawkins's forearm pushed the gun-filled hand away. The mercenary lifted one foot and snapped down, striking to crush Hawkins's instep with one of the most basic martial arts movements around. The Texan, however, was not slow with his footwork, either, spreading his legs even as the crippling stomp struck the concrete floor, its thud reaffirming that Hawkins had barely escaped with his ability to walk intact.

The gun-for-hire lashed out with his left hand, fingers hooked like the claws of an eagle, nails left long so that they could rake flesh and possibly burst eyeballs. Hawkins took a page from David McCarter's book and lunged in, forehead meeting fingertips. The skin on the Texan's hairline tore, blood trickling from the deep scratches, but the unmistakable crackle of dislocating finger joints vibrated through Hawkins's skull. The Korean pulled his numbed "talons" back and worked to step away from the Phoenix Force badass.

Hawkins would have none of that, snagging the guy by a loop on the back of his load-bearing vest. With a savage twist, he lifted the Korean and swung him around, hurling the Asian into the floor with a splat. The mercenary hit the ground face-first, likely bursting his nose or his exposed eyeball, and his body folded over, legs bending almost to touch the back of his neck. The Texan looped his arm around the upside-down gunman's knee, then pumped three snap kicks into his foe's throat and collarbone. Steel-reinforced toes met flesh and bone hard, the Korean's clavicle splintering under each kick.

Hawkins twisted again and let his opponent collapse into a boneless heap.

There were still other gunmen to deal with.

The distinctive bellow of a .357 Magnum revolver caught Hawkins's ear, and he knew that Geum and Manning had found another entrance, fighting through whoever was trying to flank them in the underground facility. The smashing Magnum slug must have struck home, as Hawkins also heard a body slam against a stack of building supplies, then spill to the ground.

A second blast from the revolver and suddenly Hawkins was able to hear the sound of Manning's voice over their communicators. "Cleared out here. You?"

Hawkins looked around. "Might be one moving around. Still searching. How're you feeling?"

"Like someone threw several ounces of steel at my ribs very hard," Manning replied. "I spot him…he's wounded and doesn't look armed."

"Got him," the Texan replied. And with that, Hawkins took off running, following the retreating shadow. While the man might not be a threat, there was also the likelihood that he'd have information about the conspiracy. Either way, the Phoenix pro didn't want to let the injured gunman escape. Racing along on ground-eating strides, he kept his other senses peeled. This might be a trap, and if it was sprung on Hawkins, it could likely make Geum and Manning far more vulnerable.

Hawkins bounded to the top of a stack of building supplies, running along a row of stored drywall.

The staggered mercenary paused, hearing the sound of Hawkins's footsteps crashing behind him. The Asian tore open his vest and let it slither to the floor. Hawkins could already see that the man's right hand was mangled, likely wrecked by one of Manning's ingenious death discs.

Either way, Hawkins wasn't going to leave himself vulnerable as he charged down the man, pulling the Glock from its holster.

"Keep your hand where I can see it," he ordered, leveling the pistol at his prisoner.

The gunman was a mess, standing on rubbery legs; head drooped from his injuries and blood loss. Hawkins could also sense a little bit of resignation from his foe, that bit of gut-wrenching loss when you were captured dead to rights and helpless.

"Look at me," Hawkins ordered.

It was a Chinese man, he recognized. Blood glistened from what light came through the incomplete ceiling and windows of the warehouse. The prisoner managed to keep his left hand raised, palm wide-open to Hawkins. His eyes were cast to the floor, though. The Texan turned on his flashlight to look for signs of a booby trap at the man's feet, then searched the area. The Asian had kicked his vest far to the side. Hawkins could see the man's side arm in a chest pouch holster.

"Sit down," Hawkins ordered. The Chinese gunman seemed to understand English well enough. He leaned against an I-beam pillar, sliding to the ground slowly, agonized. Hawkins holstered his pistol and moved closer to the injured man.

"Gary, Min, this guy needs medical help," he called to his allies.

"On our way," Manning returned.

Hawkins quickly but efficiently frisked the wounded man, checking everywhere, even his crotch. Hawkins knew all too well how many good lawmen or soldiers had been killed because they were too afraid of being called "gay" to give a proper pat-down to another man's most intimate areas. Hawkins was glad he did search his prisoner thoroughly, coming away with a small aluminum two-shot derringer secreted against the man's groin.

However, since the gun was positioned for a right-handed draw, the Texan didn't think his prisoner had been holding out or would swiftly be able to employ the miniature handgun.

Hawkins opened the latch, folding the derringer as if it was a double-barreled over-and-under shotgun. Two .38 Special rounds were in place in a gun, which was just over two-thirds of an inch thick and only four-and-a-half-inches long. It was a Chinese knockoff of an American design, right down to the double-action-style trigger. Hawkins put it in a breast pocket, just in case, then felt along the wounded man's right arm, searching for the source of the bleeding.

It was a laceration, complete with a section of the rebound ring from Manning's discs. Blood seeped around it, but it was thick and murky, not bright and arterial. It seeped all over, so Hawkins inserted his finger into the hole and withdrew the three-inch arc of fractured metal. Manning arrived shortly, pulling a pack of gauze from a vest pouch.

"Why don't you make these rings pre-fragmented?" Hawkins asked.

"Because then I couldn't do stuff like ricochet it around corners or bank it through doorways," Manning returned. "Besides, this fragment seemed dangerous enough."

"Evil and crazy," the prisoner murmured, sounding drunk because of his blood loss.

Manning maintained direct pressure on the bloody wound as Hawkins taped the gauze in place.

"Evil and crazy?" Manning repeated. "I'm not the one sinking ships for no damned reason."

Almond eyes rose to meet Manning's gaze. "Sinking ships. Sinking damned whalers, man."

"What's your part in this mess?" Hawkins asked.

All that was in the man's eyes was spite and anger. "My part in this is making these Japs pay for what they've done."

Hawkins and Manning could pick up a bit of an Australian lilt in the Chinese man's tone. Before anything else could be said, the ground shuddered violently. Hawkins turned and reached out to Geum even as the ceiling flexed, shifting as the ground surged. Rather than him grabbing her out of the way, though, she snagged him and threw him off balance and out of the way of a girder that slammed into the concrete floor, raising a gout of dust.

Manning had been on the other side of the toppling I-beam, and he gave the bar a shove, leaping beyond it. The Chinese man, however, was only a pair of legs sealed against the flat surface of the metal girder. Anything else was out of sight or hammered into the floor, the greasy mess that used to be his body hammered deep into the base below.

"It sounded like a missile!" Geum warned, pulling on Hawkins's wrist as the warehouse buckled and groaned, its support structure falling to pieces.

"We know where the last trimaran is," Manning noted, helping Geum move Hawkins along. The three of them burst through an exit door as they saw another fiery trail swooping out of the sky. Even as they raced away from the door, the Yingji-82 plowed through the wall and punched across as if it were a pair of scissors stabbing through newsprint. The ground beneath their feet shuddered violently as the warhead, 165 kilograms of high explosive, erupted inside the floor of the false front.

The wall above them, already moaning under the force of the slamming impacts of the missile, was sucked backward. The sudden excavation beneath the warehouse created a vacuum that inadvertently rescued the Canadian, the Korean and the Texan from being crushed by a ton of collapsing rubble.

What they were saved from still slammed into the trio of investigators, this time in the form of vaporized particulate, jetting outward as the implosion of the warehouse vomited clouds of dust. Manning tripped and went to one knee, but Hawkins yanked his friend back to his feet. Geum continued to lurch onward, arms crossed in front of her face.

The men of Phoenix Force finally caught up with her, steadying her as the dust cloud died down around them. Through the murky smoke, they saw a fire blazing in the distance. It was the school where both Geum and Moone had taught, flattened by another three hundred and sixty-five pounds of high explosives.

The blast force had leveled the structure completely. Another blast resounded and the main factory erupted under yet one more of the Eagle Strike missiles. Geum's eyes were wide with horror, tears starting to well in them. "Oh, my God…"

Hawkins and Manning glanced at each other. The Goisama Technologies facility was in flames, smashed by four powerful missiles. They had noted, on their way in, that a night shift was working in the factory that had been hit, while the school itself was hosting the basketball games. The loss of life would be terrible. Hundreds dead in the space of a minute, and what was worse, the only leads they had developed in the hunt for the conspiracy had vanished in those blasts. Emergency vehicle wailed in the distance, their sirens a baleful song of tragedy. The flickers of their lights were visible, even through the billowing smoke and dust of devastation.

Hawkins clenched his fists tightly. This conspiracy was going to get away with even more murders because they'd burned down the last leads they'd had. His heart sank, stomach churning with anger. No, Phoenix Force didn't let its enemies get away with slaughter. But right now, Hawkins needed to help with the rescue efforts. People could be saved here, and the Texan would burrow through concrete with his bare hands to get them to safety.

CHAPTER NINETEEN

Barbara Price took another sip of her coffee, wishing for the energy from the black, tarry caffeine to hit her bloodstream and somehow shoot her back to full strength. The phone had flattened her ear against the side of her head and nerves pinched from tightened muscles. She'd been on the line for hours, confirming the presence of "Federal Agent Jeff Geum" in the Goisama Technologies campus, as well as his partner, Garfield Roi.

Japan's Public Security Intelligence Agency had discovered the two American operatives as they were assisting in search and rescue among the badly bombed electronics factory spread.

"Yes, Ogawa-san, Jeff is one of our finest agents. He brought his friend Gar with him on vacation to visit his cousin Min-seo Geum, who teaches at a school at Goisama," Price repeated.

Toshio Ogawa sounded as if he were the same rank as Hal Brognola at the Justice Department, which the PSIA was the equivalent of. He'd taken an interest in the two Phoenix Force members as he was concerned over their presence at the scene of a horrific terrorist incident. It had been three hours since the first of the missiles struck, and so far, the death toll had reached 387. On top of that, billions of dollars of production had been lost in the destruction of the main factory, not just robotics technology, which assembled the electronics, but goods that were being assembled.

Price didn't want to mention that a good portion of all of that technology had been stolen by the conspiracy that had brought down the wrath of the Eagle Strike missiles. Their enemy had done a coldly efficient job of covering its tracks. The underground facility was nothing more than a crater, anything of worth inside the hidden command center reduced to splinters by nearly 3,000 kilojoules of force detonating in its midst.

"I was concerned simply because these men seemed to have been found in an area where several automatic weapons and other explosive equipment were discovered," Ogawa said. "When a search crew sought out Miss Geum's automobile, they found it destroyed, but there were two dead men found in the vicinity. There were submachine guns and automatic pistols in close proximity to the corpses."

Price tried to sound surprised, but her hours of liaising with the PSIA had taken their toll. Instead, she merely grunted at the information. "That is unusual."

Ogawa was silent for a moment. Whether the man was curious about her lack of astonishment, or if he simply wanted more of an explanation, Price was in the dark about what went through his mind. All she knew was that she was smoothing wrinkles that accompanied this event.

"Ms. Price, you know that some conspiracy theorists would consider the presence of two American Justice Department agents on Japanese soil as damning evidence," Ogawa observed.

"Jeff Geum and Garfield Roi have never had any animosity with the nation of Japan," Price stated. "Indeed, our department and yours are working toward the same goals. As you might have heard on the international news earlier today, the FBI has determined the real belligerents in the Pennsylvania Avenue attack."

"Yes," Ogawa returned. "An organization called the Aryan Right Coalition."

Price took another sip of coffee, waiting to hear if the assistant director had anything more to say.

"We commend our allies across the water. And, personally, I would like to thank your men for their selfless efforts in rescuing the wounded," Ogawa stated.

"We appreciate that," Price said. "But I'd rather we keep their names and likenesses out of the any news accounts."

Ogawa cleared his throat. "Yes. We'll issue a general thanks for our friends from overseas."

"That would be for the best," Price added. "Both Jeff and Gar are undercover operatives, and publicity would only serve to compromise future investigations."

"Understood," Ogawa returned. "Is there someplace you'd like us to take them?"

"I'll send a friend of theirs to pick them up. Are they still at the campus?" Price asked.

"They are," Ogawa responded.

"Good," Price said. "Thank you for your cooperation in all of this, sir."

"And thank you for the assistance of your agents," Ogawa added. He hung up.

Price hit the speed dial to another Japanese number. There was an immediate answer.

"John?"

"Barb," he responded. "I don't get to hear a lot from you guys."

"No, you don't. Luckily, this time it's fairly good news," Price replied. "I just need you to pick up Gary and T.J. at Goisama Technologies, Ltd."

"Pick them up," John repeated. "No need for a hard extraction?"

"No. Things seem to have calmed down there. We will need you to take them to the address I'll text you later," Price added. "Other than that, it's going to be quiet."

"Quiet as you can get after a factory complex is bombed," John answered. "Don't worry, I know better than to ask too many questions about these things."

"Thanks," Price responded.

With that, John Trent, Phoenix Force's friend and ally in Japan, hung up the phone.

Price could trust the man; he'd joined the team on several missions, applying his linguistic and martial arts skills to assist the team across Japan, China and the rest of Southeast Asia, as well as an occasional and rare Phoenix Force mission in San Francisco.

In the meantime McCarter and the others were still a few hours out from Japan. She got up from her desk and walked over to Kurtzman's workstation.

The computer genius was hard at work, finishing up the analysis of the data gathered from the Heathens' computer systems.

"Any luck on figuring out where those missiles were launched?" Price asked.

"We've narrowed it down to somewhere in the Pacific," Kurtzman grumbled. "Akira's busy hopping from satellite to satellite, trying to pick up the communications or GPS signals the attack boat is using. There's just one problem with that approach…"

"You mean that there have been ships on the ocean for thousands of years before we started linking them up to satellites for global positioning?" Price asked.

"You sound thrilled at that knowledge. When was the last time you got any sleep?" Kurtzman asked her.

"Sleep is for the weak," Price snapped, taking another swallow of coffee.

"This isn't WonderCon, Barb," Kurtzman returned. "Head over and rack up. At least a half hour will do you some good. Otherwise, you've got little to do but wait for David and the boys to land."

"We remembered to contact Charlie and David to drop *Dragonfin* off in the waters near the Goisama campus, right?" Price asked.

"No," Kurtzman replied. "I remembered. You're punch-drunk at this point."

"Then I hope I didn't screw up with Ogawa from the PSIA," Price said.

Kurtzman shook his head. "You didn't. He's been putting through orders as we needed them to be put. T.J. and Gary will be in the clear as soon as John picks them up. Min-seo, as well."

Price smiled. "What about what was found in Long Island City?"

"So far, the analysts from the Defense Department have identified the missiles as Iranian production. They've also dated them back to 2002, having gone missing around that era," Kurtzman told her. "Likely, someone in their navy needed some extra pocket cash."

Price nodded. She blinked slowly, realizing that, as usual, Kurtzman was right. She needed to hit a pillow. Even so, her curiosity over the Chinese-designed missiles remained strong. "Any luck on tracking where it eventually ended up?"

"Not yet," Kurtzman responded. "But we're getting a bit of information about Goisama Technologies."

Price stood a little straighter. "Give it to me."

"Six years ago, it was bought out by an Australian businessman," Kurtzman explained.

Price tilted her head. Now she was intrigued. She grabbed a chair and rolled it up so she could take a seat across from him. "Australian businessman with a Japanese electronics company shouldn't seem so interesting to me."

"No, it shouldn't," Kurtzman answered. "But said businessman, Stewart Crowmass, has been living in the United States for the past several years."

Price nodded. "The thing that made me sit up was that he bought the company and then they started building that warehouse."

Kurtzman touched the side of his nose, signifying that Price was awake and "on the nose" so to speak.

Price frowned. "Stewart Crowmass…"

"Owner of the Financial Information Network," Kurtzman concluded. "He tends to keep to himself, but he's got…"

"Three or four cable news companies, as well as some big magazines and newspapers," Price said. "And those news stations have been working both sides of the debates over Japan and its being under attack."

Kurtzman nodded. "Steering the direction of the controversy, and keeping the rhetoric just this side of a civil war. Liberals frothing at one stack of his talking points, conservatives bleating their platitudes, but all of them funneling money straight into his pockets."

Price pulled out her tablet and touched a few keys. "Give me what you have on Crowmass."

"You're supposed to be getting some sleep," Kurtzman replied. "Once this bit of adrenaline fades, you won't be able to hold your head up."

"No," Price admitted. "But look up something for me…"

"If his family ended up prisoners of the Japanese expansion?"

Price touched her nose, returning Kurtzman's earlier silent compliment.

"I'll get Carmen on it," Kurtzman responded.

Price got back to her feet. "Send everything you find to my device."

"You know I will," Kurtzman said, waving her off like a burly grandfather shooing a child off to bed.

That man is usually right, Price thought as she went to her office, setting up a pillow on her sofa. It was a comfortable couch, and as soon as she snuggled onto the cushions, sleep enveloped her in its welcoming arms.

As the Globemaster was fifty miles off the southernmost tip of Japan, Charlie Mott brought the magnificent giant jet down once more. Engines flaring, flaps raised, the tail ramp lowered for deployment, the men of Phoenix Force were in place aboard *Dragonfin,* the high-speed racing catamaran. A drag chute was attached to the tail of the boat, ready to deploy once they were only yards above the surface of the Pacific.

Mott felt a lot more secure in letting off McCarter and the others from the back of the Boeing C-17, and didn't even worry about dropping its speed below 450 miles per hour. The seas were calm and he wouldn't have to slow to less than 200 so that *Dragonfin* could catch up. The drag chute would decelerate the catamaran.

It was just like the time when he'd offloaded the boat in the Ross Sea, then flown on to MacMurdo Station to land and refuel.

This was the second time that Phoenix Force was deploying, live and in the field, with the surface rocket. But that didn't mean that either Mott or McCarter, James and Encizo were leaving things to chance. Once more, the motto of a true professional in training was to practice until you never got it wrong, not stop once you completed it *once*.

"Deployment of drag chute in ten." Mott began the countdown. He read off the numbers, ticking down the altitude. Three yards off the surface of the Pacific, that was his goal, and he kept the stick steady, already his muscles starting to feel the pressure of turbulence and wind resistance.

He didn't say good luck to the Stony Man commandos and their lightning-fast boat. They had worked enough together that he didn't want them thinking about probability and chance as they had to engage in an operation that took split-second timing.

"Two…one…deploy!" Mott announced.

Once more the C-17's balance shifted, if only slightly. He could feel the weight of the catamaran leaving the cargo hold. The armed *Dragonfin* had had its ammunition belts replaced with fresh ones, and the mini-torpedoes had been restocked in their nacelle launchers. It was at its fighting weight, and on the 175-ton C-17, the minor difference was palpable on the stick.

With the subtle change in dynamics, Mott gained altitude, putting the throttle to full and pulling away. He hit the remote for the tail ramp to rise once more. He checked his bearings and altered his course for Yokota Air Base. Okinawa and Katena were just too far to the south for it to make sense of his dropping off *Dragonfin,* especially as Phoenix Force and the customized racing boat weren't supposed to exist in the first place. The dip might attract some attention, but as long as he maintained his course, the deposit of the team and the catamaran would not be noticed.

"Splash down," McCarter said over the radio. "Our asses are still in one piece."

"Which sucks, because they're supposed to be in two pieces," James quipped.

"Cut the shite, Cal," McCarter chided.

"Hell, if you boys are joking, I can rest easy," Mott said.

"Well, don't fall asleep at the wheel," Encizo warned.

"You guys be careful," Mott said.

"Why didn't you say that before you pooped us into the Pacific?" James asked.

"Because you were doing something risky. If you were going to be careful, you'd have never gotten anywhere!" Mott responded.

That got a chuckle from the men of Phoenix Force.

"Tell T.J. and Gary I'm glad you knuckleheads are out of my hair," Mott added.

"We love you, too, Charlie," McCarter responded.

With that, Charlie Mott settled in for the rest of the journey to Yokota.

He'd try not to worry about Phoenix too much, but their success would still weigh on his thoughts until they met again.

AKIRA TOKAIDO HAD very little luck with the satellite photography of the waters where the missile assault upon Goisama Technologies could have come from. He'd been poring over seemingly every inch of the Boso Peninsula's coast, throughout Tokyo Bay and the Sagami Gulf, even swinging up as far as the Oshika Peninsula, far past the Kashima Gulf.

The Yingji-82, in its original iteration, had a range of only 120 kilometers, but subsequent upgrades of the missiles, like the C-805 land-attack variant, could stretch out a full 500 kilometers.

And that, Tokaido knew, was with *known* engine

designs for those missiles, if they even were utilized. A 312.5-mile radius was a large space to search for a Gepard-class fast-attack boat. Manning and Hawkins had given them a sliver of hope in locating the heart of the conspiracy, but in the end, their enemies had closed that door tightly, forcing the Farm's computer team on the defensive as a shotgun blast of viruses and logic bombs peppered their systems.

There might have been a hint of something real in the sudden flare of possible locations. Tokaido had thought about garnering the ship's true course and location from an ever-exponentially-increasing spray of false input, but there was no indication that there'd be anything real in the information dump.

"Still trying to narrow down where the missiles could have struck from?" Huntington Wethers asked. Whereas Tokaido was a young, wiry Japanese-American man, Wethers was a tall, dignified elder African-American, looking as if he were a professor at a prestigious university. Tokaido was fast and wild, the embodiment of the thrash-punk lifestyle that his faux-hawk mane symbolized. Wethers was calm, sedate, meticulous. He would spend all the time in the world to find the smallest shred of evidence if necessary, though his attention to detail allowed him to pick anomalies out of patterns far faster than most other people.

Tokaido nodded. "Nothing on the seas. Also, scanning everywhere for 500 kilometers, in case someone launched it from land."

Wethers nibbled on the stem of his pipe. He left it unlit, but the act allowed him to concentrate. He looked at the maps that Tokaido had brought up. "You're using satellite photography to try to track the launches. And you've been meticulous in your searches on the radii of each missile range, based off the Yingji missile sample found unexploded aboard the factory ship."

Tokaido let Wethers talk.

The elder computer genius was using words as his chalkboard, putting invisible notes in the air that he could refer back to later. "You've been going by general ranges. You've eliminated Chinese and Korean coastal areas either by dint of sheer distance or by photographic evidence correlating to the time of launch and distances traveled at the various velocities of the different models."

Tokaido nodded. He began drumming on his knee with his index and ring finger of his right hand, burning off the frantic mental energies that constantly built up in him. Tokaido didn't plod with deliberation. He charged in, snatching up what he discovered with a mind and intellect that operated like a rapid twitch.

"One thing, however, my friend," Wethers said. "The ARC intended to launch their missiles from a much shorter range. We've been working under the assumption that the fast-attack boat was the source of all of the missiles utilized to destroy the factory."

Tokaido sat up. "I could kiss you, man."

"You've made a deductive leap?" Wethers asked.

Tokaido nodded. "We kept thinking that the electronics that had been taken was to equip a third missile cruiser, as well."

"But the same suites of communications and targeting technology could be used remotely," Wethers responded. "The missiles will have launched from a land-based site only a few miles away, while the actual people behind the launch can be, literally, on the other side of the world."

Tokaido leaned back. "Carmen, do you still have the inventory missing from Goisama Tech?"

Carmen Delahunt was the intermediate member of

the group, who Aaron Kurtzman recruited to round out his staff of cybernetic geniuses. Her adeptness with electronics was further backed up by a career in law enforcement, where she'd learned to look for and trust in gut feelings and intangibles that didn't necessarily translate into computer data. Instincts and common sense were her forte, as well as the mathematical skills that the others possessed. As a team, one would assume that every one of the crew would arrive at conclusions or solutions at different times, or one would prove more efficient than the other, but historically, that wasn't the case. The redhead sent the file immediately, then walked to look over Tokaido's shoulder.

"Trying to figure how much and where this stuff all went?" Delahunt asked.

Tokaido nodded. "Pakistan ordered multiple iterations for a trimaran-style Gepard. The three went missing, but as we've been gathering data on the wreckage and video from *Dragonfin,* we're seeing elements of the Houbei-class in these designs."

"Gepard size and engines, Houbei stealth and hull," Delahunt mused. "And McCarter's been calling it a super-Houbei, to make things simpler. And yet, this Frankenstein is actually being run off, mostly, Japanese electronics."

"We can account for these two sets of systems with the ones blasted by the RAAF," Weathers pointed out. Tokaido displayed everything in the form of Venn diagrams. He immediately subtracted the two sets of operational systems into the "accounted for" circle.

"And from what we'd seen of the command center that Manning and Hawkins discovered, we could take these particular units off the list," Delahunt pointed out.

"That is what's messing with me. We've got the systems for almost a complete warship, but if we do that, we don't have launch computers for the missiles that attacked Goisama," Tokaido said.

Wethers spoke up. "We're missing one point."

The other two nodded.

"We're assuming that the Chinese naval prototype for this extra-size Houbei was scuttled," Delahunt noted. "So we split up the systems between the automated launchers near the factory and their remote station…"

"That still leaves us searching for the last ship," Weathers said.

"No, it doesn't," Tokaido replied. He pointed out the last bit of technology. "The last of the encrypted communications systems."

"Which is what the last ship would need to talk with the others or to home base," Delahunt said. "That still won't give us a way to listen in on their party line."

"No, but we know what frequencies these transmitters use, as well as their power profile," Tokaido countered.

"So we go back and listen for burst transmissions and triangulate," Wethers concluded.

"You check that out," Delahunt suggested. "Aaron's busy digging into Stewart Crowmass, so I'm going to help him check into Crowmass's holdings…"

"To see if any of them put out transmissions along the lines we are looking for, at the same time," Tokaido finished. "We're not sure he's guilty…but looking at it this way will either confirm or eliminate him as a suspect."

"And give us another handle to look for the remaining ship or ships," Wethers said. "There's also got to be some port out there to service these ships."

"There's plenty of islands for that," Tokaido answered. "Both off North and South Korea, entire archipelagos

with some substantial caverns to hide them from even
the nosiest of satellites."

The cyber team returned to their workstations. They
had a thread of possibility. And for the three of them,
that was more than sufficient.

CHAPTER TWENTY

Min-seo Geum had been asked not to go after the men who launched the missiles at the Goisama plant, at least not alone. Fortunately for her sake, she would not be alone; she had the allegiance of the man they called John. John was tall, with black hair, brown eyes and hints of Asian blood coursing through his veins. He also seemed to move with grace and efficiency of motion, as if he were gliding through the world rather than allowing his weight to settle against its surface. Gravity was a suggestion, and she would not have been surprised to seem him suddenly spring up a wall as if he were a human spider.

Geum looked over the team's catamaran racer, bristling with weapons. They'd come to this section of the coast, still relatively abandoned and showing signs of the torment induced by the tsunami that inundated Japan in 2011. Up the coast, the Fukushima Daiichi nuclear plant was still an example of a Level 7 nuclear disaster thanks to the tidal wave's flooding of three of its reactors, as well as pre-existing structural flaws in their construction.

This place was deserted enough for Phoenix Force to reunite, bringing the powerful *Dragonfin* to the shore without prying eyes noticing the armed ocean interceptor. Geum didn't know how fast it could go, but she also wouldn't be surprised if the thing took to the air and broke the sound barrier.

Manning and Hawkins had both looked delighted to

be back with their friends, and they'd taken a few moments to get reacquainted and caught up with John Trent.

They'd introduced Geum, first names only, and not a one of them was discourteous or aloof.

"You five want to get after the last of the attack ships, and you don't have time to hunt down the man responsible for launching the missiles," Geum offered. "Meanwhile, I do have a personal interest in taking down that goon, if only to avenge what he did to my school."

"Are you set for fighting?" James asked Trent.

"I've got a few of my things," Trent returned.

"And I still have the gear you lent me," Geum reminded Manning.

The big Canadian turned to address Geum. "Barb didn't recruit you to become a part of the strike teams, Min."

Geum shook her head. "No. I'm an ear to the ground, but truth be told, I feel like I should do something more for you guys."

David McCarter offered her a bit of advice. "If you're cheating in a fight, you're winning. Luckily, John here is an expert at 'cheat fighting.'"

"If you're in a fair fight, your tactics suck," Hawkins added with his warm drawl and a wink.

"Don't worry, guys, I'll take good care of her," Trent told the other members of the team before he led her to his car.

Geum took the wheel, while the Eurasian man fed shotgun shells into the tubular magazine beneath the barrel of his folding-stock 12-gauge.

"I thought Japan was a haven from unsupervised firearms," Geum noted.

Trent smirked. "My firearms are always under careful supervision. But, yes, I know what you mean. You would be surprised at the number of illicit arms here in Tokyo alone. Thing is, the criminals don't want to poison the well by getting into loud, unnecessary gunfights."

"That hasn't been the case over the past few days," Geum responded.

Trent frowned. "Really? Because except for the missiles and the reports of gunfire at Moone's home, there haven't been any notable gun battles, despite what you personally encountered."

Geum nodded. "I see what you mean. This stuff all happens out of sight and out of mind."

"The United States can't even get the record straight on shootings or firearms use," Trent added. "Because a lot of it happens where no one will see or hear it, or if they do notice, it happens where no one dares to report it."

Geum glanced to the small personal tablet that Manning had left her. Barb had forwarded the suspected location of the missile launchers that had obliterated several buildings and left hundreds dead or wounded. Actually, they were homing in on the man who pushed the trigger, as the launch site itself was in flames, destroyed as a means of closing down any hopes of tracing the bomber via forensic investigation.

The Stony Man cybernetics crew had managed to find one link to the launch site, but that was simply because they had access to the nearly limitless surveillance equipment of a half-dozen governments, and a willingness to plunge into the "deep net"—the vast bulk of sites and locations that would never pop up on a commercially available browser search engine. Tokaido, making use of the Goisama electronics and proprietary encryption systems, had been able to track down the remote control for the missile launchers and right now it was in an office building, having driven from a vantage point over the Goisama Technologies compound.

The man with this remote unit had seen that his crew of deadly cleaners had failed to uproot Manning, Hawkins and Geum from the warehouse. With that failure, the gunmen were considered expendable, and antiship missiles had been loosed to sever as many ties as possible. The killer might have gotten away with all of it, had it not been for the fact that he was up against four of the most brilliant hackers in North America who'd used every resource not nailed down or on fire to track him.

Geum watched as Trent did one last press-check on his .45-caliber pistol and then slipped it back into a shoulder holster. She spotted the handle of a sword tucked against his thigh. "You're a swordsman, too?"

Trent nodded. "My original contact with…the team… came from my being Calvin's martial arts instructor."

Geum noted that the handle looked as if it would have been to a samurai sword, but the cord wrapping it was black and plain. The crosspiece was a plain black square of metal, not the ornate carved oval of some gilded steel. Everything about this man was utilitarian, despite the gliding ease with which he moved. She had a name on the tip of her tongue at what the Eurasian man could have been. Whatever it was, they were both now speaking in fluent Korean, which indicated that John was far more than some blunt instrument.

She pulled into a parking spot near the building and they got out of the compact car.

Trent's coat hung down, concealing the folded shotgun and sword against his tall, lean frame.

Geum herself was equipped with the Glock given to her as part of her care package, but she'd replaced the compact Mk 18 carbine with the even more concealable

MP-7. With the stock retracted and the pistol grip folded, it was no larger than a large handgun. She had six 40-round magazines for when the initial 20-shot mag ran out, the 20-rounder being used to keep the gun hot while it was concealed.

Together, the pair entered the building. It was night and there was no one at the entrance, but the doors had been left unlocked. According to the PDA screen, their target was on the twelfth floor.

"Let's go by elevator," Trent said. "They won't be expecting trouble."

"I doubt that," Geum said. Still, she waited for the car to arrive. She didn't want to be out of breath when they encountered the enemy. When Trent pressed for the eleventh floor, she smiled. They would walk up one flight and then dispel the suspicions of their target, especially if it was more than one man. He then tapped the button for the very top floor.

"Get out on eleven and climb the stairs," he said. He then stood on the rail around the middle of the car and pushed up the access hatch. Within moments he'd slithered up through the opening.

She heard him moving around on the car's roof, but by the time they'd reached the eleventh floor, things had gone quiet. Geum got out, pulling the MP-7 from her shoulder harness. She snapped down the folding vertical fore grip, then extended the collapsing stock, adjusting it to her length of pull with the jacket. A flick of her thumb and the gun was set to full auto, even as she reached the nearby stairwell. She opened the door and listened for the sound of anyone on the spiral steps. Nothing. Even the smell of cigarette smoke was old and stale, informing her that no one was currently present, nor had been recently. Trigger finger on the frame, she moved up the last flight to the twelfth floor and listened at the door. Things were quiet.

She cracked open the door and the corridor beyond was dark and silent. Geum slipped through, scanning for anyone who would be on guard. The last thing she wanted to do was to accidentally shoot someone who was simply a security guard. Given the state of how quiet and unattended the offices seemed, she was doubtful there would be much of a problem with unintended bystanders wandering into this conflict. Even so…

Someone loomed into the hall behind her, bursting from a door. The man had a big gun in his fist and pushed it toward her. Geum heard the metallic click of the safety and she anticipated the roar of a bullet when the shape collapsed to his knees in the wake of a sharp, wet crack. It wasn't the sound of a gun, but she saw her ambusher, rivulets of blood seeping down his forehead and over his cheeks. There was an ugly furrow smashed in the top of his head, and for the first time, she saw John standing behind the man, sword in hand.

Geum swallowed, realizing that he had saved her life with a sword stroke that smashed the dome of the man's skull, producing a brutal pressure wave inside the cradle of bone that destroyed his brain.

Trent gripped the collar of the man's shirt to keep him from tumbling unceremoniously to the floor. "Get his pistol," he whispered softly.

Geum took the weapon and flicked on the safety latch, then put it to the side.

Trent lowered the body to the carpet, then dragged him back through the door they had both likely appeared from.

"Where'd you come from?" Geum asked.

"When the elevator stopped on eleven, I opened the

doors to twelve by hand," Trent explained. "That way, the car signal didn't make a sound."

"Anyone else up here?" Geum asked him.

"Three more men," Trent answered. "They have guns, but two are obviously bodyguards like this one."

Geum thought about the hulking shadow that had gotten the drop on her. She remembered, with some embarrassment, the incident that had occurred before she'd been introduced to T. J. Hawkins. Those men moved with the same stealth and skill, snatching Geum even as she looked down in shock at the corpse of Veronica Moone. When the dead guard had been dragged through the door, she'd seen Korean features on the would-be killer, further identifying this man as part of the same group responsible for Moone's murder.

"The others are Korean?" she asked.

Trent nodded. "Not a mix like you and the others described at Goisama."

"Take me to them," Geum ordered.

The swordsman gestured and the two of them walked down the hall. Trent walked normally and Geum found herself moving at his pace. Down a corridor, they heard a door open.

"Hey! Quit dicking around out there!" came a snarl in what Geum recognized as the same North Korean accent as the men who'd grabbed her and tried to kill Gary and T.J. Geum tightened her jaw, then shouldered her machine pistol, making sure that her companion did not cross her muzzle.

Trent gave her a wide berth, unhooking his folding-stock shotgun. The man who moved like a ninja allowed the breech to close, but didn't rack the pump as was so de rigueur in action movies. There was a quiet, stealthy way to make sure your pump-action shotgun was live and ready to fire, and Trent displayed that skill. Geum was alongside another professional, but then, she now expected nothing less of the Americans who had entered her life.

"Take it easy!" Trent called out in a different voice than the one he spoke to her in. He'd duplicated the North Korean accent, and Geum hoped the distance and echo of the darkened hall would prove to be enough to allow the illusion that Trent was the dead guard.

"What was that with the elevator?" the man down the way asked.

"Well, no one stopped on our floor," Trent said in reply.

There was a groan of impatience. "No shit, man. Did you check the stairs?"

"No. I went out for shrimp chips," Trent snapped with equal irritation.

"Quit making so much noise," another man said, entering the conversation. "Get over here!"

Geum and Trent approached at a normal walking pace. So far, they'd been well enough in the shadows that no one had noticed Geum's presence beside the taller Trent.

But now...both men locked eyes on her.

"Who the hell is she?" One spoke as the other reached into his belt for a weapon.

Geum pulled the trigger on the guy attempting a fast draw, and at 800 rounds per minute, the high-velocity little 4.6 mm German rounds leaped the distance between her and the target. Geum ran a line of blossoming destruction across the guy's chest, and she kept her finger down on the trigger. She thought of the old military saying: "do not shoot a large-caliber man with a small-caliber bullet."

Maybe the 4.6 mm was a very small caliber, but what

it lacked in outright mass and energy, Geum made up for by keeping the low-recoil machine pistol on her target for what felt like a dozen impacts, something a little short of a full second of fire. The Korean who clawed for his gun was now splattered across the carpet, his white shirt spotted all over with tiny blossoms of crimson.

The other man dived through the doorway they had been standing beside, Trent whipping up his shotgun and firing just a moment too late, blasting the jamb to splinters. Geum winced at the pressure unleashed by the powerful 12-gauge boom, but she shook it off, advancing a little more quickly, even as the glass frames adjacent to the doorway suddenly popped from within. Geum paused at the wall, hoping her opponents didn't think to try drilling their rounds through the wall, something most of the weapons present could easily do. Even as she did so, she ejected her mostly empty magazine, putting a 40-shot stick in its place.

Trent was by her side in an instant and he threw something through a broken pane of glass. It was a small, round object, nothing like the flash-bang grenades that Manning or Hawkins used, but there was a bright flare suddenly inside the office.

That blaze of light inspired another wave of gunfire, blasting the partially open door and the last of the frosted-glass windows to oblivion. Geum took a step back from the wall, using it to keep her movements and position concealed, then fired the MP-7 through the sheets of plaster and drywall. The machine pistol stayed rock-solid on target, the spread of her initial burst drilling a base-ball-size hole through the wall about four and a half feet from the floor. For once, Geum was glad for her height, because anyone else, even crouched, would still be eye-to-eye with her.

Trent threw another flash-powder burst through the broken windows. He then grabbed Geum and hauled them both to the other side of the doorway as the sheet of bright whiteness cracked in the office.

Trent's maneuver was well-timed because only instants later the enemy gunmen, aware of the flimsiness of their walls, returned fire.

Geum's ears rang from the racket unleashed during the past few moments, but she could tell that her enemy either had submachine guns or full-auto-capable carbines. Whatever it was, it was loud, and it was incessant.

The wall they'd been standing by was now hammered brutally, chopped apart by bursts.

Things were now quiet. Trent bade Geum to stay still with a hand gesture.

In the distance there was a groan, a wet, hacking cough.

"Messed me up bad." He cursed in raspy, soft Korean.

"Hang on. We'll get out of here," was the answer. "They won't catch us…"

Panic dripped from the next words. "No…don't…"

A gunshot rang out, but it didn't come through the doorway. A second gunshot followed, this time accompanied by the sound of loose limbs dropping heavily to the carpet.

Geum frowned. She looked to Trent, who nodded in agreement with her silent assessment. This was some kind of bluff.

Trent thumbed a shell into the magazine of his shotgun. He'd only fired one shot, most of his contribution to the gunfight being the packets of flash powder that had dazzled and blinded their opponents. Still, Geum was alive because of his actions, and they'd sneaked closer to their enemies than she could have anticipated.

Trent pointed to the flash-bang that had been a part of Geum's arsenal. She plucked the pin and threw it into the office. The blast resounded, the force blowing the door shut with a slam. Trent blasted the locking mechanism even as it closed, barreling through the doorway before the reverberations were done shaking plaster powder from the damaged walls. Geum was right behind him and the two saw a pair of bodies on the ground.

Trent pumped and swung the shotgun at the wounded man, staggered by the enormous wave of sound pressure that assailed the two fallen Koreans. That injured killer had his machine pistol locked in his fist, aimed at the doorway. Because Trent and Geum came in so close to the grenade's burst, they had beaten out the stream of automatic fire pouring out of the gun by inches.

Trent's shotgun boomed violently and suddenly the wounded man's arm and head were missing large chunks of flesh and bone. The Eurasian ninja tromboned the slide and fired again, making certain the man was down.

In that same instant something whistled through the air, striking Trent in the side of his knee. He buckled under the impact, nearly sprawling on the carpet. A second arcing movement came up, but Trent caught the brunt of the attack on his forearm.

Geum could make out the weapon; it was a tube of silk with something metal and heavy knotted in the center. Right now, it was the equivalent of a padlock in a sock, capable of caving in Trent's skull if it connected one more time.

Geum also recognized it as the same kind of thing that had been used to garrote Moone. However, with Trent between her and the man wielding the unusual weapon, she couldn't use the machine pistol, not without harming her ally. The North Korean scrambled to his feet, spotting Geum in his blurred vision. He brought up the pistol in his other hand, but the woman threw herself to the ground, literally diving over the stunned Trent.

She felt the burning closeness of two hot chunks of lead passing too close to her skin. Geum hit the ground, and the MP-7 jarred from her fingers.

Trent rolled back, barely getting out of the way of more heavy booms from the North Korean killer's handgun.

Geum clawed for her Glock in its holster, then winced as the whirling, improvised whip cracked loudly against her left shoulder, rendering her whole arm numb. She twisted and kicked herself beneath a table even as a 9 mm slug blasted into the heavy wooden top. She finally fished the Glock free and shoved it toward her opponent's feet.

Geum's first shot exploded across the man's shin, making him drop to one knee in pain. The South Korean agent fired again, blasting a chunk out of his knee and bursting his ankle. The communist Northerner wailed in agony, clutching his ruined thigh as he rolled to his side.

Still, the North Korean murderer, the man who had likely strangled the woman Geum loved, still had his gun in his free hand. He raised it to shoot her under the table.

A ribbon of silver flashed and suddenly the killer was disarmed. Literally. Everything from below the elbow was gone, leaving only a red, spurting stump of gushing meat. Trent brought down the sword again, this time spearing the Korean murderer through the side of his neck and impaling him to the floor of the office.

"You okay?" Trent asked, helping her up.

Geum nodded. "You?"

"He got some bad hits on me," Trent returned. "But I'll live."

Geum looked at the man sprawled on the floor. She

still had her Glock in had, and the killer spasmed, likely already dead and only twitching from misfiring neurons.

"Finish it," Trent said.

Min-seo Geum put any anger and guilt over the death of Veronica Moone to rest as she emptied the Glock into the Korean's skull.

CHAPTER TWENTY-ONE

As a younger man, whenever Stewart Crowmass was asked about his exotic looks, he would respond with a story about his mother and how she had found love in Malaysia. His mother, always described as saintly, as pure and gentle, and ultimately caring, had been a nurse who'd traveled from her native England to spread not only the word of God, but the blessings of twentieth-century medicine to the backward Malay archipelago. It was there that she'd met one of the few educated Malaysian men, a tall, handsome army officer who had been educated in Britain. Sadly, that man had died in the defense of the islands, killed by the Imperial Japanese Army in their war of expansion, the same spreading surge tide that would, in 1941, expand to engulf the United States.

Crowmass would then grow quiet and wistful. And everyone would assume that the handsome, educated army officer was his father. He did nothing to disabuse others of that notion, though it was a complete fabrication. That man might have been a handsome islander, but there was no indication that he was anything other than a torrid romance on foreign soils, the tasty wild oats sown by an adventurous woman looking for exotic locales.

Crowmass hadn't been conceived until months later while his mother was in an interment camp. It was there that she, like any other attractive female captured by the Imperial forces, was used as a depository for their sexual frustration and hostile xenophobia. Crowmass's true father was one of dozens of racist, spineless cowards who could only get a woman at the point of a bayonet or the muzzle of a gun. He thought that he might even have had the DNA of every one of those lord's accursed bigots, which he felt would excuse him from his lifelong disdain for the Japanese.

Crowmass's initial disdain for what the bastards had done to his mother, the bigotry that had been heaped upon him as a little half-slant kid in Alice Springs, Australia, only grew.

There'd been enough of his schoolmates who developed a loathing for anything Asian because of what their parents had been through in the war. As long as Crowmass lied about his paternity, though, things got better, and he'd won over plenty with his quick wit and smooth talk.

That was the lesson that Crowmass carried with him, though. People were easy to hate, but that hate was easy to divert, to steer from one target to another. Aboriginals who'd actually done nothing could end up with a severe beating just on Crowmass's glib suggestion. People moving to the city and surrounding area, even if they were native-born Aussies, were viewed with zealous separatism. They had the wrong attitude for someone inside Alice Springs; they were too "coastal." They were green, too stupid for an outback people.

Crowmass loved how the insipid apes around him could go from unfocused biases toward concentrated anger with just the right wording. That got him first writing a few articles for the newspapers of Alice Springs. Then he got his own column. Then collections of his editorial pieces in book form. He became a talking head on the news, gaining more interest there.

He rode that manipulation of public opinion hard. His closest acquaintances—he never truly had "friends," just those he was most amicable to—told him that this was akin to riding a wild bronco. Someday the horse would throw him to the ground and he would be trampled into oblivion.

Crowmass shook his head at that naive statement. A horse who was ridden that hard, that long, wouldn't throw him. It would be broken by him. A man of will could outlast any horse. And Crowmass could outlast public opinion the same way, smothering its resistance, its skepticism. In '65, he was writing for newspapers, spinning things to his profit. In '75, he was steering television and magazines. In '85, he owned four newspapers and a television station.

In '95, he bought American tabloids of repute and started his own news network.

Now, in his seventies, he ruled the world. So what if his cable news channels disagreed with each other, taking attention off of actual, vital issues and turning them into static on the outskirts of the elements that he wanted to push forward. He was a god.

For years he'd been building international opinion against the land of the Rising Sun, making Japan seem like the devil to environmentalists, between dolphin slaughters in the pursuit of tuna to their whaling, even making a hit television program about a group of anti-whaling activists attempting to stop the harvesting of the great cetaceans in Antarctic waters. He also had more fringe journalists bring up Japan's ignominy during the days they expanded their empire, including the sins committed in China, Korea and Malaysia.

Crowmass's media empire did all of this, but he was the one plucking the threads of these webs, strumming the vibrations subtly.

America, where his power had grown exponentially

thanks to the willingness to hang on to old hatreds and prejudices, the polarization and balkanization of political beliefs and stubborn denial of any cogent points brought up in opposition, had been easy to play.

Even with the Japanese government and the contingent of businessmen and politicians sent to the United States cleared of the heinous spilling of blood on American streets, there were still those who felt that those "dirty yellow bastards" still had something to do with the violence. Women's groups decried the perverse objectification of women in many areas of life, naturalist groups continued to blame the country's overfishing to crises among whale and penguin populations, and there was still anger and distrust of the country for not shutting down their nuclear reactors in the wake of the massive tsunami that had struck the country and left one of those power plants leaking radiation across the Pacific Ocean.

Crowmass felt secure in his home, and that the world at large had no clue about the truth of how easily it had been twisted and manipulated to the point of economic Armageddon. Goisama Technologies, Ltd., was named for the former governor and "colonial relations" minister who had inflicted some of the harshest repeals of reforms and persecution of Korean customs. It had been a fairly floundering company, but with Crowmass's Wall Street connections, he'd started giving them edges here and there. Finally, six years ago, Crowmass had bought a majority stake in it just before its stock rose incredibly.

The influx of money put him on, almost literally, a throne of gold. He was one of the gods, now, and with that boost six years ago, the sociopathic glee he took in twisting world views solidified.

Crowmass took a sip of whiskey after raising the glass

to a frame with the logo of GTL. "Congrats, you bastard. Without you, I never would have gotten the idea for this."

Goisama, the Minister of Imperial Colonial Affairs, had been the man who'd given the ultimate order to imprison westerners in Malaysia. His was the ear that was deaf to International Red Cross requests for leniency and mercy toward British nurses taken prisoner and left in prisoner of war camps. Goisama, the cold-hearted bastard, had no problem with sending communiques to the effect that the prison camp commanders had free reign of the women, and that the use of anyone, Malay, English, whomever, as "comfort ladies" for the soldiers was allowed and expected.

To Crowmass, that damned the minister, his family and the corporation they tried to build. The only thing that GTL would be remembered for was their involvement in producing the very weapons systems that caused the deaths of millions. Japan's domination of global technology would be the source of murder and mayhem. It wouldn't matter, in the end, that the equipment used would have fallen into the hands of a North Korean cadre seeking to spark the reunification of the split peninsula.

Crowmass gave this little assembly of maniacs all the tools they needed. He'd come into contact with them during an instance where the People's Republic of China was very nearly goaded into war. The conspiracy involved in that crisis had struck at a North Korean diplomat who was trying to be a voice of reason. There had been a group of North Korean officers who saw a lack of will to reunite the splintered nations and a wasted opportunity. Crowmass, however, thanks to some of his "independent" journalist contacts, began speaking with them.

With the influx of exiled Chinese naval officers, the Korean cadre saw an opportunity, especially with Crowmass whispering in their ears. Trimaran ships built for Pakistan in Turkey became available, especially to back up Crowmass's main toy—the super-Houbei combat trimaran that Pakistan used as a template. Combining the best of German and Chinese designs, the two Pakistani warships and the Chinese original, Crowmass had the makings of a kind of juicy crisis that was making his news channels millions in revenue.

Thanks to income from these news cycles, revenge on the Japanese who made his birth and youthful shame a living hell, and just the smug pleasure of making bigotry and intolerance reap the full rewards of economic and social chaos, Crowmass didn't need whiskey to feel drunk. At this point, he had turned the world into a pit of squabbling children. The process of American politics and debate over issues had been transformed into a joke, a mockery of intellectual honesty, thanks to his direction.

Disdain for the mewling little apes around him had brought him to this level of opportunity. Even if war did not break out because of his end song, he'd inscribed his wrath upon a world that had tormented and abused him from the moment of his conception.

It was not as if the bigots he'd recruited to make up the Arrangement and their cat paws in the Aryan Right Coalition would escape from this. Crowmass already knew that someone had made a bloody sweep through the ARC, and had gathered up intel on the men who'd inspired them. The racist maniacs had done more than enough to bring down the fury of someone, a group that had left every one of them dead.

The same had happened to the bikers who'd sheltered the ARC squad before it could move on to a safer location. These weren't law enforcement. These were trained killers, men who would make a clean sweep of everyone involved in the slaughter of innocents. The Arrangement was doomed.

Crowmass took another sip. "They're likely coming for me, too. But what the hell? I've done what I've wanted in life."

Just the same, Crowmass's estate was now teeming with guards, protectors from the Arrangement itself, sent to make sure that their sugar daddy didn't come under attack. Apparently the racist goons had encountered similar enemies, maybe even the same foes, earlier. Multiples of their ploys had gone by the wayside, dozens of groups destroyed before they could unleash their cleansing rampages, or exterminated in response to their violent fits.

And now, the fools had sent an army of trained bodyguards to protect him from enemies who had blown through countless other men like them.

"Bigots just have no clue," Crowmass said. He put the empty tumbler on his desk and took a seat on his sofa. He picked up a remote and threw on some '50s blues music. He leaned back and let the tunes flow over him.

His tweaking of right-wing coverage of a presidential election all but guaranteed a backlash that would push the first African-American president into power. His pandering to all those who felt disenfranchised because of their prejudices brought him around to an era of unmatched political power. Now, it seemed that only the most corrupt or inane of all choices were chosen by the pundits *he* put on the air or in print. And without misery or controversy, none of these sock puppets would select anything better than the worst choices available. Political parties would crumble, having degenerated into inbred royalty the way that Europe had been before the collapse of monarchies.

The Americans who bought into the lines of thought he foisted upon them, creating divisive rifts in the areas of same-sex marriage, of the parentage and citizenship of natural-born Americans, on even the war between politics and science in regard to the fate of the Earth's climate, would have been surprised to see the Australian allow himself to be soothed and refreshed by the sound of New Orleans blues and jazz.

He remembered how the country had been sundered over the horrific flooding of that city, where Presidents failed cities. The atmosphere of discourse swiftly turned to how the Big Easy was not a city that deserved to be rebuilt, in a place where "American culture" was not celebrated, that "cultural diversity" and the wonderful music born in the breast of the metropolis was unworthy of the effort to restore history.

Crowmass felt a twist of angst over that. Music was his only real sight of the true worth and potential of mankind, and New Orleans, of all cities, the birthplace of so many genres of music, such amazing cuisines and styles, was especially dear to him. And yet, any sympathy for the besotted fools who had chosen to live in a hurricane area was dashed by one of the closed-minded troupes of fools and turned into a false banner by their counterparts in his game of driving sanity from the world.

There were times when he wished that there would be an apocalypse to wash away civilization. He'd planted those seeds, as well, but humanity had fought back. There was a group out there that had intervened in these near-extinction events. They had fought to protect the world from threats that had launched kinetic rods into major cities, stopped a potential "starvation plague," and had blunted efforts to create a global war. These people seemed to have no media presence, but he could see elements of it within the reports coming out of Long Island City, as well as the deadly standoff between police and the Heathens Outlaw motorcycle club, where every one of the Heathens was found dead, blown apart in a close-quarters battle that authorities claimed was an internal spasm of self-destruction induced by meth.

Crowmass's phone chirped and he hit Pause on his music. He was glad for at least a few minutes of the soothing tunes clearing the venom, the anger, from his blood.

He looked at the caller identification.

It was Sun-shin Yi.

Crowmass smiled at the name. He knew enough of Korean history to recall Admiral Sun-shin Yi, the man who'd designed an incredible ocean war machine called the "turtle ship" and led a mere dozen of them against a fleet of 133 Japanese war vessels seeking to invade his nation. While the historical Yi had perished in the conflict, shot by an enemy sniper on the deck of his ship, the Korean turtles sank one in four Japanese invaders, and put the rest of them to rout. That was in 1597, and his name echoed on through the centuries, a standard of courage and nobility among all who aspired to be a warrior.

This new Yi had wanted the Communist North to take advantage of a crisis to reunite the shattered nation, but the "beloved leader" vetoed that plan. And so, Yi stewed and simmered. The appellation drawn from such a historical and noted warrior hero would most likely have been an assumed identity. Crowmass knew the power of names and legends was more than enough to unify disparate forces, and the use of the stolen super-Houbei as well as the hulls intended for Pakistan's navy called back to the turtle ships.

Yi even called the new war craft *Geobukseon,* after the originals. Where those sixteenth-century warships were heavily armored—especially with the shell that gave them their turtle nickname—and equipped with spikes, twenty-six cannon apiece and a sulfur gas thrower, the new trimarans were guarded with stealth and speed, able to hurtle along at fifty-five miles per hour and equipped with an upgraded variant of the Chinese Yingji anti-ship missiles. The *Geobukseon,* as Yi called his flagship, bristled with the equivalent missile pods, more than enough to obliterate entire fleets or to lay waste to a coastal city.

"You're calling at a bad time," Crowmass said.

Yi sounded disinterested. "I am informing you that we will likely never speak again, Stewart."

"Why do you say that, Sun?" Crowmass asked.

"I won't insult your intelligence by pandering or humoring you," Yi returned.

Crowmass chuckled. "I'm waiting for the hammer to fall on me. Things have gotten crazed enough here in the States. What makes you think you will be found?"

"Our port radioed us to return to base," Yi said.

"So?"

Yi's voice held a deep dread. "I left none behind to send such a missive."

Crowmass nodded. "You didn't answer, did you?"

"I did. Just long enough to give them a chance to find me," Yi stated.

Crowmass remained quiet. The Korean had the same sense of fatalism that he had now. The die was cast on his mission, but there was a sense of awareness. "Do you believe you will be able to accomplish your goals?"

"Like my ancestor, I will not live to see the defeat of Japan, or the glory of Korea, but I will see them crippled and set to flight," Yi responded. "As well, when I spoke on the radio, I spoke with a woman. An American woman."

"What did she say?" Crowmass asked.

"She gave me an opportunity to surrender," Yi related. "I declined."

Crowmass nodded. The Korean had too much on the line. "How do you know that an entire fleet hasn't been sent to seek you out?"

"We've picked up a single craft on the edge of our radar," Yi stated. "A surface ship, moving at great speed. If the military were seeking to intercept us, they would have done so as when we lost one of the copies south of Australia… They would have sent fighters with air-to-surface missiles."

"A small group, a small agency," Crowmass said.

"You find something familiar? Such as the destruction of your American gunmen?" Yi asked.

"We've both seen crisis situations dissolved without seeming intervention by large, conventional forces or mediation by diplomats," Crowmass explained. "And the Aryan Right Coalition had appeared and been destroyed in multiple incarnations. I believe that we're looking at a small agency, something that slips between the cracks, between the laws of engagement and the rules of sanction."

"An outlaw group, akin to us, but with far more altruistic motives," Yi said. "This is not outside the realm of possibility. It makes sense. They operate with the grudging tolerance or misidentification of government authorities. Just like the government has misidentified you for nearly eighty years."

Crowmass sighed. "They may have identified me appropriately, as well."

"We have." A woman's voice interjected. "Neither of you will be allowed to escape, you've ended far too many lives through your actions. But we will be fair, and not cruel."

"Fair and not cruel?" Crowmass asked. "My girl, if I were you, I would bring back the ways of Torquemada to extract a proper punishment for the likes of me. Yi, however, will be the one who will relish ending his days as a warrior. Am I right?"

"Better to die for something than to live for nothing," the Korean answered.

The woman—Barbara Price—sighed. "You've earned the worst of punishments, but we do not operate out of cruelty. We act to protect others who you or those you have gathered may threaten. You will be a message to those who think to follow in your footsteps. You will be ended. Death is the only reward, the only outcome any of you will ever receive."

Crowmass smirked. "You're truthful. And I can tell you are holding back a lot of hatred. Tell me, girl, have you ever heard of a study on emotional stimulation that correlates hatred to clarity of thought and increased thought process?"

"I have," Price returned. "The thing is, those thought processes are still garbage in, garbage out. Only if you get real data will your hate be rational. You've been putting out garbage data just to start unnecessary conflicts."

"Unnecessary?" Crowmass asked. "Look at the good that's been done just with your dealing with my little machinations."

"No amount of scum killed makes up for the lives destroyed by your hand-picked maniacs," Price returned. "We'll burn you down."

"A minor squabble of a few years until my natural death or the end of society as you know it," Crowmass said. "Have your men do their worst."

Yi grunted in agreement. "I hope you have sent your

finest warriors against me. For my end shall not be silent, or easy."

Crowmass suddenly heard something rumble on Yi's end of the conversation.

"Trust me, Captain Yi." Price's voice punctuated the blast. "You will find no more capable foes."

Something crackled outside the gates of Crowmass's mansion. "And, Mr. Crowmass, thank you for sending your house staff away."

Crowmass smirked. "I did not want them to be abused or insulted by the likes of the goons the Arrangement provided for my protection. For all you do, it'll never be enough to undo the rotting of this decaying world."

"We're just amputating the necrotic flesh. The world can heal itself," Price concluded, disconnecting the lines of communication.

Finally, Stewart Crowmass was alone in his office. He opened his desk drawer and pulled out a Peacemaker-style revolver with a bird's-head grip. It was loaded, six rounds in the cylinder, hammer down on a notch between chambers, a half-dozen Magnum slugs ready to fly.

"Amputating the necrotic flesh," Crowmass repeated. Outside, he listened to the sounds of Able Team crashing in on his mansion.

CHAPTER TWENTY-TWO

Thanks to the efforts of Min-seo Geum and John Trent, the cybernetic wizards at Stony Man Farm were able to connect to the remote link that allowed the North Koreans to open fire on Goisama Technologies, Ltd. With a link to that device, the computer experts were able to isolate the ship belonging to the North Korean naval officer who had assembled the mercenaries and ousted Chinese sailors and commanders into the fleet that had been attacking Japanese and Australian ships.

Right now, David McCarter manned the Bushmaster while *Dragonfin* hurtled to intercept the trimaran missile cruiser commanded by Sun-shin Yi. It was visible on the horizon and well within missile range of any one of dozens of coastal nuclear power plants or millions of gallons of stored fuel. If the *Geobukseon* fired one missile at one of those targets, thousands would die brutally in an instant. If the trimaran fired off its whole salvo of eight missiles in one load, the damages would be in the billions and could result in enormous environmental disasters, from spilled oil to reactor meltdowns.

"That thing is moving at up to seventy miles an hour," Rafael Encizo warned. "And according to radar, it's deployed its missile launchers."

"We're inside firing range," Calvin James said. "Any time you boys want to raise some hell, I'll hold her steady for—"

"Guns! Guns!" Gary Manning announced. Even as he yelled, the whole of *Dragonfin* tilted violently, James putting the high-speed catamaran in a violent turn. The pivot at 180 miles per hour had been a last-minute dodge as streams of 20 mm cannon fire whipped the Pacific surface to foamy froth.

T. J. Hawkins, operating the 40 mm grenade launchers on the Phoenix Force warship, cut loose with a long blast of return fire, McCarter adding the thumping punch of his 25 mm Bushmaster to the long-range grenades.

"Negative effect!" Manning called out. "I thought you said you were going to hold her steady for us, Cal!"

"You wanna get out and walk?" James snapped back.

"You know damned well he saved our asses from the cannon on that son of a bitch," McCarter growled at his friend.

"They pinged us," Encizo announced. "We've been painted."

"Missile launch!" Manning echoed. McCarter could feel the fifties fire, making *Dragonfin* shudder with an unmistakable feeling. "Not a big one."

"Anti-radiation missile," McCarter noted.

"Pedal's to the metal," James returned.

McCarter could see the missile slicing through the night, tearing across the air just past them. Luckily, Encizo picked up on McCarter's warning, killing the active radar. James, so far, had kept them ahead of the radar sweeps that were trying to light up the Phoenix Force war boat. Hawkins released a cloud of chaff from one of the top launchers on *Dragonfin*. Behind them, hundreds of yards back, the anti-radiation missile detonated in proximity to the chaff, probably mistaking it for the actual catamaran.

McCarter returned his attention to the enemy vessel.

Whoever was at the helm was fairly good. The enemy CIWS ripped loose, trying to pick up the slack of the now lost ARM. The 20 mm cannons of the Close In Weapons System were designed to target enemy incoming missiles, but also had a secondary role of blasting small craft out of the water. Considering that each of the shells was an inch thick and packed with armor-piercing explosives, the Briton was glad that James and Encizo were keeping the Phoenix boat just ahead of them.

McCarter cut loose with the Bushmaster, sweeping a line of his own armor-piercing shells across the sleek, deadly *Geobukseon* and watched flickers of light blaze on the top decks. Hawkins brought in the Mk 19 grenade launchers, as well, the long-range 40 mm shells not having the kind of penetration of the Bushmaster, but the small HEAT rounds still had enough oomph to leaving smoldering holes on the surface.

"How's she looking, Gary?" McCarter asked.

"We're going to nail the Koreans with our torpedoes. Our guns are making a lot of flash and cosmetic damage, but she hasn't slowed down," Manning returned.

"She's still apace at sixty-one knots." Encizo spoke up. "She also has a lot tighter of a turning radius than us thanks to being a little slower and three hulls."

"And no way am I slowing down," James added. "Those CIWS will shred us in a heartbeat."

McCarter grimaced. "What will you need for a good shot on that thing?"

Encizo glanced back. "Our MAKOs can't catch up with the *Geobukseon*. They can only do forty-six knots compared to her sixty-one."

"Down her throat," Manning returned.

"I'd love for a good plan of how to get that kind of a shot," McCarter said.

"We don't have to worry about a minimum arming range," James answered. He steered, shaking *Dragonfin*'s path. McCarter could see the spray kicked up by the 20 mm guns on board their enemy. Now, it also looked as if there were gunners manning smaller weapons on deck.

As soon as those guns flared to life, they became targets of streams of lead from Manning on the Browning .50s. Hawkins cut loose with another burst of grenades that tore up sections of hull around one of the CIWS cannons. Moving so fast, swerving back and forth, McCarter could make out the damage to the normal radar domes housed above each of the guns. Unless there was a direct hit, though, McCarter doubted that they could damage the weapons systems.

After all, these things were meant to absorb the punishment of being at sea, and other attacks.

McCarter decided to adjust for wind and speed, then gave the Bushmaster its head. At 300 rounds per minute, the chain gun chunked out its explosive shells with deadly abandon. Fortunately, *Dragonfin*'s velocity was enough to keep the ship level, but the rate of fire only allowed him to score near hits. Sure, each 25 mm shell punched out a fist-size hole in the deck and left a large gap in the pill-like radar cap, but the CIWS still swung and tried to connect with the nearly two-hundred-mile-per-hour catamaran.

"Goliath can't hit David, and David doesn't have the right weapons to hurt Goliath. We're outsized by—" Encizo began.

"Don't tell me the odds," McCarter returned. "Cal, swing us down on that bastard so we can shit a MAKO down his throat!"

James nodded. Encizo readied the torpedo launcher. Unfortunately as *Dragonfin* changed course to get in

closer to the Korean trimaran, the *Geobukseon* deceler-
ated, drifting on the water and changing direction. The
several-hundred-ton craft created huge swells in that
maneuver, causing McCarter, Manning and Hawkins to
overshoot their target with their heavy weapons.

"At least while they're fighting with us…" Hawkins
began.

"Don't you finish that sentence!" McCarter snapped.
He saw the smoke begin to billow from one of the launchers. "Too late! Hit that missile pod!"

Suddenly everything on board *Dragonfin* was firing,
even the M-60 turrets; a wave of slugs and shells exploding all across the side of the murderous trimaran. *Geobukseon* shuddered as blossoms of fire erupted along
its central deck. McCarter held down the trigger on the
M-242, gritting his teeth and willing the 25 mm shells to
punch through the missile rack and destroy the Yingji-82
before it could take flight. Explosive shells cracked, popping like flashbulbs of old, the flickers of their detonations illuminating the growing cloud of rocket exhaust
from the missile's charging engines.

Somewhere in the middle of the torrent of Phoenix
Force fire and thunder, the nose cone of the Yingji appeared, emerging like the head of a turtle from its shell.
McCarter's vision was whited out with a tremendous blast
in that moment, the shock wave of one hundred and sixty-
five kilograms of high explosives detonating and rolling
over *Dragonfin* even though they were still more than a
hundred yards from the Korean commander's ship. The
Chinese-built trimaran shuddered under the destruction
of its missile just out of the mouth of its launcher, but the
armored pod absorbed much of the devastation.

McCarter grimaced, cursing his luck. The pods were
designed to withstand even the explosion of the weapon

in its launcher, a safety measure that made simply blasting away at the missile racks a futile gesture even with armor-piercing rounds. Even so, there was now a burning section of deck pouring smoke into the sky, hot flames in the launch tube glowing brightly and making the *Geobukseon* much easier to see.

If an armed aircraft were available at the U.S. Air Force Base in Yokota, Japan, Charlie Mott would have a nicely visible target with that flaring marker of the destroyed missile. As it was, Yokota's craft were devoted to Airlift wings, helicopters and Hercules C-130s mostly, with C-12Js, none of which was fitted with anti-ship or anti-submarine weapons.

"Fish away!" Encizo announced.

The Mark 54 MAKO compact torpedo had launched amid the mayhem of Phoenix Force pouring fire at the missile launcher. The deadly little shark was slicing through the Pacific at forty-seven miles an hour, but it had been fired at an intercept angle to the *Geobukseon*'s course. Already rocked and staggered by the destruction of one of its missiles and the subsequent backflash, the crew of the enemy ship was now struck by the hammer blow of the equivalent of 238 pounds of TNT going off against one of its three hulls.

The detonation of the torpedo, backed up with far more explosive energy than the grenades and cannon, and focused for destroying the bulkheads of warships, created a deadly furrow through the center hull of the trimaran. Inside the craft, the detonation would have smashed machinery and turned sailors to pulp, so even if the hole in the hull didn't scuttle the *Geobukseon*, it caused major damage.

"Fox Two," Encizo called.

Above deck, Hawkins's stream of 40 mm grenades

finally pulverized the Chinese CIWS, the multiple barrels of the Gatling cannon peeled back and deforming
under the half dozen HEDP grenade blasts. The same
jets of copper penetrators that sliced through the Aryan
Right Coalition's garage doors and walls with lethal effect sliced into the CIWS ammunition belts and cooked
off the explosive shells on the belt. In addition, 20 mm
cannon rounds were ignited by the plasma lance from the
HEDP rounds, causing catastrophic sympathetic detonations that popped the radar-aimed turret off of the deck
like a champagne cork atop a bubbling cloud of smoke
and fire.

Encizo's second torpedo went up short of the target
as the other CIWS gun tracked it and hammered the explosive fish. McCarter aimed toward the bridge with the
M-242 and hoped that the cannon rounds could penetrate
deeply. The thing with the 25 mm shells and the 40 mm
grenades was that they were ideal against targets with
two inches of rolled, homogeneous steel, but the *Geobukseon* had a much heavier hide.

"Bloody turtle ships," the Phoenix Force leader
growled. He checked the ammo count on the Bushmaster
and saw that he was down to about fifty rounds. "Ammo
check!"

"My 19s are down to my last twenty," Hawkins said.
"We've laid a lot of fire, but all we've done is knock out
one hull and stop one missile."

James hit the throttle, swinging *Dragonfin* around the
blind spot of the trimaran's remaining operating CIWS.
Encizo already had the third of their MAKOs locked and
fired it before James broke off of the one hundred and sev-
enty-five-mile-per-hour charge. Once again, the Mark 54
mini torpedo struck home, spearing into the port hull of
the larger trimaran. The detonation shook the *Geobukseon*

violently before secondary blasts within the structure of the ship snapped off the wing connecting the outboard hull.

The sudden loss of the stabilizing hull made Yi's trimaran tilt. Water gushing in through the deadly wound in its center hull caused the last pontoon to rise from the surface of the Pacific.

McCarter could now see another of the missile pods opening, smoke vomiting forth through the hatch. "Hammer it!"

Hawkins was relentless while McCarter held back on the M-242. He didn't want to use up all of their explosive ordnance on one weak spot. Twenty HEDP rounds punched into the missile launcher as the deck had swung down, exposed to the guns of *Dragonfin.* Three shells struck the nose cone of the Yingji-82, shaped charges punching searing bolts of molten metal through it and into the warhead. Hundreds of pounds of high explosive on the anti-ship missile touched off, ignited by the equivalent heat of a lightning bolt cutting through it. At the same time, other HEDP shells burst other missile hatches, tearing off two of them, exposing the Eagle talons within. Hawkins's target detonated under the brutal assault.

Copper lances managed to pierce the walls separating the missiles, weakening them enough to allow the two adjacent exposed missiles to rupture and explode under the heat and pressure of the original detonation.

With the missile pod already compromised by an earlier blast and further winnowed by superheated sprays of liquid metal, the one-two punch of the three Yingji-82 missiles proved their worth as an anti-ship weapon, shattering the very vehicle that was to carry them into bloody action against the coast of Japan. The *Geobukseon* snapped in two as the combined power of more than one thousand pounds of Pentolite explosives detonated with 3.6 gigajoules of energy, an order of magnitude less than the sixty-three terajoules that destroyed Hiroshima in one single nuclear fireball.

However that sheer amount of force tore the armored Chinese-built warship apart, tearing metal as easily as if it were tissue paper. The shock wave that ripped outward from ground zero was actually palpable inside *Dragonfin,* a solid punch impulse that shook through the five men of Phoenix Force.

If there was anyone on board the *Geobukseon* right now, in close proximity to the launchers, their internal organs would have burst like water balloons. Death would be swift and painless. On the armored bridge of the ship, however, there was no sign of the superstructure, literally ripped up by the roots from its spot on the hull.

Sun-shin Yi, on the bridge, could possibly be alive.

Manning took over the FLIR cameras and scanned the water. "We've got warm bodies, but they're cooling to water temperature quickly," he announced.

"What about in the superstructure?" McCarter asked. "Anyone alive in there?"

"You think anyone could have survived that?" James countered.

McCarter glared at his friend. "We make sure they're done. I don't want anyone suffering a slow death out here, but I bloody sure well don't want Yi to pop up in the future, having learned from his mistakes."

James throttled down and swung the catamaran in a slow circle around the smoldering column of flame and smoke that marked the splintered, torn triple hulls of the *Geobukseon.*

"No mammals," Manning announced. "But subsurface, we've got sharks."

"Sharks aren't warm-blooded," Encizo noted.

"No, but they have dark muscle that generates both body heat and the power to swim endlessly," Manning answered. "Lots of sharks tearing into corpses."

"I bloody love it," McCarter added. "First, the poor finny bastards have been needing a good meal. Fat and happy, they'll stay here, rather than in closer coastal waters where they could be grabbed and finned for soup."

Hawkins wrinkled his nose. "Harvesting whales. Amputating the fins of sharks and leaving them to drown just for some soup. Why are we protecting the Japanese again?"

"Please tell me you're joking," Manning returned. "You aren't a vegan, and you've gone hunting."

Hawkins nodded. "And you're a hunter, too, hoss. You of all people ought to know the difference between a clean kill and animal torture. Or do you just lop off the legs of a wounded deer and let it bleed to death?"

Manning returned his gaze to the FLIR screen. "Logic dully noted. Good point. But what about the people working day to day? Everyone is at fault for the exotic tastes of a few psychopaths? That's like nuking Riyadh for the actions of a minority of terrorists. And let's not forget Min and John, fellow soldiers on the archipelago."

Hawkins grunted. "Eat up, fishes. Consider this a present from humans who give a damn."

"The small fires on floating wreckage are making it hard to be certain," Manning observed. "I don't see anyone clinging to flotation devices, though."

"The superstructure next," McCarter ordered.

"That's already sucked below the waves," Encizo noted. "Radar places it at twenty-five meters deep and dropping. Unless the bridge is hermetically sealed, and they have scuba gear, I don't see anyone getting out of there."

"Not to mention the superstructure flew five hundred yards when the missiles went through their chain reaction," James added. "Flying that far and that fast, striking the water is like riding a rocket sled into the side of a mountain. Anyone on the bridge is pulp."

McCarter took a deep breath. He didn't want to feel this much unfocused hate. He just didn't feel an ounce of satisfaction with the destruction of the *Geobukseon*. The huge detonation of the missiles on board *should* have killed everyone. He had seen ships struck by such blasts, and had seen the kind of death toll extant from such impacts. On top of that, the two torpedoes with their deadly payloads would have done more than enough damage belowdecks.

Sun-shin Yi, however, was a smart man. He'd managed to get the Chinese prototype, along with dozens of Chinese naval men to join him in his campaign of smearing the Japanese or inflicting agony on the country. Nearly eight decades on, Japan did its best to rewrite history about their actions across Southeast Asia, but Yi had found the embers of deep burning hatred and raked them to the surface. The blaze had resulted in hundreds dead, thousands injured. Yi might have claimed that this was an attempt to reunify Korea, though it seemed more like the petulant fit of rage by the North Korean officer.

"David, you're acting a little paranoid about this." Manning spoke up.

McCarter nodded. His instincts told him that this kind of long-range battle was just as visceral, just as deadly, as up-close-and-personal, shooting his opponents at a range of a few inches or driving a knife through their breastbone. And yet there was something else, something digging at the back of his mind.

There would always be the possibility that Yi had

survived the obliteration of the *Geobukseon*. That somewhere, below the waves, the man named for a legendary
Korean admiral still lived, if even for a moment.

"Sod it," McCarter grunted. "If anyone does survive,
we'll be there to stop 'em."

In the distance, plumes of frothy water shot into the
air as munitions and fuel tanks on board the dying hulls
erupted.

"*If* they sodding survived."

McCarter wished the hungry sharks a large, satisfy-
ing feast, and that one of the items on their menu was
Sun-shin Yi.

CHAPTER TWENTY-THREE

Carl Lyons was listening in on the conversation between Barbara Price and Stewart Crowmass, chomping at the bit like a racehorse in harness. This was a rare instance where Stony Man could have arranged for a far less violent outcome for all involved. All they needed was for Crowmass to appear in an open window and Lyons would gently stroke the trigger of the suppressed Barrett .50-caliber rifle as he lay atop the roof of the Able Team van. He had grown comfortable in this sniper's rest, a canopy of elm leaves providing concealment for him thanks to Blancanales's parking. The Crowmass estate was three acres of fenced land with another thirty spread out for ranching and other activities.

Next to him in the sniper's roost was Hermann Schwarz, utilizing a pair of ungainly seeming binoculars. As usual with the wizard of Able Team, this was his effort at improving surveillance capabilities to the point of near magic. While the binoculars looked as if they weighed ten pounds—and they actually did—they were also equipped with a suite of scanners and sensors that gave the men of Able Team an accurate count of the men on the estate. The mansion had a dozen gunmen inside and another twenty were on foot around the fenced grounds.

At the far reaches of the mansion's land sat another concern that simply added to the thirty-odd soldiers assigned to the protection of the corrupt Crowmass. Twenty-four bikers, members of the Heathens motorcycle club, were present, on their sleds. Using magnetic resonance imagery, Schwarz's super-goggles were attuned so that he could tell the make of their firearms.

There were plenty of M-16s and AK-47 variants in the hands of the assembled cadre of bodyguards.

Truthfully, Lyons was not disappointed that Crowmass said that Able Team's upcoming attack would do more good for the world. Members of the Aryan Right Coalition and the outlaw bikers were all savage predators who thought nothing of wrecking lives using drugs and illicit firearms trading. He was also glad that Crowmass had confirmed that his house staff had been sent away. Noncombatants were not the target of the Lyons's wrath, though Crowmass himself was an exception.

Crowmass's machinations had resulted in too many deaths, too much economic panic and mayhem for Lyons to allow this man to escape his capital sentence. The only lethal injection that Crowmass would see would be the introduction of lead into his brain.

"Have your men do their worst," Crowmass had challenged.

Lyons set the Barrett into the recessed storage on the roof of the van, trading it for another weapon.

"He's taking out a pistol," Schwarz said. "A Magnum revolver, single-action, according to its magnetic profile."

Lyons grinned as he shouldered the new arm, a fifty-four-inch-long tube with pistol grips and advanced optics. "He's made me a happy, happy man."

Schwarz got to his knees, preparing follow-up 83 mm rockets as Lyons would not pick up a weapon that wasn't ready to fire. The Shoulder-launched Multipurpose Assault Weapon was an upgrade from the mere grenade

launchers Blancanales had utilized against the ARC in
their garage headquarters. Here, a quarter of a kilometer
away from the main gate, the assault weapon—the only
arm actually warranting that title—was more than up to
the task of blowing up the heavily guarded and fortified
gates. The SMAW was meant to punch through bunkers
and armored vehicles, and in an instant, the 83 mm rocket
launched, spearing through the space between van and
defensive wall.

The missile was slow, only 712 feet per second, meaning the warhead was still short of its target by the time
Schwarz put in a fresh shell and gave Lyons a tap on the
shoulder informing him that the weapon was live. The
Lyons aimed for the front doors of the mansion where
he saw gunmen assembled. He pulled the trigger, and as
he did, the gates erupted under the impact of the HEDP
shell. The SMAW was designed to pass through eight
inches of reinforced concrete, a foot of brick, or nearly
seven feet of wood-reinforced sandbags. The wrought-
iron gates were mangled as if by the fist of an angry god,
the splintering bars and the disintegrating crest of Crowmass turning into shards of shrapnel that produced a zone
of death and agony for thirty yards beyond the gates.

Another slap on the shoulder and Lyons swung the
muzzle toward a third target, a van that served as a command post for the ARC maniacs assigned to guard Crowmass. The destruction of the gates was a loud precursor
to the second 83 mm rocket's impact on the front door.
Lyons squeezed the trigger on the van.

The front doors of the mansion disappeared; replaced
by a rapidly spreading cloud of brick dust, powdered
wood and burning flesh.

The ARC gunmen were suddenly down by six, going
by Schwarz's goggles. The smoke trail of the hurtling

rockets would give the riflemen on the grounds a good idea of Able Team's position, even as orders were shouted and sentries raced across the lawn. Windows were thrown open so that snipers and machine gunners could respond to the attack from their elevated position. In another heartbeat, the van serving as their command post became a pillar of roiling fire, a jetting mushroom of flame rising then spreading in the conflagration of igniting fuel and twisted metal.

One last tap. The fourth shell was in the breech and Lyons knew who would be the recipient of this rocket. "Go ride shotgun."

Schwarz scrambled off the roof of the van and Blancanales put the vehicle in gear.

Lyons stuck his arm through a nylon loop and dug his toes into footholds atop the van, anchoring himself in place for the last shot.

Schwarz and Blancanales knew that Lyons intended to dump the last SMAW shell into the phalanx of Heathens motorcycles. Even over the pitter-patter of rifles in the distance and the tap dance of bullets on their armored windshield, the roar of thunder from dozens of motorcycles revving in unison was unmistakable.

The Heathens loved to liken themselves to an oncoming storm, for their presence was always announced by the rumble of their bikes, but the outlaws didn't have a single clue who was truly an oncoming storm.

As soon as the first of the bikers rounded the mansion on the road to the front, Lyons adjusted his aim and fired at the road well ahead of the Heathens. The criminal gang should have taken the hint when their Maryland safe house had been raided and destroyed, but instead they'd answered the summons of the Arrangement and the Aryan Right Coalition. The bikers could have skated away with only minimal losses, but they'd chosen to put themselves as the line between Crowmass and justice.

As soon as Lyons fired, the van charged from its parking spot, tearing down the slope of the hill. Any other delivery van's axles would have been destroyed by the stresses put upon it, but Able Team knew what they needed in a vehicle. The suspension of the van had been sufficiently up-sized to handle the extra weight of the van's armor and equipment.

It certainly wasn't a smooth ride, and Lyons was glad for his hand- and footholds as the vehicle bucked like a bronco on its way to the enemy's gate—or rather, the smoldering wreckage that used to be the entrance. On the mansion grounds, Lyons's SMAW rocket reached the road just as the Heathens did. The HEDP round detonated and the energies designed to lay waste to seven feet worth of sandbags now unleashed itself, splashing off the asphalt the Heathens rolled upon. Burly men and bikes weighing five hundred pounds or more were hurled from the road, swept aside like seeds by a wind.

"That's a damned waste of good bikes," Schwarz growled, seeing the column of smoke rise from the detonation, a grisly shadow of the burning souls exiting their bodies. Either pulped by the overpressure of the warhead, or simply smashed beneath the weight of their own motorcycles, Schwarz didn't think they were going to be dealing with too many enemy bikers.

Even so, four rockets wouldn't put their enemy to rout. When Lyons told Schwarz to ride shotgun, the electronics genius went actually one better with a Mk 46 Mod 0 compact light machine gun. Essentially a commando version of the old M-249 SAW, the 46 was pounds lighter and inches shorter, making it a relatively handy and mobile weapon while giving up little of the firepower only a 200-round attached belt could provide.

The Able Team van zoomed over the crumpled gates and onto the grounds.

Schwarz kicked open his door, seeing that the lawn was full of men who had ducked or were seeking cover from the rain of doom Lyons had unleashed moments before. With a laser sight along the barrel, the Able Team wizard could direct the withering stream of 5.56 mm mayhem across groups of men while keeping himself braced in the passenger seat.

On the roof of the Able Team van, Lyons switched to M-67 fragmentation grenades. The former high school and college football player had a fairly good arm that had been specialized in anti-personnel throwing by his years as a Farm commando. Even from the shifting platform of the van's roof, he was putting the munitions within five yards of running gunmen, well within the fatality radius of the hand-held bombs. As the fraggers detonated, not only the initial target was hit by a wall of shrapnel, but others within a fifteen-yard radius received splinters of steel or deadly pieces of notched wire that sliced into flesh, producing injuries.

Schwarz triggered a short burst from the shotgun seat, the Mk 46 stuttering out its message of death that brought down an M-16 armed ARC gunner with haste. This wasn't some action movie where the hero only had to hold down the trigger to bring down swarms of opponents. Instead, Schwarz nursed the 200-round belt on the machine gun, loathe to waste precious bullets with little result. Thankfully the laser pointer allowed him to burn off a third of the payload while putting down every target he aimed at.

Schwarz looked through the windshield, noting that

the glass was smeared with reddish gore. "Are you aiming to run over these people?"

"The suspension is that good you didn't notice us rolling over a dozen of these reptiles?" Blancanales asked in response.

"Score one for the Stony Man motor pool," Schwarz said with a grim, cold chuckle. He focused a laser dot on a pair of bikers who staggered away from the pileup of wrecked Heathens. "Should've stuck to the open road, maggots!"

The 46's roar preceded Schwarz sweeping the pair of outlaws from the face of the Earth with a dozen 5.56 mm rounds.

"We're almost to the mansion!" Blancanales shouted. His voice was raised despite their hands-free communicators. He regretted the volume, but luckily the radios had built-in filters to prevent him from blowing out the eardrums of his compatriots.

Lyons grunted with the effort from another grenade toss. "Good, I'm tired of throwing goodies to these brats. Let's get a little face time."

"How's the situation with the snipers on side one?" Blancanales asked, referring to the face of the mansion.

"We've been chasing out splashes," Lyons returned. "They're trying to lead us, but you're too fast for them."

"Great," Blancanales announced. "But once I put on the brakes…"

"Gadgets, you take the west windows. I'll aim for the east," Lyons said.

"Gotcha," Schwarz responded.

Blancanales brought the van to a screeching halt, hammering the smoke trigger on the dash for good measure. Gouts of tear gas and thick chemical smoke burst from nozzles on the roof of the vehicle. Lyons would be surrounded by hot spouts of spewing gas, but those same thick clouds would make it hard for the window gunners to see them, while the burning capsicum would keep men on the ground at bay.

Sure enough, with the van stopped, Blancanales heard the thunder of Lyons's shotgun putting out blasts of buckshot into windows where gunmen sought to stop Able Team. Schwarz was on the ground and raking the windows on the other side of the mansion entrance with short, controlled bursts.

Blancanales exited via the driver's-side door, bringing his M-16/M-203 with him. The Honey Badger had done an admirable job in the first few engagements, but Blancanales was a man of old habits. He was the over/under man in his platoon, and he appreciated the balance of the full-length rifle and the 40 mm grenade launcher mounted under the barrel.

He came around the front of the van and targeted the smashed remnants of the front doors. An ARC rifleman lurched into view and Blancanales put him down with a burst of 5.56 mm death. There were more sounds of movement to the left of the doorway, so he switched to the M-203 and triggered a 40 mm shell through the doorway, hooking that shell through a doorjamb. The grenade detonated, shaking glass from the front windows, a severed foot tumbling into the open.

Blancanales opened the breech, threw in a fresh shell, then closed it. "Good girl."

He slipped through the gaping hole, seeing dazed ARC gunners sprawled around in the wake of the blast. One started to rise and Blancanales told him to rest by slicing open his torso with a stitching line of high-velocity rifle bullets. Another fumbled for a handgun, but Blancanales blew his face off before he could level the weapon.

It was a slaughter, shooting the guards down like this, but Able Team had never had any doubts about the guilt of those who'd taken on the name of the Aryan Right. These were killers and bank robbers, maniacs who had tried to poison the water supply of Manhattan, and bigots who tormented people over the color of their skin. They'd stolen guns and utilized them for wholesale slaughter in an attempt to take over the drug trade in Louisiana, and knocked over armored cars in gun battles that left bystanders wounded or dead.

If the ARC men expected mercy, they had sided with a group that never spared such kindness for others. Blancanales left the parlor after making certain all were dead within, then aimed the M-203 up the stairs. There was movement in the hallway up above, but the grenade launcher spat its load. Blancanales watched the blossom of flame and smoke at the top of the steps, then watched as a bloody torso, shorn of its head and one arm, toppled down the stairs.

Outside, Lyons twisted a new tube magazine into place before he hammered out another pair of 12-gauge thunderbolts into Heathens who had reassembled themselves. Eight of their own had been killed, either by Schwarz or by Lyons with the SMAW. Those who remained were angry but cautious, keeping cover behind the mangled remains of some of their motorcycles, while others sought the protection of concrete planters. Since the smoke dispensers were now dry, Lyons slid off the top of the van and landed on the ground. He put out a couple more shotgun blasts and then pulled the quad tube from its mounting. He brought up a second quad from its quiver and snapped it into place, grateful for the Doric columns bracketing the front of the mansion.

Rifles and handguns barked and crackled, seeking

out Lyons's flesh. This was not an ideal situation, as he was now on the defensive.

"Pol! Do you have a better angle on the Heathens?" Lyons asked.

"I'm cutting through to the dining hall now. Tired of trading shots with them?" Blancanales asked.

"Blow them up," the Able Team commander ordered.

Suddenly one of the first-floor windows burst outward. Before the shards of glass could even begin to fall, Blancanales's grenade detonated behind the barricade of mangled motorcycles. Men screamed in agony as they were torn asunder, limbs and heads ripped from their anchors on torsos, while others died from overpressure crushing their ribs.

In the wake of the shattering bolt, Blancanales followed up by switching back to the M-16 and emptying tribursts into bikers who were still up and active.

Lyons swung out from the other side of the column with his SRM 1216, pumping four shells into three outlaws scrambling from the ambush through the window.

Lyons switched to a fresh tube, jogging to where the Heathens had made their last stand, but Blancanales had been cruel and efficient with his M-16/M-203. Grenade and gun took out the other men, at least those who'd chosen to stand their ground.

From the rear of the Able Team van, Schwarz was tracking the fleeing bikers with the Mk 46, this time holding the light machine gun as a proper weapon, stock to shoulder, both hands on it, looking through the sights. The five Heathens who thought that discretion was the better part of valor found that Able Team had no intention of allowing any living thing to escape the grounds. There would be no retreat or surrender allowed now.

"Prosecution to the max," Lyons repeated under his

breath as he turned back and went into the brutally hammered mansion. The top of the stairs in the grand entrance was a mangled mess of bodies and shattered furniture, a sure sign of the devastation Blancanales could unleash with his chosen weapon.

"How many still outside?" Lyons asked.

"Four or five," Schwarz answered. "They're scared and keeping to cover."

"Use the SMAW or something to dig them out of their holes," Lyons ordered.

"I have just the tool for the job," Schwarz returned. "Go in and clean out the mansion."

True to his word, Schwarz did indeed pick the proper implement for the task at hand, grabbing up the stand-alone launcher with which Blancanales had unleashed such hell on the enemy back in Long Island City. He scooped up a bandolier of shells and jogged to flank the dug-in gunmen.

The name of the game now was total extermination. Able Team knew that the best means of ensuring the return of a violent group of bigots was judicious and liberal applications of high explosives and firepower. "If violence isn't the answer, you're simply not using enough."

From his left, Schwarz heard the boom of Blancanales's rifle-grenade-launcher combo sail a 40 mm shell into a gunman who'd taken refuge behind a fountain. The raggedy corpse of the man cartwheeled across the lawn, sent spinning by the detonation of several ounces of high explosives.

"We give up!" another man shouted, waving a white rag as a sign of surrender.

"Fill your hands!" Schwarz challenged, knowing it was a ruse. He didn't quite give the ARC thug a chance, however, immediately pumping a 40 mm round into the guy before he could aim. The HEDP round from the M-203 struck and burst the Heathen like a bubble.

Curses arose from the remaining two men hiding.

Schwarz fed a fresh round into the breech of the grenade launcher.

The way things looked, Lyons wouldn't have much of a cleanup.

Of course, even just that thought was more than enough to make things go tits up.

CHAPTER TWENTY-FOUR

Blancanales had cleared the first floor, so now Lyons went up; skirting a grenade-mangled corpse sprawled upside down on the stairs. It wasn't a matter of queasiness, but the Able Team commander wasn't keen on slipping on a greasy, disgorged organ from a burst torso. Fortunately, his boots had more than enough traction on the blood-sticky carpeting of the steps. Carl Lyons had eight rounds for his 12-gauge, so he took a moment, feeding fresh shells into the mostly empty tubes. It was no slower or faster than replacing the rotating magazine tubes, but going into battle with seventeen shots was much better than only with nine. He put the last round into the breech of the SRM 1216.

He reached the top of the stairs, the big shotgun leading the way, and he saw a corridor. The area closest to him was strewed with broken furniture and two more mangled bodies, silent testimony to the brutal efficiency of a 40 mm grenade launcher. Lyons and Schwarz had done a lot of damage to the gunners on the upper floors of the mansion with their weaponry, but there wasn't any confirmation of kills so much as a cessation of enemy gunfire from those windows, so Stewart Crowmass was not going to be the only challenge on this level of the mansion.

Lyons could feel the presence of hatred, angry men who were also desperate to survive. The Aryan Right Coalition had its back to the wall, pressed there by Able Team and its quest for justice. The Able Team leader didn't presume to think that this fight would be the last between his battle squad and the army of bigots that continually rose from the ashes, but he would take it one war at a time. Able Team had stopped them before, and they would put the next batch of maniacs down. This was an eternal struggle, between those who would protect civilization and those who sought to allow their barbarian prejudices to run rampant.

Lyons couldn't think of an enemy that wasn't a pack of bigots, from Muslim extremists who lashed out against peaceful followers of Islam with the same zeal as they murdered Christians and Jews, to criminal organizations that aligned along racial lines—Colombian cartels, Mexican heroin gangs, even various flavors of outlaw motorcycle clubs. Greed and hatred were incestuous lovers, having mated again and again to give birth to such murderers as the Mafia, the Zetas or the Crips.

Lyons pulled an M-67 grenade from his harness, one of his last three, and rolled it through a doorway without pulling the pin. Even as the deadly little egg bounced on the carpet, he heard screams of surprise and curses at the sight of a fragmentation bomb. Lyons turned the 1216 to the wall and fired through it, blowing massive holes through Sheetrock and into one of the screaming men on the other side. Buckshot smashed through drywall easily thanks to its mass and speed, and subsequent rounds slithered through the first hole made. Lyons dropped to a knee, ducking beneath the gunfire that came through the wall.

As he was out of sight of the man behind the wall, he pulled a second bluff.

"Agh!"

And with that cry, he slammed against the far wall, clutching his shoulder. It was a risky gamble, but the sound of him hitting the wall and the floor might make these gullible gun thugs think they had slowed him down. One gunman came out of the doorway across from him, while a couple more heads poked out from the door adjacent to Lyons. The Able Team leader wore an anguished grimace, spurring the men from the doorway beside him to step out. One of those two was wounded, but had a revolver in his hand, while the other had a sniper rifle.

Lyons looked up, faking a look of fear that didn't require too much acting. As a cop, as a federal agent, as the leader of Able Team, one wouldn't have thought the big blond man to be someone who felt terror and panic, but nothing could have been further from the truth. The thing that made Carl Lyons such a powerhouse was that he used that fear to keep him smart and sharp. This was a rare instance where he allowed his internal feelings to show on his face, and the sniper lowered the stock of his rifle from his shoulder, but kept the muzzle close to his face.

At this range, the bullet from the bolt-action rifle would cut through Lyons's body armor with ease.

"Why ain't there blood?" the wounded gunner asked as the third ARC gunman stepped to their side. That man was in condition white, letting his weapon hang on its sling, hands empty and eyes wide.

"I hit him!" Lyons's initial bluff target sputtered.

Lyons gurgled, wincing and squirming farther into the wall. "No, no don't…"

"Blow his face off," the revolver guy ordered. "It's a trick…"

Lyons shot his left hand under the rifle's muzzle, pushing it hard up and back into the jaw of the sniper. The rubber recoil pad might not have made much of an impression on the mandible, but it did make the sniper step back in surprise. Lyons ripped his .357 Magnum from its spot in his shoulder holster, swiveling around the six-inch barrel of the silvery hog leg.

The revolver shooter fired, his bullet slamming into the chest plate of Lyons's armored vest. A ceramic trauma shell, chain mail and Kevlar blunted the power of the hand gunner's initial shot while Lyons put his first .357 slug through the ARC thug's groin. The 158-grain hollowpoint connected with solid pelvic bone, shattering it at near contact distance and folding his opponent nearly double.

The boastful gunman fumbled to bring his assault rifle up into action, but Lyons pushed the muzzle of his Ruger GP-100 straight at him. His second Magnum missive smashed into the bare throat of that easily tricked bigot. Windpipe crushed, neck bones pulverized, spinal cord severed, the gullible ARC soldier toppled backward against the wall, eyes staring lifelessly as he trailed a wide smear of gore from the Magnum's exit wound.

Lyons hurled the sniper rifle aside with his off hand as he returned his attention to its owner. The marksman went for a pistol in his chest holster, but Lyons smashed his wrist to a pulp with a third lead hollowpoint. The 158-grain hollowpoint had more than enough power to slice through the sniper's wrist, breaking bones into powder, and still leave a dent in the gunner's body armor. Lyons lifted his aim and stroked the trigger a fourth time, vaporizing the sniper's nose and creating a blossom of skin flaps and spraying brain chunks in the back of his target's skull.

Lyons grabbed the crippled survivor of this brief melee, using his shoulder as leverage to bring himself back to his feet.

"Can't feel my legs," the man with the shattered pelvis said, voice rough, tears flowing down his cheeks.

"Can't give a damn," Lyons returned. The hot muzzle of the Ruger brushed the ARC soldier's temple and gunshot number five roared in the close confines of the hallway. The bigot would never have to worry about being confined to a wheelchair, his life exiting through the same cavern that his brain left his body.

Lyons was about to holster and go to another weapon when a latecomer stepped out into the hall with a shotgun of his own. Lyons felt what it was like to be the target of a burst of buckshot, his armored vest holding against the pellets punching through his skin, but the impact was still as bad as a baseball bat to the ribs. Lyons fired a single shot toward his opponent, but an odd metallic clang resounded.

The shotgunner was wearing some kind of plate armor, and as soon as Lyons put out the sixth shot, he lowered the muzzle of his shotgun, laughing. The ARC thug was wearing a helmet, as well, complete with a visor that covered half of his face, from his nose up.

"Ha! You're empty!" the living juggernaut shouted. He pumped the action of his 12-gauge, looking down at Lyons's own shotgun on the floor. "And don't even think about going for that shotty on the floor."

Lyons still aimed the Ruger at his opponent. "I'm empty?"

"I counted your shots. Six," the shotgunner said, stepping closer. "I'm going to enjoy taking you apart slowly. You've got armor, too, but I don't think that'll protect your hands and feet…"

Lyons stroked the trigger of the modified GP-100. Round number seven in the customized cylinder launched in a fireball and struck the heavily armored thug in his open, braying mouth. The shot went through the back of his head. The shell-like helmet his foe wore was twisted violently off his face, smashed aside by the passage of 158 grains of .357 Magnum fury.

Lyons stuffed the empty Ruger into its holster and swiftly picked up the SRM. He looked at the juggernaut that had collapsed to the floor, facedown, blood pooling underneath his head from the torrent that flooded out of his still open mouth. "You should've learned to keep your mouth shut."

Lyons stepped over the defeated human tank, thumbing new shells into one of the partially spent tube magazines. He could see now that the man had cannibalized some of Stewart Crowmass's collection of ancient armors to give himself a brief edge over the men who dared attack the fortified estate. And yet, like his beliefs in "racial purity," the Aryan warrior was completely wrong.

"Stewie! Where are you at, boy?" Lyons asked facetiously. He already knew that Crowmass had been in his office and was armed with a handgun, thanks to the super-goggles with which Schwarz had swept the estate. There was no indication that Crowmass had moved, and the big oaken doors were closed.

He walked up to them and gave the handles a test.

Locked.

Didn't hurt to see if Crowmass would make it easy for him. Lyons looked below the handles, seeing that they looked like brass. He emptied a tube from the 1216 into the locking mechanisms, four rapid rounds that showed the office doors to be heavier, sturdier and far more secure than they appeared. He tested the doors again. They were still locked.

"Well, isn't that something?" Lyons mused.

"You think I wouldn't have anything to deal with people trying to kill me?" Crowmass's voice came over a hidden speaker.

Lyons looked around and remembered that despite the carnage and wreckage, the billionaire had plenty of cameras and microphones watching the whole of the estate. The battle might have caused some of his panic room systems to have blind spots, but Crowmass's taunt told him that this spot was well observed. It was also likely that Crowmass would have a panic room that not even armor-piercing shells could penetrate.

"Actually, I thought you would have cast your lot with these walking bags of cement with guns. Apparently, I was wrong," Lyons answered.

Outside, more grenades detonated, informing the Able Team leader that his allies were finished, or nearly finished with the last survivors of the defensive cadre. Lyons wondered why Schwarz's magnetic resonance sweep hadn't picked up these doors, but he dismissed it as he dug his knife into the splintered wood of one of the doors and found that while he could go through the pane, there was a steel shutter behind it.

Lyons narrowed his eyes, blowing out the hinges of the one door he'd made a hole through, and looked to see that the shutter descended from the ceiling. It was segmented plates, flat and flush with each other. He tried to slip between two of them, but they were beveled, interlocking. Nothing would go straight through the slats of the panic door. He couldn't even gauge the thickness of the metal, or its approximate composition. He stood back, examining the frame around the door.

"Gadgets, you about done with the pests outside?" Lyons asked through his com set.

"Sure. What do you need?" Schwarz returned.

"Give Crowmass's office a quick look again. He's

got some kind of blast doors you didn't notice," Lyons explained.

Schwarz was quiet for a moment before issuing a soft rumble of concern. "Yup. Blast doors. Judging by the density on the MR scan, it's at least three inches thick."

Lyons sneered. "Three inches."

"Yeah. Sadly, our HEDP rounds can't punch through steel that thick," Schwarz told him.

Lyons grumbled. "I know."

"For someone who calls me a nerd, you study even more than I do," Schwarz said.

"Focus, bro," Lyons snapped.

"Yes, 'Gadgets,'" Crowmass's voice interjected into the radio communications, something that irritated the Able Team commander no end. Still, Crowmass had built a television and internet media empire atop the foundations of print. To expect any less than a top-of-the-line security system would have been stupidly underestimating the billionaire.

Underestimating your foes, Lyons knew, was deadly to your health. He couldn't forget all the friends and allies, even the lovers, who had been killed because they hadn't brought enough response to bear upon an opponent.

"So, you can hear what we're talking about," Lyons said. He walked out of the corridor, and looked at the wall. He gave it a test stab with his combat knife and the Sheetrock cracked, four inches of steel cutting through. With a wrench and a twist, he pulled open a hole. He then took the last two of his M-67 grenades and pulled the pin on each, dumping them through the hole. Within a second, he'd run back into the hallway to stand in front of the armored doors.

In another second the two grenades went off like a one-two punch, a double blast that filled the room he'd entered with plaster dust. The drywall was gone, and when he came back, he noted that he'd shattered the lowest section of the wall, having splintered the timbers. There would be a space large enough to get through the wall with just a little extra effort.

Lyons blasted away, fragmenting wall studs and lumber with the SRM 1216. Fist-size holes weakened the barrier between him and the old man who'd sought to set the people of the world at each others' throats and to attempt to destroy Japan's reputation and economy. Seventeen rounds of 12-gauge later, splinters fell from the last bits of wall. He could see the leathery wallpaper, and kicked at it.

There was a bookshelf or a cabinet on the other side that resisted his kick. Lyons slashed at the wallpaper, then stepped away for a running start. At two hundred pounds, he was ready to get through to Crowmass no matter what. He charged, recalling his football days, and struck the last barrier between him and the old murderer with all of his strength. The shelving, whatever it was, toppled then crashed to the floor.

He saw Crowmass standing at his desk, eyes wide with shock.

"Should have armored all the walls of your office," Lyons said. "Those blast doors would have helped against most people, but you're fighting us now, Stewie."

The six-gun in Crowmass's hand roared, a .357 Magnum round striking Lyons dead in the chest, his body armor once more catching the bullet before it caused severe internal damage. Even so, the toll of these past days of battle was wearing on the Able Team commander. He coughed and experienced a knifing pain in his lung area that felt exactly like a fractured rib.

"What does it take to stop you people?" Crowmass asked.

Lyons glared, rubbing his sore chest. "Call it the extermination of every maniac and fanatic on the planet. Then I'll take some time off, drink a beer and look for a woman with good birthing hips and a taste for battle-scarred, brooding Vikings."

Crowmass looked at the revolver in Lyons's shoulder holster. "Ah. You like six-guns?"

Lyons tilted his head.

"Let's do this like men," Crowmass continued. He twirled the cowboy gun in his hand, then slid it into a hip holster. "Like they did in the West."

Lyons took a deep breath. "I need to reload. I emptied it in the hall."

"Oh…right. It'll be fairer than that monster gun. That's empty, too," Crowmass stated.

Lyons tossed down the 1216 and drew the Ruger from its sheath. He thumbed the cylinder release and emptied the spent brass onto the carpet. He reached under his right armpit and pulled out a speed loader designed for the seven-shot cylinder. Pushing it in, he twisted the release knob and the cartridges were now nestled in the seven little charge holes for the Magnum. With a deliberate push, he swung the crane shut and then tucked the six-inch barrel back into his shoulder holster.

"We're doing a *High Noon*-style duel because it's fair and honorable?"

Crowmass nodded.

"I do have a question for you, Stewie…"

"Stop calling me that."

"Like I said, Stewie, I have a question."

"What?"

"When have you ever been honorable?" Lyons asked.

The window to Crowmass's office suddenly exploded, armored glass disintegrating under the impact of a 40 mm grenade launcher. The anti-armor shell had been launched by Blancanales, suddenly opening the office to the outside world.

Crowmass turned toward the destroyed window. Even with the grenade explosion, the armored panel had done its job, smothering the blast and protecting the old man. But even as he looked through the torn hole, he saw Blancanales and Schwarz on the roof of their van, a hundred yards distant, just far enough back to have a good angle on the office.

And Schwarz was behind the scope of the biggest rifle Crowmass had ever seen.

"Now wai—" Crowmass began.

He didn't even finish the word as his rib cage imploded on one side, his back bursting open with a disgorge of internal organs and a gallon of blood spray.

Crowmass was on his back, trying to breathe with lungs that were spattered across the far wall of his office. He blinked, realizing that his brain had enough oxygen, enough life, to keep operating for at least twenty seconds. He worked his lips, trying to speak to Lyons.

"We now conclude our broadcast day," the Able Team leader growled.

The last thing Stewart Crowmass saw in his existence was the tread of Carl Lyons's boot smashing down into his face with terminal force.

"Nice shot, Gadgets," Lyons said.

"Nice sign-off, boss," Schwarz returned.

"All this racket, I'm pretty sure the law will be on its way," Blancanales added. "Of course, we do have one last bit of business to conduct."

"Yeah," Lyons said. "Did you at least offload the damn thing at the front door?"

"Of course," Blancanales replied.

Lyons signed off and was down the stairs, walking slowly past a quartet of 55-gallon drums. He knew the drums were filled with a mix of nitrate and TNT, and made to look like something a home-grown terrorist group would assemble. In fact, it was the same explosive formula that had crushed the facade of the Murrow Building in Oklahoma City more than two decades earlier.

The setup was a fuel-air explosive. One of the reasons why Blancanales and Schwarz had opened up the office wall of the corrupt media mogul was to make certain that the fuel-air explosion would spread into the building and get Crowmass himself.

The last thing that Stony Man Farm needed was to have the owner of a conservative news conglomerate become the victim of a top-secret government death squad. It wouldn't matter to the paranoid maniacs that Crowmass's power in the liberal news media was just as insidious and powerful.

However, this would make it seem as if the Heathens and the Aryan Right Coalition had made an effort to strike one final blow.

THE ABLE TEAM van drove past the shattered gates and the mangled corpses of the ARC guards stationed there.

Blancanales paused, but Schwarz eyeballed the distance. "Leave them, we'll need verification that the bigots were on the grounds," Schwarz stated. "Everything else will be burned clean of forensic evidence in the Daisy Cutter."

Lyons looked out the rear window of the van as Blancanales took it onto the road. As soon as they were far enough away, Schwarz thumbed the trigger on his detonator.

The white-hot ball of fire formed a perfect dome, more than eighty feet tall and eighty feet in diameter. The hemisphere of plasma was hot enough to melt metal, and Crowmass's mansion and a score of bodies out on the lawn were subjected to vaporizing fury. Any physical evidence of Able Team's rampage would be lost in the conflagration. Out of more than fifty bodies on the premises, thirty would be reduced to ashes by the thermobaric blast, including everything inside the estate.

Remaining bodies would be charred and hurled around, puzzle pieces to be collected by forensic technicians later.

This wouldn't bring back dead policemen or Japanese sailors. It wouldn't ease the pain of families who'd lost loved ones to this conspiracy.

But Stewart Crowmass was correct. A lot of dangerous people would never harm another human being again.

The Stony Man commandos and cyber wizards would have to leave the healing of international relations and Japanese economics to diplomats and businessmen. Evil had been avenged and the innocent had been protected.

Lyons turned back toward his partners and took a seat behind Blancanales. "Take us home, Pol. I'm sick of the smell of burning flesh."

* * * * *

The Executioner
Don Pendleton's®
ARCTIC KILL

White supremacists threaten to unleash a deadly virus...

Formed in the wake of World War I, the Thule Society has never lost sight of its goal to eradicate the "lesser races" and restore a mythical paradise. This nightmare scenario becomes a terrifying possibility when the society discovers an ancient virus hidden in a Cold War–era military installation. Called in to avert the looming apocalypse, Mack Bolan must stop the white supremacists by any means necessary. Bolan tracks the group to Alaska, but the clock is ticking. All that stands between millions of people and sure death is one man: The Executioner.

Available August wherever books and ebooks are sold.

GOLD EAGLE®

The Executioner
Don Pendleton's
DEADLY SALVAGE

A power-hungry billionaire dredges up sunken Soviet missiles in the Caribbean

A rich American businessman is behind the secret excavation of a sunken Soviet submarine off the Caribbean's coast. He's found nuclear weapons on board and intends to use them to dupe the U.S. into attacking Iran—and to strike at America's heart in the process. With international peace and millions of lives at stake, Bolan must race to put an end to the billionaire's deadly scheme. Every man is an island, and the Executioner plans to blow this one off the map

GOLD EAGLE

*Available September wherever
books and ebooks are sold.*